MIRACLE BOAT

Endorsements

"I loved *Miracle Boat*. It is a magical, thought-provoking story that reminds the reader of how God works differently in each person's life. I found myself examining my faith and wondering how I might have missed God trying to talk to me. I also enjoyed the character development, especially the backstories of the couple Dalton and Eileen and their friend John who gifted them the boat that became such a special part of their lives."

Mara Hamner

"Through a simple story of a man, a friend, and a boat, Dean Johnson points us toward hope, healing, and help. For anyone who has experienced the depths of grief when a loved one dies by suicide, this story can bring comfort in the raging storm and calm to the troubled waters of the soul. Hope floats on every page. *Miracle Boat* is a gift to anyone who wants to better understand the tragedy of suicide or bless someone who endures after such a loss."

Brent McDougal

Pastor First Baptist Church, Knoxville, TN

"Dean Johnson has crafted a compelling narrative which takes the reader from paralyzing despair to a magnetic hope. Johnson, drawing from his own experience, plumbs the depths and heights of the human spirit. You will be hooked by riveting reading."

Gary Burton

Pastor of Pintlala Baptist Church, Hope Hull, AL

DEAN ALLAN JOHNSON

MIRACLE BOAT

A NOVEL

www.ambassador-international.com

Miracle Boat

ISBN: 978-1-64960-214-5
eISBN:978-1-64960-322-7
Library of Congress Control Number: 2022938917

Cover design by Hannah Linder Designs
Interior typesetting by Dentelle Design

Robinson, Phil Alden, director. *Field of Dreams.* Gordon Company, 1989. 1 hr. 47 min.

AMBASSADOR INTERNATIONAL
Emerald House
411 University Ridge, Suite B14
Greenville, SC 29601
United States
www.ambassador-international.com

AMBASSADOR BOOKS
The Mount
2 Woodstock Link
Belfast, BT6 8DD
Northern Ireland, United Kingdom
www.ambassadormedia.co.uk

The colophon is a trademark of Ambassador, a Christian publishing company.

Dedicated to my mother Frances Baker. You gave me life and taught me how to live. You have been there through the bad, the good, the extraordinary, the ordinary and the everyday. Thank you for cheering me on to shine!

Author's Note

When I was thirteen, my dad's suicidal death was a pivotal point in my life. It deepened my relationship with Christ and thrust me into leadership roles within my Boy Scout troop. I began talking to groups about overcoming depression, avoiding suicide, and how to comfort your loved ones who are grieving. Through all of this, there remained unanswered questions, though. This led me to write *Miracle Boat* to tell the story of overcoming grief of suicidal loss of loved ones and to help those who have had loved ones who have crossed over the threshold of death. My hope is that *Miracle Boat* helps the reader escape from the ongoing drama of life and will serve to remind us that we have Hope.

Chapter 1

My father's suicide spun my life 180 degrees. I was thirteen years old. Daddy's death devastated me but didn't surprise me. Daddy battled depression for six long years. Numerous times, I heard him make threats of taking his life. Every son needs his dad. How would I survive without mine?

God began to bring people into my life to fill the void left by my dad's death. The summer of my dad's death, I met John Millington. He became my best friend. At first he was a minister to me, then a mentor and a father figure. Our friendship went a step deeper—he was my best fishing buddy. As fishermen, we shared a passion passed onto us by our dads. It linked us with a shared passion passed on to us. It made us lovers of fishing vessels, lakes, rivers, and oceans.

John was the one person with whom I could talk about all things important to me—career, relationships, love, Jesus, the Bible, science, nature, miracles, and music. Our time together in a fishing boat was our mutual therapy session. Jumping in a boat, pushing away from the shore, and floating on water were release, relief, and restoration. When I needed guidance and direction, John provided it. When John needed support and encouragement, I provided it. It was back and forth—all connected by rod, reel, lure, and boat.

Then one day, I got the news that John had taken his life. John's suicide knocked me to my knees. Gone! Just like that, I was a survivor of two suicides of two dear people in my life.

From where did this come? I was not aware he was depressed. He did not tell me his pain, despair, his frustration, or his wanting a way out of this world.

When John Millington died, a part of me, Dalton Russell, died. John's death left me lost, confused, and laden with guilt. I prayed, *God, give me a chance to talk with John, to discover what went wrong to release my burden*

That's what I need! I want one more conversation with John and my dad. I ache to hear my dad's voice and have one last chance to tell him what he means to me. It's agonizing to need to have one more conversation with John and get answers to my questions.

But this is not how it works. Once a soul leaves this earthly world, we can talk to them, but we can't hear them or see them. Those conversations are gone. I wake up every day in Alabama grieving my loss, still trying to make the most of today.

Today is a homecoming. Homecoming for an old friend. Homecoming for a piece of my life history. Homecoming for a work of craftsmanship. A miracle is about to happen, and it looms on the horizon, coming to me on the shoulders of a trailer.

Today, John's boat is returning to Huntsville, Alabama. It was here in Huntsville that my fishing buddy, John Millington, bought his boat and made it his own. With his own hands, John turned the basic hull of a boat into a fishing machine. It was on this boat that John and I shared many fishing adventures. We ventured across Guntersville Lake to catch bass, black drum, and bluegill.

We drifted below the tailrace waters of Wheeler Dam, fishing and talking. Always talking.

About twenty years ago, John and his family moved from Huntsville to Idaho Falls, Idaho, to take a job and promotion with a counseling agency. Then about fifteen years ago, John and his family had moved back to Nashville, Tennessee, to be near family.

That's when things went downhill. I wasn't talking to John as much as before, and he had been back in the South a few months when I got a call from his wife, Joyce, telling me John had passed away. He had taken his own life by locking himself inside his car and letting the carbon monoxide painlessly take him out of this world.

Over my years, I have lost people close to me. I have lost grandparents, aunts, uncles, cousins, in-laws, and friends. My dad to suicide. And then two months after Daddy died, I met John. He was a new marriage and family counselor, with a specialty in marriage counseling, who joined the counseling agency where my mother worked. He greeted me that August day with a broad smile, shook my hand for what seemed like ten minutes, and said, "Dean, it's so nice to meet you." In a short time at the agency, he was highly regarded for restoring the relationships of husbands and wives. His greeting to me that day began a connection—from a connection, to minister, fishing buddy, mentor, and close friend.

The shock of why he took his own life hadn't worn off even though ten years have gone by since his passing. It made little sense to me. I did not know he was battling depression. He never told me. Why did this happen?

Though my dad had died decades before John, I had seen the progression of my dad's depression. I had even heard him insist to my mother that we would be better off if he just shot himself. I hadn't wanted to lose my dad, but it wasn't as much of a surprise as John's death, which brought renewed trauma.

Now, a piece of John was coming to my house—a gift willed to me by John himself, a gift given to me by his wife and children. John's boat was coming back to Huntsville.

In 1997, John sold his pop-up camper and bought a brand-new boat. It was a sixteen feet long SeaArk boat painted flat olive green. It was an aluminum shell with a bench seat in the back, exposed ribs in the middle, and an elevated casting deck in the front or bow. A friend of John's sold him a used outboard motor with twenty-five horsepower. John decided to use his carpentry skills to customize the boat in order to save money. That winter, John went to work transforming his boat shell into a customized fishing vessel that became the boat where John and I would share many fishing memories.

John cut plywood to make a flat floor over the ribs and create a raised back deck casting platform. He welded in a metal frame to extend the front deck and covered it with solid plywood. The decks and floor were covered with green marine carpet. Hatches were added for storage under the front deck. Padded swivel pedestal seats were placed on the front and rear deck. An electric trolling motor was placed on the bow with a hands-free foot pedal to steer the boat forward, backward, left or right while fishing with a rod and reel.

Over the course of weekends and holidays, John's wife, Joyce, and his two children, Patton and Amber, watched him in the garage spraying sawdust as he cut wood to build his craft. They told me a smile was always on his face while working in the garage, and he was always eager to show them the boat's progress.

The following spring, John invited me to join him at Guntersville Lake for the maiden voyage of his very own John Millington customized bass fishing boat. We met at a concrete ramp along the lake. John was standing on the wooden dock.

John said, “What do you think of my boat?”

“My goodness,” I said. “It’s wonderful!” It gleamed under the clear morning sky.

The hull was painted a flat olive green, similar to a World War II tank, and looked brand new. It also smelled new, with the scents of fresh cut wood, new carpet glue, and fresh vinyl seats.

“Get in,” said John, “and check out all of my storage.”

We got in the boat together, and John opened up every hatch for me to peer inside. There were two hatches on the front deck that were the length of my wrist to elbow for under-deck storage. It’s a fisherman’s dream to have all equipment stowed out of sight to keep the decks clear of anything to trip over.

Our fishing rods were placed in the horizontal foam cushion holders on the side gunnel. We were ready for our first adventure in the SeaArk. John started the outboard motor, and we were on our way across Guntersville Lake. The cool spring air raced over us as we sped over the open water. Across our faces were smiles as wide as a child on a Christmas morning. John’s chest stuck out with pride. He put in a tremendous amount of his time, creativity, and ingenuity to build something uniquely and solely his.

Lost in the scent of blooming honeysuckle flowers, I exclaimed, “Congratulations and great work on a finely built fishing boat. We’re going to have some fantastic adventures in this thing.”

Many years have passed since that maiden voyage in John Millington's boat. And many years have passed since our last fishing trip together.

One day, a shiny, blue dual-wheeled pick-up truck turned onto my street, towing a boat on a trailer. I was in the front yard trimming bushes when the truck, boat, and trailer stopped in front of our house.

"I have a delivery for Dalton Russell," said the truck driver as he got out of the cab.

"That's me," I answered.

"Great to see you, Mr. Russell," said the truck driver. "I'm Bill."

I shook his hand as we exchanged pleasantries and Bill glanced around at the surrounding hills. "This part of Alabama ain't what I expected it to be—all mountainous and such."

"This your first time to Huntsville?" I asked.

"Yes, sir," said Bill.

"Welcome." I smiled. "Most people think of Alabama as flat, rural farmland. They don't know that the Appalachian Mountain chain ends here—or begins here, depending on how you look at it."

Bill handed me a clipboard with a white invoice and a yellow check list behind it.

"Here's a note that came with it from Mr. Millington and a packet of information on the boat," said Bill.

I took the two manila yellow envelopes from him—one looked like a notecard, and the other large envelope contained owner's manuals and documents for the boat.

"Mr. Russell," said Bill, "let's take a walk around the boat and check off this list to make sure it arrived in the same shape it was in when I picked it up in Valdosta, Georgia."

"This is the first time in years that I have seen this boat," I said as we began our walk around. "It's not in the same shape as it was twenty years ago."

I noticed spots of wear and tear on the boat. The bow had a dent as long and wide as a soft drink bottle where the green paint was worn, exposing bare aluminum. Along the side were dents and dings where the boat had scraped against a rock or boat dock. The green carpet looked old and was peeling away from the plywood. The scent of mildew wafted up from the carpet. A silver drain in the floor had a screw missing and was loose. I pushed on it, and the drain sank through rotten wood. The trolling motor was secure to the boat, but the plastic motor head was cracked and held together with black duct tape. The outboard motor decals were peeling off of the cowling cover. Electrical tape held together wires on the steering tiller. There were spots of rust on the trailer. The inside of the boat looked and smelled like it had been left uncovered and drenched in rainwater. It was long past its shiny newness that gleamed in the spring sunshine on the lake the first time I saw it.

"That was all there when I picked it up from Mr. Millington," said Bill. "I've even got it checked and noted on the walk around with him down in Valdosta."

I completed the checklist, signed the white invoice, and handed the clipboard to Bill. "Mr. Russel, where ya want me to park it?"

"Put it in the backyard," I replied.

Bill backed the boat and trailer onto our concrete slab behind our house. As I unhooked the trailer from Bill's truck, my wife, Eileen, came out the back door with our eight-year-old son, Ned, bouncing along in front of her.

"Daddy, is this Mr. John's boat?" asked Ned.

"Yes, it sure is," I said.

My wife came up beside me and put her arm around my waist. Her shoulder-length, dark brown hair brushed my arm. "Dalton, it's here. You've been looking forward to this."

I put my arm around Eileen as Ned encircled my leg with his arms. "Yes, it's here. Bill, this is my wife, Eileen, and my son, Ned."

"Nice to meet you two," said Bill. "Mr. Russell and I are about done passing on the delivery of this boat here. I sure hope y'all will enjoy it."

"Thank you for bringing it to us," I said.

"Glad to," replied Bill. "Now, it's time to head back to Valdosta."

"Hope you have safe travel gettin' back home," Ned chirped politely.

"Well, thank you, Ned." Bill shook Ned's, Eileen's, and my hands. He got in his truck and drove out our driveway.

I looked at the boat and told Eileen and Ned, "Well, looks like I have a bit of a project on my hands to make some repairs to get this thing back into running condition."

"Can I get in, Daddy?" asked Ned. I picked him up and placed him on the floor of the boat.

Eileen walked to the back of the boat as her eyes gleaned when she saw the outboard motor.

"This is an outboard from the mid-eighties! This is an easy project to get running right! Dad would have loved to see this. I can take care of that for you." Eileen grew up the daughter of a marine mechanic on Guntersville Lake and eventually became employed in the family business. Like father, like daughter, and now it looked like her skills would come in handy with our new acquisition.

"It's all yours," I said. "What do y'all think of the boat?"

"I like Mr. John's boat," proclaimed Ned.

"Me, too," agreed Eileen.

"I guess it's our boat now," I said. "You know, John went by John B. Millington. Most people don't know his middle name—Bruce. What do you say we call this boat *Johnny Bruce?*"

Eileen looked at the boat, and then at me, smiled, and said, "I think that's fitting. It looks like a *Johnny Bruce.*"

"Yeah, Daddy," said Ned. "Our very own *Johnny Bruce.*"

Little did I know that in naming this boat—this hunk of metal, wood, and wires—we had awakened its soul.

Chapter 2

I was alone in the backyard with the boat.

Twenty-five years had passed since I had last seen *Johnny Bruce*. I opened up the hatches on the front casting deck. Water stood inside the hull. I cranked up the trailer tongue to raise the front of the boat to allow water to drain out the back. Nothing was coming out the back drain. Opening up the rear deck hatch, I saw water pooled an inch above the boat floor.

I poked a stick into the drain hole and cleared trash clogging the drain. Water started pouring out the drain like a wide-open kitchen faucet. The familiar scent of oil, gasoline, and grease hit me. To a boat person like me, it was the scent of many adventures on the water running an outboard motor in the days of two-stroke outboards. John's outboard motor ran a mix of oil in the gas tank to lubricate the parts. The smell took me back to my childhood, running my dad's 1956 Evinrude outboard. I breathed in slowly. It smelled like home.

The mildew scent smelled like a boat that had been sitting all summer in the rain. Patton had kept the boat covered in a driveway in South Georgia; but a heavy windstorm ripped the cover, and water seeped in over the summer. The front storage compartments were stuffed with water-soaked gear that endured those rainstorms. I pulled out the contents that were inside the storage locker. I felt like I was cleaning up a trusty dog that had been playing in the rain and mud. Just as I would do with a dog, I began talking to *Johnny Bruce*.

"Guess I better get the garbage bin over here and start cleaning you up," I murmured to the boat.

Into the trash went old rags, a yellow hat, rusty fishing lures, water-logged bags of plastic worms, and . . .

"Look down here," came a whisper from within.

"What?" I said out loud as I looked left and right. "Somebody here?"

"See the box," came the whisper again.

Beneath the deck was a familiar plastic box. The handwriting on top read, "Crappie Lures." It was John's handwriting. "Our old standby and go-to crappie lures," I spoke aloud as I grinned.

Inside the box were about ten sealed plastic bags with different plastic lure colors. It was a mix of pink, aquamarine, chartreuse, watermelon, silver, deep purple, green pumpkin, solid white, and flaked orange. This was *the* box John would pull out when we got serious about catching crappie. We attached those plastic bodies to jigs and dropped them near bridge pilings of Guntersville Lake. It was *the* box we used when we wanted to bring home a bunch of crappie to fry in oil for dinner. The box was still in good shape, but the rainwater ruined the lures inside. I opened the box; pulled out all the bags; got a whiff of the old plastic, gasoline, and mildew; then threw the bags away.

"The plastic box I can salvage," I said toward the whispering voice.

"Salvage more," whispered the voice.

"Who are you? Where are you?" I whispered softly. No answer came, just a gentle nudge to look further and deeper.

I dug further, filling the garbage bin. There was a good amount of extra weight on board with things not necessary for every fishing trip. I stretched out ropes across the length of the boat so they could dry in the sun. The carpet was in rough shape. With my bare hands, I pulled back the rotting carpet and saw the plywood underneath. It was turning brown from its exposure to sun and moisture. I would have to pull up all of this carpet and replace the plywood decks and floor.

"Learn from me," came the whisper.

"All right," I replied. Inspiration entered me lightning fast. "Rather than cover the decks with carpet, let's paint the plywood. It will drain and dry faster." No reply from the whisper. I guess this is a one-way conversation.

I opened the hatches as wide as they would go. The weather forecast predicted several days of hot, dry, and clear weather. No rain in sight. That would give time for *Johnny Bruce* to dry in the sun. I walked back to the house, turned, and looked at the boat—this boat I longed to have in my yard—and realized he was talking to me. He was guiding me. How would I explain this to Eileen?

That was enough work on the boat for today. "Dry out, my friend."

Chapter 3

I walked into the house and found Eileen standing near a window. The afternoon light created a backlit halo effect around her dark brown hair that was pulled back in a ponytail. Her green eyes met mine with a smile. For the first time in a while, I saw her look at me the same as the day we met on the lake dock of her dad's marina. She even had a black smudge mark on her cheek.

"Hey, Eileen," I said, "you look lovely with that black smudge on your left cheek."

"What?" she asked, "Oh, I guess I got that on me when looking at the outboard. You know me—I love old outboards. I like the boat, Dalton."

"I'm glad it's here," I said, "I'm glad *he's* here."

"John—is that who you mean?" asked Eileen.

"Yeah, I can't explain it." I looked around to see if the children were within earshot of listening, stood right next to Eileen, and whispered into her ear.

"*Johnny Bruce*, uh, the boat," I whispered. "I feel like it's talking to me."

"Huh?" asked Eileen.

I grabbed her hand and pulled her aside to the empty dining room and sat her down.

"What's going on, Dalton?" Eileen asked. "I haven't seen you this giddy for a long time!"

"Hear me out on this." I looked at Eileen with my eyebrows lifted and a half-smile on my face. "This is a little unbelievable, and you may think I'm crazy for what I'm about to tell you."

Eileen nodded at me, her eyebrows lifted, eyes wide, and head tilted to the right.

"*Johnny Bruce* . . . uh the boat," I said. "It's . . . well . . . it's talking to me."

Eileen's head snapped back with a look of astonishment. "It's talking to you? What does it sound like?"

"It's a hushed whisper," I answered. "It's like, 'Look over here.' I wouldn't be able to hear it if there was much of any other noise nearby. I had to put my ear toward the center compartment to hear it best, but the voice didn't repeat itself. The first time it repeated, I guess it got my attention, since I wasn't expecting it. It said, 'Lean in. Look over here.'"

"So," replied Eileen, "it's speaking to you *and* watching you." Her face told me she doubted me.

"Hmmm, I hadn't thought of it like that," I said. "So, it's a live presence. What in the world?"

"Does it sound like a male or female voice?" she asked as her head tilted to the left and her ponytail twitched.

"Male," I replied.

"Is it a voice you recognize?" Eileen asked. Her face crinkled up with her chin low, looking at me like I was a lunatic. Her eyes slightly squinted, and her eyebrows pushed down low.

"No, not at all," I answered. "It's like the voice in the movie *Field of Dreams*. I know it sounds cliché, but how else do I describe it?"

"You don't believe me. You think I'm crazy, don't you?" My voice rose, and my head tilted.

"Shhh, keep your voice down," she scolded me. "No, I believe you. Well, maybe not. I mean, it does sound pretty ridiculous. A hunk of metal and wood whispering to you? Come on, I've heard you tell lots of stories, but most of yours are exaggerated. And I'm definitely not ready to plow up our backyard and build a fishing pond and a dock large enough for a bass fishing team to gather."

"Okay, maybe I am crazy," I said, "but it sure seems real. I'm tellin' ya, I'm not making this stuff up. I heard a soft voice whispering to me. Then when I did what it said, I found something from my past—from *our* past. I told Eileen about the boxes of lures and how often John and I used them to catch crappie. I told her about the vision that had come to me to rebuild the boat, to make it better, and to make it our own.

"I feel compelled to follow the voice; it's guiding me. Do what it says, within reason, and go from there. We don't have a cornfield in our backyard. I'm not a farmer; I'm a marketing guy from an electronics company. I help build, sell, and promote electronics. Now, my experience with God has taught me to go with His flow. If you go against Him, guess Who will win?"

"It ain't going to be you." She grabbed my hand. "We've learned our lessons." She looked at me and her mouth relaxed into a warm smile.

"Yep, we sure have," I said as I squeezed her hand. Her touch and her eyes reminded me we were in this together. We may not know what was around the corner, but we felt we needed to make the first step. Eileen peered out the window. "So, what's next?"

I exhaled. "It's time to take apart the boat, repair, rebuild, and restore it. Get the motor running, get on the water, and see where *Johnny Bruce* takes us. Let's keep this to ourselves for now. I don't even think the kids are ready to hear this. My gut is telling me not to doubt or question, yet believe, follow, and trust."

For years, this woman was supportive in endeavors to make things better for our family. However, now, she was much more realistic and added caution to my dreams and ambitions. We both had been hurt by people who squashed us when we thought things were going well. I knew when I pushed too far into a fantasy that couldn't become reality.

"Agreed," said Eileen. "Now, Dalton, look at me. This isn't you making a career change; this is you fixing up a boat. It's like a hot rod in the garage that needs rust removed, carburetor cleaned, and fresh paint. Let's get to work on your hot rod—just not right now. It's time to eat dinner."

Chapter 4

On Monday, I was back at work at Rocket City Technology as director of marketing. As part of my job, I traveled the country connecting with our clients and speaking to prospects who were looking for computer systems that could withstand vibration and moisture exposure. The parts and connections had to be stronger and resist one thing that electricity doesn't like—water. Much of my time was speaking, but it was usually one-on-one or one-on-four with decision-makers. Occasionally, I would speak to groups of fifty or more people. I loved it because I was able to engage more people in one setting. The larger the audience became, the more encouraged I felt to keep going because there was more audience reaction.

When I was a college student, I was on a team that gave weekly Bible studies or sermons to lunch gatherings at a Christian student group. I then joined a traveling drama group, where we spoke to youth groups across the state. I mixed humor into the skits to illuminate Bible stories. Sometimes, people said, "Dalton, you would make a great preacher. You are a talented storyteller, and we connect with what you are saying."

The opportunity presented itself when John moved to Idaho. He left a vacant spot open at the small, local church, where he served as a bi-vocational pastor in addition to his full-time counseling practice. John told me I should apply to be their next bi-vocational pastor. He would give a favorable reference. I applied, interviewed, and preached one Sunday. They hired me. It provided extra income and allowed me to exercise my gift of public speaking. I honed my craft of storytelling, preaching, and teaching. To me, preaching and teaching was the fun side of church work. It's like the ride operator at an amusement park. You get to see the anticipation and excitement of the children as they line up and get on the ride. Then, you see their smiling faces when their ride is complete. The most delightful response is hearing a child say, "Let's go again!"

What you don't notice at an amusement park are the people arriving early to oil the machines, clean dirty restrooms, and take out the trash. It's necessary, and someone has to do it. People are hired and paid to do this work. Now, imagine replacing the mechanics, janitors, and waste engineers with volunteers. Add to this that everyone has their own idea and opinion on how the operation works and believes their method is better than others, and these volunteers get to vote on who their leaders are going to be. Do we keep the park director, or do we replace them with who we think would be better?

Welcome to church work—the art and craft of operating a church business in a local community! I did not enjoy the church work of weekday evening committee meetings, the business of running a building, or the politics of keeping people happy like you do business customers. Since I was a bi-vocational pastor, every church member pitched in to be the Body of Christ, doing their part to keep the church going. We had a team that came in weekly to clean the church, mow the grass, and maintain the facility. As in most churches, the deacons and elders joined with me in serving the community by doing in-home visits and hospital visits to the sick and maintained the communication network.

In my time as pastor of Valley Church, I planned an idea for a story I hoped one day would become a book. I just never made the time to write it down. Instead, it just sat in my head as an idea that gathered dust.

After my first child, Eva, was born, it became too much for me to work full-time, be a pastor, and be a dad to a baby girl. It was putting a strain on my family life. The church expected Eileen and Eva to be at every event when the church doors were open. Sometimes, Eileen and Eva needed to be at home or elsewhere, and that bothered some people. Lovingly, the people of Valley Church understood that my choice was best for my family. I resigned as their pastor to narrow down to one job so that I could better focus on being a dad. This meant I had to step away from preaching. I missed it.

Professionally, I channeled my talents and gifts to be a marketer with Rocket City Tech. I was a marketer who helped somebody else build a business, a product, or a brand. It provided a decent living for my family; but it left me unfulfilled, especially when I traveled away from home, missing out on Eva's dance lessons or Ned's t-ball practice. I put my head down and gave it my best because my purpose was to take care of Eileen, Eva, and Ned.

"Good mornin', Cathy," I greeted our receptionist at Rocket City Tech.

"How was your weekend?" Cathy asked as she peered up from her desk with a warm smile.

"It was good—a little extra time with the kids." Behind her desk was a photo of a smiling toddler in a blue, plastic wagon, and my heart swelled. "Aww, is that Claire's new wagon?"

Cathy's eyes lit up with pride as she turned to pick up the photo. "Yes, she loves this wagon. She rode in it and played all weekend. She is fond of wheels and loves 'go-go,' as she calls it."

"Love it! She is a cutie," I replied as Cathy's desk phone rang. I waved to Cathy and went on to my office, barely sitting down at my swivel desk chair when I got a call from the production floor.

"Hey, Dalton," said Herb Ericson through the speakerphone. "Are you here?"

"Yeah, Herb, what can I do for ya?" I answered.

"We need you to look at this thing we're building for AeroWorks out in California."

I told him I would be there in a moment, arose from my desk, and headed down the brightly lit hallway with almond-painted walls. The hall was lined with framed photographs of clients using our products.

After a short walk, I entered the high bay production section—high on anticipation. I enjoyed working with the men and women out here. They were the innovators, the tinkerers, and the quality control of the products we sold for Rocket City Tech. Herb Ericson and Clyde Williams were two mechanical engineers who had the mind of engineers but the fix-it nature of wood carpenters and auto mechanics. They reminded me of my grandfather, who was a carpenter, and my dad, who was an engineer and tinkerer.

Clyde was from the small town of Lineville, Alabama, which is in the shadow of Mount Cheaha, the highest point in Alabama at an elevation of twenty-four hundred feet. Clyde spoke with a distinct Southern accent from his region, where a word ending in the letter *a* was spoken as an *r*. When Clyde talked about his daughter,

Linda, he would say, "Lind*er* and her family are coming to see us this weekend. You know they like to go to the races down there at Talladigg*er* Speedway."

Herb Ericson hailed from the small Alabama town of Scottsboro, which is in the shadow of Sand Mountain and touches the banks of Guntersville Lake. These two guys in their late fifties had been the dynamic duo of ingenuity at Rocket City Tech for quite some time. In typical fashion, they were leaning over their wood-topped workbench, peering through their reading glasses perched on the end of their noses. They looked toward me as I approached their bench.

"Dalton, old boy," greeted Herb. "Would you call AeroWorks and tell them we have a problem. Ask if we can apply our fix to it? Their design works, but our improvement will make it last." They showed me the problem they were having, and the durability fix they discovered.

"Sure, I can do that," I answered.

"If you need to, Clyde can explain it to them," said Herb. "He's the communicator between the two of us back here." The shop roll-up door was open nearby, and I saw an old outboard motor mounted to a static tank of water.

"What's this y'all got here?" I asked.

"Oh, that," answered Clyde. "That's a minor side project me and Herb are working on."

"I love old outboard motors, you guys," I answered. "I just got a an outboard from the mid-1980s. I'm in the process of fixing it up to get it running again. These old machines are easier to work on than the new models."

"Yeah, me and Herb here are motorheads, and we've always enjoyed working on outboards," said Clyde. "When we have some downtime, we tinker on this old outboard. One problem with them is they mix gasoline and oil. Most of today's stuff has separate oil and gas tanks, which puts out less smoke and doesn't dump unused gas or oil into the water."

"Yeah, I know about that blue smoke that comes out," I said. "I used to see it all the time on my dad's Evinrude from the 1950s."

"Then you know what we're talking about," said Herb. "Clyde and I can't afford one of the newfangled outboards with all of its fancy electronics, but we can work on these old outboards and keep them runnin' for years. Those new machines cost thousands, and you have to hire an electrical engineer to work on them if they have a problem. They sip gas, though."

Clyde interjected, "We got to thinkin', can we make these old motors run cleaner? Our tinkerin' led us to make this here computer chip valve to mix the oil and gas with just what the engine needs with no excess thrown into the exhaust."

"Lookie here," said Herb as he pulled on the outboard's starter cord and cranked up the engine.

"There's no smoke!" My eyes widened in amazement. "How'd y'all do that?"

"Just a bit of mountain rocket engineering." Herb chuckled.

"Me and Herb have been testing out the little thing this spring when we've been bass fishing," said Clyde. "Our motors aren't leaving a greasy oil trail like they used to, and the motor's still runnin' fine. We worried we would burn up a power head. Instead, we're burnin' less fuel than ever and buyin' less oil than we used to."

"It's our fun project," said Herb. "Aerospace industry may be our bread and butter, but for me and Clyde, our passion is fishing on a budget. Neither of us is the church-goin' type like you, Dalton, but ain't our responsibility as humans to be caretakers of this world we live in? Aren't we supposed to take better care of our resources?"

"Excellent point, Herb," I said. "Have you shown this to Milo or Bob?"

"Oh no," Herb replied. "This is a fun project. Besides, Milo ain't gonna listen to us, and Bob's too busy countin' the money already flowing in to look at something new."

On the bench was one of the outboard chip valves Clyde and Herb had built. I picked it up, turned it around in my hands, and looked at it closely. It was a sealed aluminum block about the size of a matchbox. On one side was a plastic computer chip sealed with a waterproof, plastic cover.

"Gentlemen, I'm impressed. It would be great to get more of Rocket City Tech into the marine industry."

"Hey," said Clyde, "you like to fish. When you drive to the lake, you pass many houses, yards, and marinas that have old boats that are sittin' around. Families can't afford a new boat and can't fix the old one. They stop boating altogether and lose interest."

Herb chimed in, "We've used our own money for materials, and Rocket City's tools and shop to make several of these things for some friends who have old boats. We probably have ten of them out runnin' on boats. They are our test group, I guess." Clyde and Herb laughed.

"So, what's the verdict?" I asked.

"Our test group has given us feedback, and we've made some modifications," answered Clyde. "We probably have over one hundred hours of use out of it. No one has blown an engine, and everyone tells us they are buying less gas with this thing."

"We found a way for people to get those old motors up and runnin' again for cheap," said Herb.

"It won't ever amount to anything," said Clyde. "Dalton, you're the first person who's come out to look at it."

"Gentlemen, thank you for showing this to me." I shook my head in admiration for what these two engineers had created. "I'll get back up front and call AeroWorks. Clyde, I will conference call you in with me. So, why don't you join me up front in fifteen minutes?"

Clyde looked up from under his ball cap with only one eye showing. "Okay, let me clean up from this oil and grease."

Chapter 5

Clyde came into my office, and we made our call to AeroWorks. After the call, I told Clyde, "Come with me for just a moment."

We walked over to Milo Whitney's office—the chief of operations at Rocket City Tech. I knocked on his door.

"Come in," said Milo, barely looking away from his computer screen. "Hey, Dalton and Clyde."

"Morning." I pushed open the half-closed door. "Hey, you got a minute?"

"A minute is about all I have. What's up?" asked Milo.

"You know how I've been saying Rocket City Tech should do more in the marine industry?"

"Yeah, Dalton, I remember." Milo exhaled as his shoulders dropped while he kept looking at his computer screen.

"Clyde and Herb have stumbled across something that would be beneficial to the marine industry," I said.

"Oh yeah?" asked Milo. "How so, Clyde?"

"Well, sir, Herb and I have this electronic chip and valve we've come up with to use on old outboards to . . . "

"Wait a minute," said Milo, finally looking away from his computer screen. "A part for *old* outboard motors? We are a high-tech firm working with aerospace manufactures and innovative defense equipment manufacturers. Why would we want to step back and work to build parts on vintage engines?"

I excitedly arched my eyebrows. "It's a brilliant market that we haven't tapped; plus, we make great electronics that seal out water and moisture. That's what the marine industry—"

"Let me stop you right there, Dalton," said Milo. "We already have a line of products in the marine world. There is no need to introduce anything new. What we have is selling. You keep promoting our existing product line to our customers. Clyde, you get back to the shop and keep on doing, er, what you do. Now, please excuse me, gentlemen, but your minute is up."

"Thank you, sir," Clyde and I answered in unison.

I walked Clyde down the hall back toward the production area.

"We told you, Dalton," said Clyde. "They ain't interested in anything different around here."

My eyes squinted, and my lips pursed in thought. "They used to be. You and Herb keep me up to date on your testing. Can you make me one to test on my outboard?"

"Sure," answered Clyde. "Send me an email with the year and horses on it."

"Will do. What do y'all call this thing?" I asked.

Clyde smiled and said, "We call it the Green Wave."

For a moment, I was getting excited again about working at Rocket City Tech. I could see the amazing potential and a chance to work with companies that would be fun for me. Finally, something beyond the stale, same old, same old. Idea shot down again.

In his role as operations chief, Milo and I had a cordial working relationship. He had been in this role when I came aboard Rocket City

Tech, but we never hit it off. Milo liked being the boss and kept himself distant from the employees. He was jealous of how well I got along with everyone in my relationships beyond the workplace. I couldn't shake the pastoral skills of connecting with people and being likable. That's why I was in sales and marketing, and he managed the operation.

I was hired by Bob King, who was the owner of Rocket City Tech. He and I hit it off from the very beginning. Bob was a car guy who loved muscle cars from the 1960s and 1970s. He and his family went boating on a regular basis. Our families gathered together on his boat for relaxing summer weekends and barbecues.

When I came on board, I had ideas for new products and improvements to our existing products. I told Bob about them, and he always said, "Run it past Milo and see what he says. He is the one who has to get the crew to build it."

The first time I brought an innovative idea to Milo, he made it clear that I must follow the proper chain of command. I didn't go to Bob and *then* Milo. I ran any ideas past Milo first, then *he* would take it to Bob. "Stay in line, follow the rules, don't rock the boat, Dalton."

Over the years, not a single new idea has been carried out. One afternoon, I was walking down the hallway near Milo's office and overheard him on the phone with Bob, who was in his office. He would not even step out of his office to see Bob in person. Milo's office door was open about an inch as I heard him say, "Dalton's up to his schemes again; you aren't interested in creating a new actuator switch for ailerons are you?"

With that kind of presentation, Milo was setting up Bob to say no.

As much as I missed my family when I traveled, I became frustrated the more time I spent at the office. That's how I got to know Clyde and Herb because they showed me how our products worked, which helped me present them to our customers. Milo seemed happier when I was away from the office. Thankfully, a good number of our customers were here in North Alabama with such a prominent aerospace industry presence with the Department of Defense. I learned to be cordial with Milo by keeping our interaction to a minimum. Rocket City Tech provided a healthy stream of income for my family, so I stayed. I got along well with the rest of the people at the company. I wasn't going to let one sour person ruin it for the rest of us.

Chapter 6

The last father and son memory I had with Daddy was of us fishing together. It was a June Sunday morning that we ventured to Town Creek on Guntersville Lake. I was thirteen years old, and my passion for fishing was growing; I was eager to try out my bait-casting reel for the first time. After reading about bass fishing in *Bassmaster* magazine, practicing my casting from our back patio, and polishing the gears on my new round bait-caster, I was ready for the real thing.

That summer day many years ago exemplified every fishing trip with my dad. We hooked up the boat and motor to the car the night before. We awoke at dark thirty, ate breakfast, and headed out the driveway before sunrise. In the morning darkness, I looked back from the passenger seat to watch the boat motor pivot as we turned onto the street.

Two-lane roads took us from Huntsville toward Guntersville. The streets were empty as sunrise brightened the sky. The air smelled crisp with a mix of river water and wafts of bacon being cooked inside nearby kitchens.

We traveled through a tunnel of trees carpeting the short, stubby mountains of North Alabama as ripples of sunlight danced through the windshield. We rounded a curve and broke into the open sky as we crossed the Town Creek Bridge to our beloved Guntersville Lake, Town Creek, and launch ramp.

Many times before, Daddy and I made this same journey, and it was always special. The boat and motor spent more time in the yard and garage than on the lake. We only went fishing in the boat about three times a year. The more I read *Bassmaster* magazine, the more I wanted to fish and be in a fishing tournament. You can't catch fish if you don't have a hook in the water. In my backyard, I was catching twigs, leaves, and crabgrass—but no fish. On this day, at a lake instead of the yard, I had the opportunity to catch fish.

We launched the boat for one last fishing adventure together. Daddy cranked the Evinrude, belching out a cloud of blue smoke that emitted a scent of burned oil and gasoline. This scent comforted me because I have an admiration for the internal combustion engine. I had played in the garage around the gas cans, quarts of oil, and grease guns. My nose associated this as a pleasant aroma.

We were off on our magic carpet, zooming across the glassy water. Mist blew across my face like soft, tiny water needles splashing my skin. Three feet vertical, circular columns of fog rose from the water like ghostly shaped silver traffic cones awaking to meet the sun's warmth.

We went under the bridge at idle speed and then throttled to full power—not much for a motor with less than ten horses but faster and more direct than we could walk there. We motored into a cove, and Daddy turned off the engine.

"Well, let's see what we can catch," said Daddy. "I see some willow flies beginning to hatch. I believe I'll try a popping bug on-the-fly rod."

"Okay," I said. "'I'll try a spinner bait."

Daddy cast the fly line and caught bluegill, pumpkinseed, and shell cracker—part of the whole bream fish family.

At the front of the boat, I cast and reeled, then cast and reeled with not a single bite. Bait-casting reels take practice learning how to slow the revolving spool with your thumb. The spool spins, rolling out the line through rod guides with the weight of the lure. If the spool spins too fast, the line may roll back onto the spool, creating a tangle of line on the spool that looks like a bird's nest. I call it a backlash. Feeling the line with your thumb, you apply pressure on the spool of the line to slow it down or feather the spool. I wanted to get better at my feathering the spool skill.

"You sure you don't want to try some crickets and catch some bream?" asked Daddy. "They're all around us."

"Yeah, I know," I said. "I'm happy with my bait-caster."

Daddy was smiling as he caught fish, and for the first time in years, I saw a glimmer in him that was missing. He was enjoying fishing again.

Depression had fallen over him over the past six years and stolen his enjoyment of life. At thirteen, I didn't know if it was me he didn't enjoy being with or if it was me getting older and learning more about life than that of an innocent boy who saw the world with endless optimism. At that moment, my daddy was back.

With each fish caught, the wider Daddy smiled and the louder he laughed. His joy was contagious, a relief.

"You happy, Dalton?" asked Daddy.

"I am, Daddy," I answered, eyes gleaming as I reeled in my chartreuse spinner bait.

"That's all that matters," he replied.

As the sun rose higher in the sky, the shade of the trees diminished; the heat rose; and the fish catching slowed down.

"Well, I guess we should move. Maybe some deeper water," said Daddy, and I agreed.

Daddy turned around, pulled on the starter rope on the Evinrude. Daddy put it into forward gear, and we idled out of the cove.

"Sounds different," said Daddy. The engine pitch was higher than before, but not as loud. He turned the throttle to full power, but we weren't moving much faster.

Being the mechanical engineer, Daddy said, "She's running on only one cylinder instead of two." He shut off the motor, popped open the engine cowling, and checked the spark plug wires.

"They are snug. Not sure what's wrong," he said. While he did that, I cast some more to maximize my time to fish the lake.

Daddy closed the cowling. "Let's see how she runs now."

He started the motor, put it into gear, and throttled up no faster than before.

I saw his face, and the despondent look had returned.

Throttling back to idle speed, he said, "I think we may have a bad electrical coil. I fixed them about eight years ago. I coated them with epoxy to seal the cracks. Guess they have run their course. Those are the original coils from '56."

"Dalton, I don't think we will get around the lake too fast. It's getting hot, and lunchtime is coming. I think we should head home."

I was disappointed. I could stay out there all day. However, 4:30 in the morning was two hours before my usual wake time, and I was feeling drowsy.

We secured the boat to the trailer and drove home from Guntersville Lake. Daddy was quieter on the trip home; I wished he would talk more.

On the ride home, Daddy said, "Dalton, I want you to know that I love you very, very much. I want what is best for you, and it's all because I truly love you."

"I know," I said in quiet, teenage-boy fashion. "I love you very much, Daddy." I stared straight ahead at the road, uncomfortable with the emotional talk between father and son. I appreciated him saying it, as a comfort blanket fell over sensing the meaning in Daddy's words.

"Dalton, I don't know how much longer your mother and I will be together," he said. "I guess you can tell we have been fighting a good bit."

Hearing this, my emotions fell flat, and I stared straight ahead. "Yeah, I have," I said. "Y'all still talking about divorce?"

"Yeah, we are." Daddy sighed. "I don't know that your mother can keep putting up with me, but it may be for the best."

"Will you still take me fishing?" Tears welled up behind the lenses of my black polarized sunglasses. I didn't want him to know I was crying.

"Of course, I will," he said. "Spending time with you and your sister will always be important to me. I love you."

This was not the first time this topic came up. I could truly feel that Daddy loved me and that he wanted what was best for me.

When we got home, we unhooked the boat, put the motor back on its stand in the garage, stored our tackle, and went inside to tell Mother of our day's adventure.

Within the next week, Daddy began to unravel, and he and Mother argued constantly. It got ugly. I don't even want to think about it, much less write about it.

One week after our fishing trip, he left this earth. After a six-year battle with depression and suicide threats, the depression won.

I can still smell the exhaust surrounding the car in the woods where he had taken his life. A piece of garden hose stretched from the exhaust pipe to a crack in the front driver's side window. Daddy's body had already been removed from the car when I arrived there with my mother. To this day, when I smell that exhaust from any other car, I am instantly taken back to that moment staring at the car—the same car we took to the lake a week ago—where my daddy's final moments were on this earth. I didn't like the smell of this exhaust and the memory that it emitted.

My life was never the same after that. In some ways, 180 degrees for the good, and in some ways, 180 degrees for the bad. Every child needs *both* of their parents to raise them. I missed my dad. When a parent dies before his child hits adulthood, the child's life is radically disrupted. Some growth will always be missing.

God would bring into my life many more dads to help fill the gap of the one I missed.

Chapter 7

On Saturday morning, I opened up the garage door and felt the cool spring air fill as sunlight shone on *Johnny Bruce* parked inside. Rich was rolling his truck to a stop in our driveway. Today was a new beginning.

"Ya ready to get started on this boat project?" asked Rich as he got out of his truck in our driveway.

"Yep, ready to go." I reached out and shook Rich's hand.

After being married to my dad, my mother had been in no hurry to remarry, and I can't blame her. My mother is a saint. However, Rich is my stepdad after she finally remarried. Rich is a wonderful man, and he takes excellent care of Mother. We also get along pretty well.

"Let me get my tools," said Rich.

The boat had been sitting in the backyard for about a month. I took some time to gather resources and come up with a plan on how to restore *Johnny Bruce*. Over that month, I spent time around the boat and continued to hear the voice whisper some guidance.

"I think I have everything we need to put in some new floors and decks," I said.

I focused my free thought moments on how to fix the boat. At one point, I told Eileen, "This thing is therapy for me. It's helping me deal with losing John."

After losing John, I put my emotions on a shelf and tucked them away to make it through the daily routine of life. We had a child during that time. He started elementary school while our daughter Eva started high school.

When I talked about the boat with Eileen, she would look at me with a gleam in her eyes. "Your spark is returning. It's good for you. You are talking about the good times with John. It's nice to see you smiling more. I think he is in this boat, and you are reconnecting. You are getting back some of what the two of you had—a connection to the water. A connection to fishing. A connection to boats."

"Yeah," I replied, "but it feels even bigger than that, and I can't put my finger on it. I can't describe it. It just feels bigger."

Now, we began the labor of demolition. Rich and I pulled out the screwdrivers, wrenches, sockets, crowbars, and hammers. We removed the trolling motor and every exterior part so we could remove the floor on the front and rear deck. We pried up the plywood to expose the framework underneath and removed the old wiring.

Meticulously, we took apart the interior of the boat John built. Instead of throwing things in the trash heap, we used the old parts as templates to cut new wood decks and guide us where to install new wiring. This was the gift John left for us. He did all the measurements, cutting, and installing. All we had to do was see what was there, test it to see if it was still good, and replace or reinstall.

It was a blur of activity for Rich and me. Eileen came to check on us. My son, Ned, came to see if he could work with us.

"Daddy, can I help?" asked Ned.

"I would love for you to help," I answered. "But for now, we are using some pretty sharp and dangerous tools. Let me and Grandpa

Rich get out all the old, and then you can help us put in the fresh stuff. How does that sound?"

"Okay, Daddy," said Ned. The rest of the day he was in and out of the house. He rode his bike in the driveway, played with his toy helicopters and gliders, rearranged his yard spinners, and monitored what we were doing. He wanted to be near the action, just as I always wanted to be near the action when Daddy and Granddaddy were working on their projects. I learned how to use tools by watching them.

As we dismantled the boat, not once did I hear the whisper. Not once did the boat speak to me. I said nothing to Rich, wary that he would think I was crazy. *Maybe it's said everything it needs to at this point. Maybe it's just waiting on us to get this part complete. Been noisy, too—hard to hear a whisper,* I thought.

We installed the new wiring. We cut fresh wood, drilled new holes, and prepared to secure the floor and decks to the aluminum boat ribs and frame. Instead of solid plywood, we used ten-inch-wide planks that were one-inch thick with spacing between each plank. It looked more like a backyard deck than a solid boat floor. Instead of laying carpet, we varnished the wood to make it waterproof and allow the natural wood to shine through.

The varnished decks and floors were drying on sawhorses. They would sit overnight to be ready to receive another coat of varnish in the morning.

"Well, I'm exhausted," I said. "Let's call it a day. Besides, do you smell that?"

"Oh yeah, smells like an Italian restaurant," said Rich. A door was all that separated the garage from the house. On the other side of the door was our kitchen, which was emitting an aroma of tomato sauce, cooked onions, garlic, and oregano. We breathed in this delightful, mouth-watering bouquet.

"I think Eileen has cooked us up some spaghetti with meat sauce to recharge our batteries," I said as a blue car pulled into our driveway and parked next to Rich's truck. It was my mother. She got out of her car wearing an orange, cotton top and brown capri pants with sandals on her feet.

"Hey, Mother," I called.

"Hello, gentlemen," said Mother.

"Great to see you, sweetheart."

Eileen invited me to dinner," Mother explained as she reached out for a hug.

I hugged Mother, "I'm sweaty, so not sure if you want to hug me or not."

"Oh, I'm happy to get a hug from my son, anyway." Her hair was short and gray, but her eyesight was still strong.

Mother looked to her left and to her right to make sure no one else was around and whispered to me, "I've got something to tell you about a visit I had."

"A visit?" I asked. "Who came by to see you?"

"Not that kind of visit," she said. "It was a visit from your dad."

Chapter 8

Mother opened the door into the house, and we came in behind her. Ned was coloring at the table when he saw his grandmother.

"Grandma!" Ned ran to give his grandmother a hug.

"Well, hello, sweetie." Mother wrapped her arms around her grandson. "It's great to see you."

Rich and I inhaled the delightful aroma of an Italian meal.

"Eileen, whatever you've made smells wonderful," said Rich.

I nodded in agreement.

I looked at Eileen. "As much as it pains me to step away from this wonderful meal you are preparing, I gotta take a shower. Be back in a jiffy."

Eileen looked at me with a grin and nodded. "Yeah, Dalton, you stink, and there is sawdust in your hair. Dinner should be ready when you get back."

While getting dressed after my shower, I noticed our jewelry box lid was open on the dresser in our bedroom. The four-drawer wood box contained Eileen's rings, earrings, pendants, and necklaces. The bottom drawer contained my tie tacks, lapel pins, and cufflinks. I went across the room to close it when I felt a nudge to open my drawer. A silver pin caught my eye. It was a one-inch silver pin of Snoopy dancing in a space suit.

I smiled when I saw it and said, "Daddy, from the hands of Frank Borman to your hands is how you told the story."

NASA astronauts handed out Silver Snoopy Awards to people who made significant contributions to the space program.

Daddy led a team of people that built the swing arms on the tower gantry for the *Saturn V* moon rocket. Yes, that rocket—*the* rocket—that launched all the missions to the moon. Daddy was very proud of his work on NASA's Project Apollo. The swing arms were the red, metal structure that held the rocket in place until it lifted off the ground and began its flight toward space. As soon as the rocket began to rise from the launch pad, the swing arms had to move away from it within seconds to avoid snagging it in flight. That would have led to an explosion—or, as Daddy calmly called it, "A bad day."

Daddy worked long hours for months on end to get the swing arms to perform perfectly. There was no margin for error.

After *Apollo 8's* first mission to the moon in December 1968, the astronaut crew that flew the mission—Frank Borman, Jim Lovell, and Bill Anders—came to visit Huntsville's Marshall Space Flight Center—the NASA facility responsible for building NASA's mighty rocket.

In January 1969, the crew made its rounds to thank the people who made their mission possible. Daddy's boss invited him to meet them. Inside one of the high-bay buildings at Marshall Space Flight Center, Frank Borman was walking around shaking everyone's hands and saying, "Thank you for your service."

Astronaut Borman stepped out in front of the crowd and spoke to all of them. "Is Sanders Russell here? Come on up."

Daddy walked in front of Borman, who said to Daddy, "Sir, what is your role in Apollo?"

Daddy said, "It's not a big one, Colonel Borman. I helped make the swing arms."

Borman looked straight into Daddy's eyes and said, "I understand that you led the team that made the swing arms. Thanks to your work, they pulled away from the rocket right on time and let us fly to the moon. Here."

Borman reached into his pocket and pulled out the silver Snoopy award pin.

"This is for you, Mr. Russell," said Frank Borman.

"Thank you, Mr. Russell," said Borman while shaking Daddy's hand.

Daddy told us the story for years afterward. "I received this pin from the hands of Frank Borman. It's small but a significant recognition for my team's hard work on the greatest adventures of the twentieth century.

"Frank Borman probably handed out a bunch more of these lapel pins, but there are only four hundred thousand Americans that were worthy of receiving it, too. That's how many worked on Apollo."

After Daddy died, Mother gave it to me to keep because I was the space history nut in the family.

There was a knock on the bedroom door.

"Come in," I said.

The door opened, and Mother said, "Dinner is ready. Come join us, Son."

I put the pin back in the drawer and joined my family for dinner.

"Smells as delicious as an Italian restaurant!" Seated around the rectangle table were Rich, Mother, Ned, Eva, Eileen, and myself.

"Thank you. Now, let's thank God for our food," said Eileen as we all joined hands.

We gave thanks and passed around the dishes, filling our plates with spaghetti pasta, marinara meat sauce, garlic bread, and corn niblets. From Eva's childhood, whenever we ate spaghetti, she always wanted corn niblets. It was an odd mix, but it helped her eat her spaghetti.

"Thanks for making the corn, Mom," said Eva.

"Eva," I began, "what have you been up to today?"

"I've been working on my physics class project," said Eva. "It's not my best class, but I'm really trying."

"Is there anything we can help you with?" asked Eileen.

"No, Mom, not now," answered Eva.

"Your mom is great at anything to do with math," I said. "You want to make her day, ask her to help with a math problem."

Eileen started bouncing a little in her seat and said, "Oh, yeah, I can show you more ways than one to come to a solution; how to build a bridge out of toothpicks that will stand up to some heavyweight and . . ."

Eva's chin dropped; she sighed and peered at Eileen through half-closed eyes. "Mom, calm down. Don't worry—I'll let you know if I need some help."

Eileen looked deflated, and we all laughed seeing her being shot down with a chance to utilize her math skills.

"Your mom has a gift for math—thank goodness because I don't," I said.

"But your dad is great at history," said my mother.

"Hey, Eileen," I said, "hang on because tomorrow I need your help if you have time."

"Oh?" asked Eileen.

"How would you like to get the old outboard running?"

"Great!" squealed Eileen. "Grease under the fingernails? Carburetor rebuild? Replace the impeller?"

"Yes, yes, and yes," I answered. "Make your dad proud!"

We ate our dinner together. Then the kids excused themselves to play in their rooms. That left us adults at the dinner table.

My mother leaned over and spoke in a soft voice. "Let me tell you what I experienced over the past couple of days. I think y'all will find it interesting."

"Okay," said Eileen and I in unison. We looked at each other and laughed.

"Do y'all believe in ghosts?" asked Mother.

Eileen and I looked at each other as Rich and Mother looked at us to gauge our reaction.

"Yeah, Diane," said Eileen, "we do. I've had some experiences with them, I guess. Dalton thinks I'm crazy when I tell him about it, but maybe it's the Cherokee in me. Dalton always comes around to believe me, though."

"If it's the Cherokee in you, Eileen," said Mother, "maybe it's the Irish in me." A smile spread across Mother's face. "Two nights ago, I woke up with a dry mouth, so I went to the kitchen to get some water. I didn't turn the lights on, so I wouldn't wake myself up too much. There was enough glow in the house from the outside streetlights to find my way. I shuffled into the kitchen and next to the refrigerator was a white figure hovering there that was just about as tall as the fridge. When I entered the kitchen, he turned and looked at me, and I saw a smile on his face. Then he vanished. At first, I was shocked. But that immediately went away, and I felt a sense of peace. He—well, the ghost—looked to be male and was wearing this gray-and-black checkered shirt. Looked like a flannel shirt."

"Reminds me of a shirt Granddaddy wore in his carpentry shop," I said.

Mother looked at me and pointed her finger at me as she closed one eye and said, "That's what I thought, too."

"That's amazing, Diane!" said Eileen. "Did it—I mean, did *he*—say anything?"

"No. I got the smile; and I saw him look at me; and that was it. I don't know what he was doing there in the kitchen—getting a drink or just waiting for me to see him. When I showed up, I think I scared him, and he disappeared. Daddy has been gone for a while now, but I always feel like he and Mother are around me. Now, I have visual proof that he is there."

"What a story," said Eileen. "You know, shortly after Eva was born, I was here at home by myself with her while Dalton was at work. Eva was sick and struggling to breathe while she lay in her crib. I heard her on the monitor struggling and ran to her crib to pick her up. I placed her on my shoulder, and she immediately sounded better. But worry and fear were flowing through me. Suddenly, in the corner of my eye, I saw a figure. I thought it was Dalton, but he wasn't here. The figure was standing in the doorway watching us. I jumped back at first, but then peace washed over me. Almost as soon as I saw the figure, he disappeared, just like you said your dad did in the kitchen."

"When I got home," I said, "Eileen had this big, bug-eyed look. As soon as I walked in the door, she ran to me, hugged me, and said, 'I'm so glad to see you.' I said to her, 'You kinda look like you saw a ghost.' She said, 'I believe I did.'"

"I couldn't wait to tell him," said Eileen. "And sending it in a text message or phone call just didn't seem to do it justice. I told Dalton the figure I saw seemed to wear a red and white shirt with short sleeves."

"Sanders!" said Mother. "It sounds like Sanders."

"Yeah, I thought the same thing," I said. "I thought it was Daddy. Remember that photograph we have of Daddy with the sunglasses on the top of his head, smiling, wearing a red-checkered shirt?"

"That was him," said Eileen. "Dalton pulled out the photo and showed it to me, and I said, 'That's him—that's who I saw today. Your dad came to watch after his granddaughter.'"

Rich spoke up. "I can't believe it. Dalton, you identified the ghost your mother saw as being Diane's father. And then, you, Diane, identified the ghost Eileen saw as being Dalton's dad."

We shook our heads hearing what Mother and Eileen saw.

Mother then stared at me and said, "That's not all. There's more, and it happened last night."

Chapter 9

My mother looked at all of us and then fixed her eyes on me and said, "The visit from my dad, well . . . it was for me. It prepared me for what happened next. Rich, I haven't even told you about this yet."

"This oughta be good." Rich grinned.

Mother looked around the table at each of us with her body language in a familiar motion I had known since childhood. I called it Mother's "I'm about to tell you a story" stance. She was a talented storyteller—whether she was reading A. A. Milne's *Winnie the Pooh* to me and my sister or telling us of the latest oddity happening at a family reunion.

"It happened last night while I was asleep. I was deep into my sleep, probably in the REM stage of dreaming. In my dream, I had gone for a walk in our neighborhood, except it was next to Guntersville Lake.

"I am walking along beside the lake when I see a man leaning against our mailbox. I get closer and realize that it's your dad. I smile at him and ask, 'Sanders, what are you doing here?'

"'I came to see you, Diane,' he said.

"He looked just like the last time I saw him, except his clothes were fresh; his hair was combed; and he wasn't sweating."

I looked at Eileen and Rich and explained, "Daddy had a rough night before he left this earth."

"Rough is the mild way to put it," said Mother before continuing.

"I looked at Sanders and asked, 'How have you been?'

"'I've been good, Diane. How have you been?'

"'I've been doing well. I've married a man named Rich. It took me two decades after your death before I was ready to marry again.'"

Mother took another bite of spaghetti and then continued. "That's when I realized, this conversation wasn't normally how it goes in my dream—this was a conversation I would have if I were fully awake. I asked Sanders, 'Where are we, Sanders?'

"'We are in your neighborhood. I've been keeping up with Rachel and Dalton. They make me proud.'"

Mother took a sip of water, smiled at our eager faces, and then continued on. "A peace suddenly fell over me. I said to your dad, 'Rachel has a great husband who treats her right, and Dalton has a wonderful wife full of love. Sanders! You should see your grandchildren; they are such delightful children—full of life and curiosity, just like we were. They are such excellent students with great imaginations. They look so much like their mommas and daddies. Little Ned looks a lot like you.'"

I wiped my suddenly teary eyes, thinking about how much Ned really did look like my dad. Mother took my hand, then began again. "Sanders smiled and said, 'I'm delighted you found Rich; he is a wonderful man, who is taking excellent care of you. Will you tell Rachel and Ned that I love them and I'm proud of them and the parents they have become?'

"I said, 'It will delight them to hear from you.'"

Mother looked at me as she said this. Eileen placed her hand on my knee as tears welled up in my eyes.

"Sanders looked out toward the lake, which magically appeared next to us—like we were sitting on the bank of Town Creek. Must be the miracle of dreams—you can move wherever you wish in a flash.

"Then Sanders said, 'Let them know that the lake will always be special for all of us. I'm always with them. I will always be with all of you.'"

"I told him, 'We all love you, Sanders. I love you and always will. We will always be with you.'"

"I think that is what he needed to hear. And then I woke up."

"Oh my goodness, Diane!" said Eileen with her eyes wide in amazement. "That's amazing! You received a blessing from God. You got to have a visit with your husband who died decades ago. You got two blessings—Sanders and seeing your dad!"

Mother tilted her head and grinned. "Yes, a blessing—that's a good way to put it."

I didn't say much, but I kept shaking my head slowly, filled with astonishing delight of these experiences combined with the whispers from *Johnny Bruce*. I was too tired to talk about it tonight.

When we wrapped up our dinner together, I asked, "Rich, are you coming back tomorrow to finish the boat?"

"It's Sunday, but I'm up for some more sweat equity," he replied, flexing his arms. "I'll come, too," said Mother. "I feel something special about that boat, and I'm sure there is something I can do to help."

I glanced at Mother and then Eileen. *She has a feeling about it? Where did that come from?*

Chapter 10

We started work that morning right after breakfast. Saturday was demolition day. Sunday was restoration day—dare I say, resurrection day? It was a flurry of activity as the entire family pitched in to help. Eva and Ned coated the new plywood decks with marine spar varnish that was mixed with tiny rubber pieces for anti-skid footing.

Eileen brought her mechanical talent to the outboard motor of *Johnny Bruce*. Her dad was a mechanic and taught her how to repair lawn mowers, car engines, and outboard motors. Growing up next to Guntersville Lake, she knew her way around marine vessels.

Eileen replaced the water pump impeller, spark plugs, fuel tank, and fuel lines and cleaned the carburetor. Eileen called Eva over several times to give a helping hand and to pass on the mechanic trade to her daughter.

"Eva," said Eileen, "it's important for you to learn how to use a wrench, socket set, and screwdriver. I want you to know how to do things yourself. That way, you don't have to depend on a man in your life to do these things for you."

"Listen to your mother, Eva," I piped up. "When I came to pick up your mother for our first date, she was under a pickup truck replacing the oil filter. That was one sign that said, 'Yeah, she's special—this is *the* one.'"

"Ah, Dad," came the teenage girl's response to talk about the romance of her parents.

"Oh yeah, Eileen," I said, "I've got an additional part for you to add." From a zip top bag, I pulled out a small, black box.

"What's this?" asked Eileen.

"It's called Green Wave," I answered. "It's a little something that the guys at work gave me to test out. Here's a little oil tank to connect it to, along with the fuel line."

"Okay," said Eileen. "Neat! So, I splice the fuel and oil line out of the gas tank and oil tank and then connect them to this valve?"

"Yeah," I answered. "It's something Clyde and Herb came up with that they've been running on ten other outboards."

"What does it do?" asked Eileen, her face perplexed.

"It's supposed to reduce the amount of oil and gas that exhausts into the lake," I answered.

"Okay, sounds good," said Eileen.

Rich and Mother worked together on the electrical workings of the boat. They put in new wiring from bow to stern to power the trolling motor, running lights, bilge pump, and live well pump.

Ned was doing a grand job of getting the varnish on the roller and coating the decks. Eva helped him in between moments where she watched her mother at work on the outboard. I could see how much better Ned had become at painting because he had less on himself and more on the plywood.

"Don't worry, Dad," said Eva. "I'm checking, and it's plenty thick with coating."

"How's it drying?" I asked.

"Quickly," answered Eva. "I bet it'll be dry enough after lunch to install in the boat."

Everything was coming together smoothly. Our family team had done great work.

As we were munching on a lunch of roast beef sandwiches, Mother said, "You know this day reminds me of a story. Eva and Ned, do y'all want to hear a story?"

"Yeah, Grandmother," said Ned, and he came and sat down in front of his grandmother. Eva nodded and looked toward her grandmother with a smile.

Mother told the story of Noah building the ark. "Many years ago, there was a man named Noah, who was favorable in the eyes of God. Noah raised a grand family, but the world around him was in trouble. God wasn't pleased and told Noah, 'I will clean things up in this world. I want you to build a boat—an ark—big enough to carry all two of my animals aboard.'

"Noah thought this was crazy, but he knew *not* to go against God. When God wants you to do something, you better go along with it, because God will win and you will lose if you go against God."

All of us adults laughed because we knew exactly what she meant.

"Noah's wife and children helped build the ark. Building materials showed up next to their home. God told him the exact length and width to build the ark."

"Was the ark made of wood or alum . . . almin . . . ammonium, I mean metal like our boat?" asked Ned.

"It was all wood." Mother chuckled. "The people in the village thought he was crazy and said, 'Noah says there's going to be a flood.

That God told him to build the ark, even though there's not that much rain.' But Noah ignored them and kept right on building."

She spoke of the animals loading onto the ark two by two. "The rains came. There was a flood. The ark floated through forty days and nights of rain. The sun came out, and a rainbow appeared."

Mother's eyebrows raised, and she waved her hands into an arc. "A rainbow appeared as a promise sign to Noah and God's people that He wouldn't do that again. God felt sad about all the people who perished in the flood.

"God told Noah, 'I will start over with you and your family, my faithful Noah.'

"The waters went down. The ark rested atop a mountain, and Noah released the animals back into the wild. Noah was obedient, and the world continued, thanks to the ark."

Hearing the word "obedient" caused me to look over at Eileen, and our eyes caught each other. With no words spoken, we understood that obedience to God came first.

"Years later, Jesus was teaching by the lakeshore. He was tired, and the sun was setting. Jesus told His disciples, 'Let's cross to the other side of the lake.' So, Jesus and His disciples got into the boat and headed to the other side of the lake. Jesus was napping when a storm came up and the boat tossed about, frightening the disciples, who woke Jesus.

"Jesus awoke, stood on the boat's bow, and shouted at the wind and waves, 'Quiet! Be still!' Immediately, the storm calmed, and the lake became glassy smooth. The disciples marveled at this miracle aboard the boat and said, 'Who is this man? Even the wind and waves obey him!'[1]

---

1 Mark 4:35-41

"Eva and Noah, I wonder what kind of experiences and miracles y'all will see in this boat right here."

"I hope we see lots of wildlife," said Ned, "and catch lots of *big* fish."

"Me, too, Ned," I said.

"Thanks for the story, Grandmother," said Eva.

"Thanks, Diane," said Eileen.

Suddenly appearing in the open garage doorway was our next-door neighbor and handyman, Ed Bartwell.

"Hey, everybody!"

"Hey, Ed," we greeted.

"Last week, Dalton told me y'all are working on restoring the boat," said Ed. "What can I do to help?" He was wearing a toolbelt with a hammer and screwdrivers hanging in the pockets. He had come to work.

"I can use your help getting the floor installed," I said.

With Ed on one side of the boat and me on the other side, we lifted the varnished plank flooring from the sawhorses into the boat. Together, we bolted the floor onto the boat ribs.

In no time flat, we installed and secured the floor, front deck, and rear deck. We were about to install the side panels, which covered the ribs on the inside sides of the boat, when I noticed two wires sticking out.

"Hey, Rich and Mother?" I asked. "What is this wire for?"

"Oh yeah," said Rich. "I'll be right back."

Rich went over to his truck and pulled out two gift-wrapped boxes and handed them to me.

"Surprise!" said Rich and Mother in unison. "While you were focused on getting replacement parts and wood, we wanted to add two special modern features to your twenty-year-old boat."

"What is it, Daddy?" asked an excited Ned.

Unwrapping the box, I exclaimed, "Oh, my goodness! You didn't. It's a brand-new fish finder! I didn't think I could get this for a while. Thank you *so* much."

"Open the other box," said Rich. I opened it up, "We got you *two* fish finders—one for the bow when you are fishing and one for when you are running the outboard."

"Daddy," asked Ned, "will this help us find fish to catch when we go out in the boat?"

"It sure will," I explained. "It's like having an underwater camera or radar so we can spend more time casting to where the fish are, rather than just casting into clear water."

"Don't you think that's cheating?" asked Eva.

"Not one bit." Rich chuckled. "You don't go to the meat section of the grocery store and feel your way around with your eyes closed, do you? Then guess, 'Hmm, this feels like a chicken, or is it the shelf?' You want to see what you are getting, grab it, and go collect the rest of your groceries."

"I used to think the same thing," responded Eileen. "Growing up around the lake, we used to spend a lot of time trying to find fish to catch. That was our dinner. Then, my dad got a depth finder of sorts—or fish locator, as he called it. We started spending more time catching fish rather than trying to find them."

Eileen handed me a purple cloth bag. "Got something else for you."

"Diane and I got these stones for you to keep aboard the boat."

Eileen opened the bag and emptied several stones and a shell into a plastic, waterproof box that was sitting on the workbench. "The mussel shell Eva picked up from Guntersville Lake several years ago—a part of *Johnny Bruce's* home lake. See the pearly inside? A symbol of wisdom being born of the water. We have a small nugget of gold Dalton got from a Boy Scout trip to Colorado from years ago. Here is Ned's pick of turquoise, which symbolizes a shield of protection. The rose quartz is my favorite, representing love, compassion, happiness, and forgiveness. We are placing them in this waterproof box to keep aboard *Johnny Bruce*."

"Wow!" I said. "This is tremendous. Pieces of the created world aboard a vessel created by John and now all of our hands, too. I hadn't thought about this being a spiritual project, but I feel the healing going on here." I looked at each person there in the garage and smiled. "Thank you for all of your help."

Eileen announced, "Let's see if everything works and start this outboard motor."

We put the batteries in the boat, connected the wires, and flipped the switch. All the lights came on.

We cheered.

I turned on the power to the new fish finders, and they chirped to life.

We cheered again.

"Rich, lower the trolling motor," I said. Rich pushed the power button on the trolling motor foot control. The propeller spun to life.

We cheered a third time.

"*Great*! The electronics work," I said. "Thanks, Mother and Rich. Now, let's roll the boat into the sunlight and hook the hose to the motor muffs." We rolled *Johnny Bruce* out of the garage into the afternoon sun.

Ned got the hose and brought it over to the motor. "Here you go, Mom."

"Thank you," replied Eileen. She connected the hose to the motor muffs—because they look like rubber earmuffs—to the lower unit. They were used to cover the outboard's lower unit water pickup.

"Y'all ready?" asked Eileen.

"Ready," we said in unison.

"Ned," said Eileen, "go turn on the water." Ned ran to the outside water faucet and opened the valve. Water started pouring out the side of the outboard's lower unit to cool the engine once I cranked it up.

Eileen looked at me and asked, "Do you want to do the honors and start the engine?"

I answered, "You did the work on the motor. You start it."

In a flash, a feeling came over me. This was the last step. As a team, we had come together to restore *Johnny Bruce*. I dreamed of this moment when it—no, when *he*—came back to life, fully operational.

We stood back from the boat almost in reverence for what was about to happen. Mother stood near the bow, reached out her hand, and placed it on the gunnel. Eva saw her grandmother's hand and did the same. Eva reached down and grabbed Ned's hand to place on the side of the boat. Rich, Ed, and I did the same near the back of the boat.

Eileen was at the stern and pressed the starter button. "Here goes!"

The starter moved to spin the flywheel. The outboard sputtered and then fired up. He was running!

Cheers and applause erupted from all of us.

"You did it, Eileen," I said. "Back to life!"

The floodgates opened with emotion. I wrapped my arms around the cowling of the outboard and gave it a hug. Tears streamed down my face.

"It's running! You are running again!" I said as I held on to this hunk of metal. Eileen came up behind me and hugged me. I stepped away and buried my face into her shoulder and wept. "Thank you so much! I feel like we have brought a part of John back to life. I know it's just metal, wood, wires, and oil; but a piece of *his* soul is in this boat."

"And now, ours, too!" announced Eileen as she pivoted her head and looked at our family gathered around the boat.

Everyone surrounded us in a hug. Our family came together, connected through an inherited gift from a friend—a brother—who had passed on to the other side.

"Ah, well," said our neighbor, Ed. "I'll join in the hug, too." Ed wrapped his arms around us, and we laughed.

"You are a part of this, too, Ed," I said. "You willingly brought your tools and put your hands to work to restore *Johnny Bruce*."

In the corner of my eye, I saw a white glow coming from the center of the boat from inside where we placed the box of crystals and gems. I shook it off as nothing, and my mind soaked in this hugging moment.

Soon, I would find out how alive *Johnny Bruce* was.

Chapter 11

The day was finally here. *Johnny Bruce* would be launched into the water again. For his first launch after renovation and restoration, I headed to Guntersville Lake's Town Creek.

I took a vacation day on Friday to have time alone with *Johnny Bruce*. Town Creek reminded me of my childhood and fishing with Daddy, Granddaddy, and, today, John. I was alone for this first trip.

The fog was thick that spring morning. The air was cool, and by late morning, it was perfect weather.

I carefully backed the boat and trailer down the ramp. Through my back window, I saw the water lift *Johnny Bruce* off the trailer. I put the truck in park, got out, and grabbed the rope tied to the front of the trailer. I guided the boat to the dock, tied him to the piling, and parked the truck. He floated peacefully as I walked onto the dock. I untied the bow rope and stepped down onto the new boat floor. That was enough motion to launch *Johnny Bruce* free from solid moorings of earth. He was floating free on the water for the first time in many years. The reins of solid moorings were released, and he was in the fluid environment in which he was designed to live.

"Okay, John," I said aloud, "let's see if your baby can run on the water. We'll go out toward the main lake where I can throttle up."

The fog was lighter toward the mouth of the creek but looked thicker going up the narrow creek. No other boats were around, and my truck was the only one at the launch ramp.

"Here goes," I said as I pushed the start button. The mechanical sound of gears touching sliced the silence, and the outboard started. Amazingly, no exhaust smoke wafted up from the back of the motor like I was used to.

"You're back! Yes!" I shouted.

Johnny Bruce swung around with the bow pointed to the mouth of the creek. A thin fog veiled the creek aglow with the boat's navigation lights. On the tiller arm, I twisted the throttle to wide open. The bow lifted above the surface. The boat sped up, leaving only four feet of the boat hull in the water. The front portion all the way to the bow was scooting over the water's surface. We were "on plane," as boaters call it.

"Woohoo!" I shouted. "Back on Town Creek. Back where it all began!" I did not care if anyone heard me or not as a wave of elation washed over me. I was alone, but I felt John's spirit with me.

Johnny Bruce scooted across the water, slicing through the glassy surface with a wake from the boat and motor. It felt warm and natural. It felt like home.

Once I passed an island, I throttled back. As much as I wanted to head out to wider water and do some 360-degree turns to celebrate this moment of recovery and restoration, the fog was too thick. I didn't want to risk colliding with another vessel or land.

I turned the bow straight toward the bridge veiled in the fog. I throttled up and drove to the bridge. I passed the launch ramp, and I throttled back, settling *Johnny Bruce's* hull back into the water. I idled under the bridge, so there was no wake of water behind the boat.

The fog was thicker on the other side of the bridge. It looked like a thick cumulus cloud had descended on the lake and engulfed everything around it.

My conversation continued between me and *Johnny Bruce* as if John were riding with me. "My goodness, look at that! It's thick. John, it reminds me of Isaiah, chapter six, when God's smoke filled the temple in Isaiah's vision." I felt a nudge and a whisper back from *Johnny Bruce.*

"God's presence fills every void," said the whisper.

I passed under the bridge and saw two fishermen on the limestone rocks. They were crappie fishermen who braved early morning to gather dinner from the twenty-feet deep water. We waved at each other.

I moved past the bridge. The bright white of fog engulfed the boat so much it diminished my visibility to fifty yards beyond the bow of the boat. I looked at my fish-finder, which indicated the water was twenty feet deep. I throttled up a little—still at idle speed but fast enough to create a wake. The fog lightened enough for me to see the bank nearby, but I didn't want to risk colliding with rocks. I fixed my eyes on the compass mounted on the front deck and used it to guide me to the first cove where there was a sandbar. Inside, I felt this tug to reach this spot, and there I could turn off the motor to await the fog lifting. I would safely be away from the risk of other boats colliding with us, yet far enough away from everyone else to soak in the quiet beauty of this day. I don't know why, but throughout the journey, I felt like I was not alone.

Suddenly the fog thickened to where I could not see the bow of *Johnny Bruce*. I throttled back to drift.

"My goodness, John," I said into the fog, "it's gotten thicker like a warm jacket. Oddly, I don't feel the warmth on me."

That's when it happened. On the front deck, the fog turned into a solid form, like water droplets assembling into a figure. The air filled with the scent of lake water and honeysuckle—the scent of spring fishing adventures from my childhood.

A person suddenly appeared sitting on the front deck of *Johnny Bruce* wearing a navy blue baseball cap similar to what Lou Gehrig wore on the day of his retirement. I noticed his light blue shirt and then a familiar face. Immediately I shut off the outboard in shock over who appeared before me.

"Daddy!" I tensed up in my seat.

"Don't be afraid," he said. "Drop the anchor, Son, and take a breath."

"What?" I inhaled in disbelief.

"Drop the anchor," he said again softly.

I twisted the button on the bow to lower the stern anchor into the water. As soon as I felt it hit bottom, I locked the rope stopper. *Johnny Bruce* stopped moving.

"Daddy, is it you?" I asked.

"Yes, it is Dalton," said the figure. He looked solidly present, just as a live human being would. I wanted to reach out and touch him, but I resisted.

"How is this possible?" I asked as nerves relaxed.

"You made this possible, along with others who love you," he said. "And God Himself."

I sat and stared at my dad sitting in a boat on Town Creek with me decades after his death.

He laughed. "You can close your mouth; this *is* happening." Then, he waved his left hand over his right hand; and a round, red Garcia reel appeared in his palm.

"My reel!" I said. "I used it for the first time on our last trip together here."

"This moment is happening because you were obedient, just like Noah," said Daddy.

"Is a flood about to happen?" I asked.

"No." Daddy chuckled. "Not in the sense of what Noah experienced. But there may be a flood of people who want to be on your boat if they hear about your experience. The flood you will experience is the people you will meet on this boat. We wanted to create a way to bridge Heaven and your world together so these folks that love you could speak to you in the way you recognize. First, God wanted to make sure you were listening, so He whispered through the boat. That was one person's idea, and I supported it."

"So, this came about because . . . " I peered at him through slightly squinted eyes. My muscles were still tense.

"Because we saw the struggle you were going through with the losses in your life. You weren't recovering. You weren't healing. You stopped fishing. We had to restore Dalton to how God created you," said Daddy.

"You mean, from John's death?" I asked.

"Yes."

"You saw that, Daddy? You knew about him?" I asked.

"Yes, I knew about what you were going through. I can't explain everything so you will fully understand. Son, on this side of Heaven, once you pass over from the earthly realm, your soul is different. We don't feel pain and suffering anymore, but we watch out over the ones we loved and cared about from our earthly days. God and His Son felt the pain and suffering along with you. You are a dad; you know what it's like when you want the best for your children. You can't always be there to protect them from things happening."

My body began to relax as I thought about being a dad to Eva and Ned. I dropped my head and nodded. "Oh yeah, I know," I said. "I watch Eva and Ned in pain, and I hurt for them. I may cry more than they."

"Son, you are blessed, and we made a request on your behalf," said Daddy. "Very few humans get to experience this—being in a two-way conversation with those of us who have passed on to this side of Heaven. Oh, you are right, Heaven is *all* around you."

"I knew it!" I shouted, punching my fist on my knee.

"You felt it, and that's more important sometimes than knowing," said Daddy. "You can't see it or hear from us, but we are all around you. We hear, see, and intercede. What you don't realize is how deep Heaven is as it goes far beyond this great big rock of earth."

"How deep?" I asked.

"Ah, ah, ah, there are some things you won't learn," said Daddy. "Some things will remain a mystery for you, but at the right moment, those things will be revealed to you. Already, I may have told you more than I should have."

Suddenly, the scent of honeysuckle filled the air. I breathed it as I watched Daddy's eyes shift to the trees nearby and then look intently back at me. His eyes were full of love, the love that warms you and comforts you. I knew this moment was Heaven-sent.

"Dalton, you need to know I lived my life doing everything I could to protect you, raise you right, and give you as much love as I could."

"I know, Daddy, thank you," I said.

"At the end, I was deeply troubled. I was fighting demons that were trying to get a hold of me. I didn't like it and it took all of my strength to fend them off. This battle had been growing slowly over the years. In some ways, it is what my father experienced. I didn't want it repeated. I didn't want to hurt your mother, but I did. I didn't want to hurt you, but I did. I didn't want to hurt Rachel, but I did. It was hard for me to forgive myself."

I sat there and stared intently at my dad.

"You know your mother is a saint," he said.

I smiled, and my eyes filled with love for my mother. "Yes, I do."

"Dalton, the two forces of light and dark are very real. As you know, light is the way to go; and God defeated darkness at the highest level, thanks to the Son of Light. But the enemy is not happy about how that came down, so he takes it out on the weak, the ones who don't have the knowledge or ability to see what is going on. He is conniving and destructive. Do you remember the story I used to tell you about the frog in the kettle?"

"Oh yeah, you told me that many times from when I was little," I said. "If you get the water hot and put a frog in the boiling water, it will immediately realize it's in danger and jump right out. If you place a frog in warm water, it will stay. As you turn up the heat, the frog doesn't notice much of a difference, and eventually, it will kill the frog who doesn't realize it's in danger."

"There are many times it's like that, but the opposite," Daddy continued. "In this battle between light and dark, the water starts warm—it feels good—then it slowly gets colder to where frostbite sets in, and the frog goes to its sleepy death.

"That's what can happen if you let the enemy win. You have to fight against it, and I was fighting hard. You couldn't see it; but when the enemy started hurting the people I love the most, that's when I had to put a stop to it. You, your mother, and your sister—all of you were getting hurt."

Daddy told this story to me in such a calm and peaceful way. There was very little inflection, and his voice was low, but I felt every word.

"Demons are destructive, and I put an end to it so the hurting would end. I know it wasn't the right way to handle it, but I could not allow your health and well-being to be at risk. I knew if I perished, the demon would perish, too. So, I removed the demon from all of you by allowing myself to perish, and with that, y'all had a life restored without the continuing presence of torment."

"Daddy," I said, "you sacrificed yourself so we could continue living?"

"Yes, I did it because I love you," Daddy said.

"All those years you threatened to shoot yourself, but you didn't," I said. "Why now?"

"They tormented me. It hurt me to see you hurting. Jesus sacrificed Himself for those He loves—every human being. Rather than you, your sister, and your mother having to continue to suffer or risk being attacked by the demons. What happened was enough. I put an end to it. But as soon as I opened my eyes in Heaven, I realized what I had done and how I hadn't saved you at all. Only God can save. I'm so sorry for how I wronged you, your mother, and your sister."

Tears welled up in my eyes. "Daddy, I love you so very much. You know that, right? Because I didn't tell you that the last time I saw you and I'm so sorry."

"I've known that all along," said Daddy. "Do you remember the fishing trip you took by yourself here, and you saw that squirrel come out and grab the one acorn out on the tree overhanging the water?"

"Oh yeah," I said. "It almost fell in and was hanging by its front legs."

"I was here that day," Daddy said. "I knew you were sad and missing me, so I sent the squirrel out on the tree."

"I remember the squirrel," I said, "and thinking, 'Sure is bright-eyed and bushy-tailed.' Which is how you described me, many times!"

"I was here with you; I've continued to be with you," said Daddy. "Do you remember your Boy Scout court of honor where you made Eagle and a hymnal fell off a chair in the choir area behind you, but no one was in the choir area?"

I nodded my head.

"That was me letting you know I was with you and proud of you."

Tears streamed down my face as I listened and absorbed this moment.

"There was a time when little Eva was sick. Eileen was at home by herself taking care of her. She was scared and asked for God's help. I stood in the bedroom doorway and brought His Spirit of healing with me."

"Eileen told me about that! She thought I was in the doorway, but when she turned to look, no one was there. But she saw an outline of a figure about my size. She told me the figure wore a red-and-white checkered shirt. When I showed her a photo of you, she said, 'That's him. That's who I saw.' You came to watch over your granddaughter!"

"Yes, I continue to be with you because He is with you," said Daddy. "Dalton, because you have heard and followed God's leading, this boat has allowed us to connect with you in a way that you can relate to. I am the first visitor to appear to you, but I won't be the last."

"What do you mean?" I asked.

"God is allowing this boat to be a portal between earth and Heaven. There will be times when key people who have passed over will visit you. I cannot say when it will be, but I can tell you that the situation must be right for a visit," said Daddy.

"What makes the situation right?" I asked.

"I cannot tell you that; even I don't know," answered Daddy. "You will just know when the moment is right. Remember this day and how I appeared to you. Remember that the boat, *Johnny Bruce,* is a key part of this. It's your heart in the right place and focused on the right things. It is an honor that you are receiving this communication, and it is because They want to help you."

"Who is this *They,* Daddy?" I asked.

"They are the ones who love you, God, the Son, and the Holy Spirit. They all work together to guide and direct you. There are beings—you call them angels—who are working on your behalf. These angels have only been in the heavenly realm and never been mortal. They have been God's dedicated servants for eternity."

Daddy continued, "The best way for me to describe them is in moments that you need protection, angels are sent to surround you, your family, your car, or even the building you are in to protect you from endangerment or the enemy messing with you. You cannot see this; you just keep moving on with your day, but They know you are paying attention."

"How?"

"Because it's followed by you or your loved ones asking each other, 'Are you okay?' and saying 'Thank you, God.'"

"I . . . er . . . I am . . . ," I stumbled to say. "I'm amazed. I don't fully understand this . . . "

Daddy interrupted. "It's not up to you to understand everything, only to accept it. Son, it is time for me to go," Daddy said gently.

"Not yet. I have so many more things to ask you," I insisted. "There is so much I want to share with you, Daddy. It's been over thirty years since we've gotten to talk. There was that time I had a dream that felt like I had a real talk with you, but that's been it."

"Yes," said Daddy, "that moment was just what you thought it was. I visited you."

"Daddy, I want my children to know you," I said as tears streamed down my face again. "My wife and kids have only known you through the stories I've told about you. They haven't met you."

"Dalton," said Daddy softly as he looked me in the eye, "they know me; they have met me because of you. They know you, and because they know you, they know me, too. You are a part of me and carry me in the earthly world."

Then, Daddy did something that he had not done on our entire visit. He reached out and placed his hand on mine. I felt warmth and a glowing sensation spread from my hands, up to my arms, to my heart, and up my neck to my head. He rested his hand over mine, and at that moment, I felt the power of Heaven.

"I've been with you this whole time," Daddy said, "and will continue to be with you, your mother, your sister, your wife, and your children—*all* of your families—all of my family."

"Now, Dalton," Daddy whispered, "it's time to pull up the anchor and allow this boat to keep moving. Go ahead: raise the anchor."

"Will I see you again—I mean—like this?" I asked.

"It's not up to me, but . . . " Daddy paused as if waiting for an answer. "I'm thinking you probably will."

I raised the anchor, and the boat drifted forward. The fog was still thick, and just as Daddy appeared on the front deck, he disappeared in the fog with his smile being the last thing showing.

My body shook like a warm tremor went through me. It brought me back to reality. How much time had passed since this visit began? The fog hadn't risen and was as thick as before. I looked at my watch, and it still said 7:30 in the morning.

What? How was this possible?

A whisper came up from this magic boat. "Remember, knowledge is not as important as acceptance and belief."

I looked around the cove and noticed the fog and mist beginning to wisp away upward—like smoke rising from a fire. I inhaled the scent of cedar.

"Maybe this is what Isaiah experienced when he came into God's presence," I said aloud. "What now?"

"Try the trolling motor, make some casts, check out your restored vessel," whispered this miracle boat, *Johnny Bruce.*

That is what I did. I checked out all of the working parts of the boat. The fog arose from the water and unveiled beautiful sunshine. *Johnny Bruce* passed his test to be back in full operation.

Chapter 12

"Eileen?" I called as I rushed into the house. "Eileen, where are you?"

"I'm in the living room," said Eileen. "I just finished replacing the gasket on the bathroom sink." She enjoyed getting her hands dirty and grease under her fingernails.

I burst into the living room with sweat pouring down my face.

"Wow, look at you! Are you okay?" she asked.

"I'm more than okay," I answered. "I'm amazed!"

"I guess that everything is working on the boat," she said.

"Oh yeah, beyond belief," I said. "Eileen, where's Ned?"

"He's across the street playing with Eric," she said. "He had a wonderful day at school today. They came home together, and Eric asked him to come over to play."

"Great," I said, "Eileen, this boat, *Johnny Bruce,* it's alive! It's . . . uh . . . well, it's a miracle boat."

"What do you mean?" she asked.

"Eileen, I don't know why I keep saying your name," I said. "So much has happened today, and I'm excited. Remember what we were talking about the day the boat came home and how the boat whispering to me reminded me of *Field of Dreams*?"

"Yeah," she said.

"We have our very own miracle ballfield in our backyard," I said. "Except, instead of a baseball diamond, it's a boat on a trailer that we can transport anywhere."

Eileen looked at me perplexed, and she asked me slowly, "What happened today, Dalton?"

I got down on my knees in front of Eileen, looked directly into her eyes, and said, "I had a visit with my daddy today . . . in the boat . . . on Town Creek."

It took a moment for it to sink in, but when Eileen saw the smile on my face, she knew. "How did this happen? What did he say? What did he look like? Where did he appear?"

"It was foggy on the lake today," I began. "I went under the bridge, and Daddy appeared on the front deck of the boat as white as the mist. But he didn't stay that way. He was wearing a blue t-shirt, jeans, and the blue cap that he wore the last time we went fishing. It was Daddy. There. In the boat. With me! We talked for a while, and he told me what happened at the end. He told me how he has been watching over our family. He told me about you, Eva, and Ned. Eileen, he knows what has been going on."

Eileen remained quiet and reached out and placed her hand over mine, and I took that as encouragement to continue.

"Daddy said that God is allowing the boat to be a way for him to cross over from the heavenly world to this earthly world and communicate with me. Daddy said, 'God is allowing this boat to be a portal between earth and Heaven. There will be times when key people who have passed over will visit you. I cannot say when it will be, but I can tell you that the situation must be right for a visit.'"

"Wow!" said Eileen. "Can I go out in the boat right now?"

"Well," I continued, "he said the time has to be right for a visit. I'm not entirely sure what that means, but I guess every trip in the boat won't always be a portal visit."

I paused and took a deep breath. Eileen rubbed the back of my neck.

"You had quite a day," said Eileen. "What do we do now?"

"We enjoy it and make the most of it," I said. "It makes me excited to go out again, but I also still want to fish and take you and the kids in the boat. That's the miracle I was looking for."

"Our very own ark," said Eileen. "Now, we don't tell anyone about this. We keep it to ourselves."

"Oh yeah," I said. "We've been down that road talking openly to some folks who don't see the unseen world the same way. Unless . . . "

"Unless what, Dalton?" asked Eileen.

"Unless we should open it to others," I said. "But I am sure He will be a guide to us when that time comes."

"Yeah, I think that's why Jesus told the people after He performed a miracle, 'Don't tell anyone.'"

Our hands locked together.

Chapter 13

"It's Saturday. Let's get to the lake!" I said as I jumped into the driver's seat of our pickup truck. *Johnny Bruce* was in tow.

"Yeah, we are taking the boat out!" said Ned from the backseat.

Truck and trailer rolled as the Russell family departed Huntsville and made our way to Guntersville Lake.

"This is exciting," said Eileen. "It's been a while since we went to the lake together, much less had a chance to be out in a boat on the lake. It's such a beautiful day. Blue sky, low wind—couldn't be better."

I glanced at Eileen, and we shared an enormous smile. Glancing in the rearview mirror, I saw Ned and Eva smiling with their eyes glued to the windows.

In less than an hour, we arrived inside Lake Guntersville State Park's launch ramp.

"I want to keep us near clean restrooms to make your mom happy," I said.

"Thank you!" replied Eileen and Eva in unison.

We launched the boat, parked the truck, and jumped aboard for a family ride together. Eileen and I sat on the bench seat while Eva and Ned sat on the floor atop two floatation cushions.

"I know it's a little cramped," I said, "but I'm glad we can all be together for this first ride. We'll return to the picnic area for lunch. Grandmother and Rich are bringing us lunch."

We idled away from the dock, then turned the bow toward the main lake. *Johnny Bruce* zoomed across the water. The air smelled like sunscreen, Eva's fruity body lotion, and Eileen's cucumber hand cream mixed with crisp lake air. Eva and Ned laughed as the breeze shifted and lifted their hair. Ned sported red sunglasses and Eva a pair of white ones, while Eileen warned them to not drop their sunglasses in the lake.

Eileen's dark hair blew in the wind, and her perpetual smile reminded me of how white her teeth were. She looked at me and quickly leaned her head on my shoulder and then sat back up.

"This is fun!" Eileen yelled over the roar of the outboard.

Suddenly, Eva's arm pointed to the right toward an osprey atop a navigation post. Following his sister's lead, Ned pointed up as we all saw an eagle soaring overhead.

Eileen pointed straight ahead at a gathering of waterfowl.

"Are those what I think they are?" asked Eileen.

The boat came off plane, and we idled our way up to the black waterfowl.

"Yes, it is!" I said. "We found the loons!" About twice a year, once in the spring and again in the fall, common loons make a stop on the Tennessee River on their flyway either headed north for the summer or south for the winter.

Ever since seeing the movie *On Golden Pond,* loons have been one of my favorite birds to watch. Sightings are rare because they are only here for about a month before they fly out again. We idled up slowly behind them and marveled at their wide necks and jet black backs, as they yodeled to one another.

"Wow, Daddy!" said Ned. "They sound funny." One loon near the back dove beneath the surface. "Where did it go?"

"Ned, it's swimming under the water," said Eva. "Watch for it to pop up."

"Look! I see it," said Ned, "right there next to the boat."

Magically, the loon popped its head upright off the bow of our boat. He yodeled at us and then, frightened by the strange humans, darted below the surface and swam away from us. We all looked at each other and grinned. There was no need for words; our body language said enough as we soaked in this rare sight. I turned off the outboard and jumped to the bow to lower the trolling motor. Eva pulled out a set of binoculars to view the loons. With the trolling motor, we kept up with the flock of loons as they swam across the water feeling safe in a mass together. There must have been twenty loons. Now and then, a loon darted underneath the water and went for a swim.

This boat crew passed the binoculars and kept watch.

"Okay, Daddy," said Ned, "can we go fast again?"

"Yeah, we have gotten a good look," said Eva.

I stowed the trolling motor, sat back down on the rear bench seat, and cranked the outboard. We throttled up and were on our way.

More adventures lay ahead for us aboard *Johnny Bruce*—even more than we realized. Soon, more of the family would experience something out of this world.

Chapter 14

We ran back to the dock near the campground and picnic area. Mother and Rich were on the dock waving at us as soon as they spotted us motoring toward them.

Idling up to the dock, Rich grabbed the bow that Eva handed him.

"Well, hello there," said Rich. "How's he running?"

"Great, Grandpa Rich," said Eva. "We saw some loons."

"Loons, oh my," said Mother. "Can I go see them?"

"Absolutely, Mother," I said, "I'll take you out to see them after lunch."

"That would be lovely, Son," said Mother. "Besides, lunch is ready, so y'all come eat."

We sat down at a picnic table and Mother surprised us. "I've got some fried chicken. Nothing says Southern picnic more than Kentucky Fried Chicken, coleslaw, and sweet potato casserole. I made the casserole myself."

"Wow, Diane," said Eileen, "you went all out."

We ate our lunch as Eva and Ned chatted with their grandparents about the boat adventure. Eileen and I looked at each other knowingly. It had been a while since we had heard this much out of Eva after she entered into the world of teenage girls. Eva and Ned were getting along famously, with Eva taking the role of protector and babysitter to her young brother. Ned leaned his head against his sister. Eva put her arm around him as Ned looked up at her with loving eyes and said, "I love you, sis."

"Love you, too, little bro," said Eva.

Johnny Bruce was at work as restoration continued to take place among the Russell family. I sat at the picnic table facing the lake, staring at John's gift—a boat for our family to enjoy. Together, we worked to get it running again. This was the first day of many family adventures, all thanks to *Johnny Bruce.*

"Hey, Dalton and Eileen," came a call from a nearby picnic table.

I looked over and saw some familiar faces. It was the Dresden family—Mark and Jan along with their children—our neighbors down the street.

"Hey, Mark," I said as I waved. Just as I did, the unpleasant smell of dead fish hit me.

"Y'all smell that?" asked Mark. "I think there's a dead fish near the beach."

"What are y'all doin' over here today?"

"Just getting our ski boat out to get it runnin' for the summer," said Mark. "I saw that you got a boat this spring. My dad used to have a SeaArk, and it lasted just about forever. Something special about them."

"Yeah, there's something special about this SeaArk, too," I said. "We inherited it from a friend of mine who passed away a while back. We got it all repaired and restored. Running good, though."

"That's great!" said Mark. "Good to see you out here today. Enjoy your lunch."

I turned and looked at Eileen, and she had a questionable look on her face. The Dresdens just always made me feel a little uncomfortable, and I wasn't sure why. They seemed like a nice family, but Mark was always coming over and borrowing tools from me and rarely returning them unless I asked. He would come into my garage and ask me questions about a lot of the things we had in the garage. It felt as though he was taking inventory of our things; I said nothing, though. Eileen knew of my suspicions. It was unusual that they would be at the same spot on the lake today. I told myself, *Just be neighborly and helpful.*

We finished our lunch, and I could tell that Mother was anxious to see the loons after hearing the tales of Eva and Ned.

"Let's go, Mother," I said. Rich stayed at the table, and the rest of us walked to the dock. Mother grabbed Ned's hand with her left hand and Eva's with her right, and the three of them practically *Tophered* their way to *Johnny Bruce.*

"I'm so glad to have been here with my grandchildren," said Mother. "Sure makes it a special day. Eva, grandmothers never grow tired of holding their grandchildren's hand."

They looked at each other and smiled.

I grabbed Eileen's hand and mimicked their *Topher* in front of us. Eileen laughed.

I helped Mother into the boat. Eileen and Eva untied the ropes.

"See y'all back here soon," I said as we all waved. "Okay, Mother, are your feet free from any rope?"

"You sound just like your dad," said Mother, "who was always the safety marshal."

We idled past the no-wake zone buoys, and we were on plane in no time. On our way out to the main body of the lake, we saw a figure atop one of the marker posts. Mother stared at the figure. The figure was sitting atop the telephone pole-size marker post with a fishing rod in hand.

"Dalton, that looks like your dad!" Mother pointed as she nearly stood up in the boat but immediately sat down. The figure waved at us and then faded away like smoke as we passed. Mother looked at me, and I just smiled.

"It sure did, Mother," I said. Up ahead, the loons came into view as they were on the water swimming away from us. "There they are!"

I stopped the outboard and jumped to the front deck to lower the trolling motor, so we could ease up on the loons. Mother marveled at the loons and how close we got to them. Then, she heard the yodel, and she clutched her heart.

"Oh, how marvelous—just like in *On Golden Pond,*" Mother said.

I handed her binoculars, so she could get a closer look. We circled the loons and kept a safe distance to keep from spooking them.

"You've made my spring, Dalton," said Mother. "Thank you for this treat, one of God's miracles."

"Funny you should say that, Mother," I said, "because this sure seems to be a miracle boat. Remember when you thought the figure atop the post looked like Daddy? Well, I believe it may have been his ghost."

"What?" asked Mother with surprising curiosity. I told her how *Johnny Bruce* whispered to me. I shared the story of my recent visit to Town Creek, my conversation with Daddy, and how he disappeared in the mist.

"Daddy said, 'Rich is a wonderful man.' He is happy for you."

Mother's eyes sparkled at me with her head tilted to one side and said, "All of this happened once the boat arrived?"

"Yes," I answered.

"I felt something," she said, "the day we came to dinner and while we worked on the boat. It was like a surge of electricity when I walked next to this boat. It felt like John was there in the garage with us. I know how hard it has been for you to lose your dad and grow up without a father to guide you in the ways of becoming a man. I did my best, but I am so grateful that John entered your life when he did. When he died, the wind came out of your sails. But now, with *Johnny Bruce* in your life, I'm seeing wind lifting your sails again. This truly is a miracle boat." She patted and rubbed the boat gunnel.

"Absolutely," I said with delight, nodding my head and a smile spreading over my face.

"Hey, Mother," I said, "let's head back to the dock. Would you and Rich mind watching after Ned and Eva so I can take Eileen out for a boat ride?"

"Of course! That's my boy," Mother said lovingly as she wrapped me with a hug.

Chapter 15

Afternoon sunlight dappled across the lake's surface and reflected onto Eileen's face. Her brunette hair shone in the light of the western sun. She was more beautiful today than the day I met her. We met alongside the lake about twenty years ago when my boat—a small boat with an eighteen-horsepower engine rented from the state park—broke down.

* * *

It was Eileen and her dad who saw me paddling along trying to get to shore. They motioned for me to come to their dock. When I saw Eileen in blue shorts and a purple t-shirt, I was mesmerized. She was in her twenties and me in my thirties. A shock of electricity went through me when I paddled up to their dock. I was intimidated and nervous.

"Why aren't you running the Evinrude outboard?" she asked.

"Well, er, it just stopped on me," I said sheepishly, "and I can't seem to find out why it won't run. Sun's getting low, so I started paddling toward shore."

"You came to the right place, didn't he, Eileen?" called a smiling man from the dock.

"You sure did," she said. "My dad can fix any outboard, lawn mower, or chainsaw."

"I'm Jake Snellgrove. This here is my daughter Eileen." Jake shook my hand. When he did, he pulled me and my boat right next to the dock. "Don't let Eileen fool you—she's a chip off of the old block. She can fix just about everything, too."

"Looks like you got this boat from the state park. They don't always take the best care of their engines. I love these old Evinrude outboard engines. Simple design and they last forever if you treat them right. Let's have a look," said Eileen with a twinkling smile. "Permission to come aboard?"

"Permission granted," I welcomed her.

She jumped into my boat near the outboard. I shook her hand. "Nice to meet you, Eileen."

"Nice to meet you, too, um . . . " She shook my hand.

"Oh, it's Dalton. Dalton Russell," I said.

That's when I smelled her. It was a mix of cucumber and strawberries—a refreshing scent that mixed with the air pleasantly.

She turned her head away from me and looked at the engine. "It's time to get some grease lotion on these hands. My hands get so dry from being in the water or working on engines."

She disconnected the fuel line and opened the cowling. I couldn't keep my eyes off of her shoulder-length hair.

"Find anything there, Eileen?" Jake's voice shocked me back to reality. *Oh, yeah, remember, dummy—her dad's right here.*

"Dad," said Eileen with her eyes fixed on the outboard engine, "I think the carb is clogged. Let me take the glass bowl off. Hey, Dalton, see right here, underneath the carburetor? That's gasoline."

"Oh yeah," I said as I peered over her shoulder. "I've never taken that off."

"Well, that may be your problem right there," said Eileen. "The gas looks discolored, so I'll remove it, drain the gas out of it, spray the carb with some cleaner, and put some treatment in the fuel tank. The gas looks old."

Jake handed her the tools, the carb cleaner, and the gas treatment bottle. In no time flat, Eileen removed the glass bow, drained the gas into a little cup, handed it to me, and said, "Yep, see how dirty it is? We'll get it fixed."

I decided then that I needed this beautiful talented mechanic in my life.

Eileen emptied the old gas from the bowl and cleaned the carburetor, then added gas treatment to the fuel tank. Removing the spark plugs, she ran a wire brush over the electrodes and put them back in.

As she closed the cowling, her warm eyes looked at me. "Hey, paddling boy, Dalton dear, give the fuel tank a shake to mix the fuel treatment."

I shook the fuel tank. Eileen reattached the fuel line and pumped the primer bulb to pressurize the tank. "Here goes nothing."

She pulled on the starter cord, and the Evinrude sputtered. Another pull and the Evinrude fired up.

"That's my girl!" yelled Jake.

Eileen throttled up the engine, and it sang as it ran. She shut off the engine.

"There ya go, Dalton," she said with pride> "We gotcha runnin' again. It should get you home."

"Well, thank you so very much, Eileen," I said with delight and amazement. "What do I owe you?

She handed her dad the tools and the chemicals and tilted her head to the side. “Hmmm, you know, we charge by the hour; so a half-hour, dockside service will be sixty bucks.”

I quickly did the math in my head and thought, *You get paid $120 per hour? Yeah, I need you in my life!*

“Can I write you a check as soon as I get back to my truck?” I asked sheepishly.

Eileen laughed and broke the tension. “I’m just kidding, and for a cute guy like you wandering up to our dock on a Saturday afternoon needing to work on one of my favorite outboards, I’ll strike a deal with you. How about dinner from Docksides in Guntersville?”

“It’s a deal!” I said excitedly. “When’s the best day? Next Friday or . . . ”

“Hey, just in case you *Topher* out on me, let’s go today—this afternoon—tonight!” came an assured response from Eileen.

I couldn’t believe the confidence from this woman, and I nodded my head. “It’s a date—er, I mean, a deal.”

“Daddy, do you mind riding back to the launch ramp with Dalton here in case the motor breaks down?” asked Eileen with her eyes on me. “Plus, I don’t want Dalton runnin’ off on me. Guess you could ride in his vehicle back to our house to pick me up.”

“Sure, Eileen,” said Jake. “I’d be glad to. I’m sure you want to clean up a little, too.”

“Yeah, maybe.” *He might be worth it.*

Off I went in my boat with Mr. Jake Snellgrove, my future father-in-law, riding along. I nervously prayed the whole way. *Please, Evinrude, don’t stop on me now.*

We made it to the state park and turned in the boat to the park office. Jake told the park rangers about the repair to the Evinrude.

Then, we got into my truck and headed toward the Snellgrove house and shop. When we got there, we saw an old Ford F-150 up on jack stands with a pair of tanned legs sticking out from underneath.

"Eileen, whatcha doin'?" asked a surprised Jake.

"Dad, I forgot I was in the middle of draining the oil on my truck," said Eileen, muffled by the engine bay between us. "I took a break to go down to the dock to let all the oil drain out and got sidetracked working on Dalton's Evinrude. Y'all back so soon? I just 'bout got the oil filter on. There. Done."

Eileen rolled the creeper out from under the truck. Grease marks streaked across the flat belly of her shirt.

"All that's left," she said, "is to fill it with fresh oil."

"Tell you what," said Jake, "you go get cleaned up and head out to Docksides with Dalton. I'll replace the oil."

"Oh," she said with appreciation. "Well, thanks, Dad. I must be a mess. I'll be right back."

"Give me a hand, Dalton," said Jake. "We'll have six quarts of oil in this truck in no time."

A woman who repairs outboard motors, changes the oil in her truck, drives a truck, lives near the lake—yeah, I gotta have her in my life. Let's just hope that she likes me half as much as I like her.

Jake and I poured six quarts of oil into the F-150, cranked it up, checked for leaks, turned off the engine, and checked the dipstick.

"It's back to full level," I said.

"Great!" A voice sounded from behind. It was Eileen freshly showered, wearing a sleeveless, purple top, khaki shorts, and purple sandals. She looked stunning with her dark brown hair looking almost black since it was still wet. Her skin glistened with a bronze tint.

"I hope you don't mind," announced Eileen. "I decided to *Topher* makeup, since I'm running behind and hungry."

My eyebrows lifted as I tilted my head in surprise. "I would never have known. You don't need it; you look wonderful without it."

Jake looked at Eileen. "Just like your momma, you don't need it. You can thank your Cherokee grandmother for that gift."

"I must look a mess," I said, glancing at my clothes. "I've been out here with sunscreen on, fishing for bass, and working on engines."

"Nah, don't worry about that. Let's go eat. I've worked up quite an appetite fixing your boat," responded Eileen.

"Okay, you two," said an embarrassed Jake. "I think I've heard enough. Y'all have a nice dinner." Jake stared at me as a protective father, and I caught his drift.

"Yes, sir," I said, almost standing at attention out of respect for my elder. "Thank you for all of your help today, sir."

"Hmmm . . . " said Eileen. "Where do you live, Dalton?"

"Oh," I answered, "in South Huntsville."

"Well," she said, "to save you time and distance, I'll follow you in my truck to Docksides, and afterward, you can head on back home and don't have to come back out here. Besides, I don't know if I can trust you not to kidnap me."

"I respect and appreciate that," I answered. "I want you to feel safe and comfortable."

"See ya at Docksides," said Eileen.

"We'll see you there," I replied. Off we went.

* * *

Suddenly, I felt the bow of the boat lift as we went over the wake of a passing ski boat that was much faster than us. It snapped me from my memory from years ago back to the present of sitting next to Eileen. That long ago meeting flashed through my head in seconds while we motored along Town Creek.

Years have flown by. Eileen's parents have died, and we have two children together. She's even more beautiful to me today, as the mother of my children, than that first day at her parents' house. I still am drawn to her mixed scent of cucumber and strawberries, and I still catch myself looking at her hair laying on the back of her neck.

Lately, I haven't given her the attention she deserves, and today is a splendid day to change that. With my left hand on the tiller, I scooted right next to her, reached my right hand around her, and drew her close. My dear wife rested her head on my shoulder. Her hair lifted and blew in the wind.

A warm glow spilled over us as we neared the bridge and its familiar limestone walls covered in moss. Two people are fishing under the bridge from either bank side. I heeded the bright orange warning sign, "No Wake Zone. Idle Speed Only." It hovered over the center of the bridge, telling me to slow the boat to a crawl so that I was not sending out waves to rock nearby boats or disturb the people fishing under the bridge.

A beautiful adventure awaited us on the other side.

Chapter 16

"Let's go to the sandbar." Eileen turned her head and looked at me as she held her arm out, pointing to the left.

"Sounds good to me." I nodded my head.

Johnny Bruce skated over the water in the canyon of Town Creek, where short, stubby mountains bordered the creek on both sides as part of the long, skinny state park boundary of Lake Guntersville State Park. Northeastern Alabama sits in the foothills of the Appalachian chain. The mountains are carpeted with the fresh, green leaves of an intermix of hardwoods—maples and oaks mixed with cedar and pine. Maple leaves look like a five-finger hand, while oak leaves look like a mitten. Cedars are dark green with needles instead of leaves. The rich scent of cedar filled the air. The carpet of green reflected in the water, making it look like a tunnel and floor of rippled, green water.

We were silent, but our hearts spoke volumes. My arm's grip tightened around Eileen, and she squeezed my leg, which told me she was in a cheerful place.

We neared the sandbar cove. No other boats were in sight. Usually on a warm Saturday, several boats were beached at this sandbar. Today, it was all ours. Well, I thought no one was around, until I spotted two people sitting on a log. It was an older couple. The man wore a casual, light blue, button-down shirt tucked into his khaki pants. His gray hair peeked out underneath his black baseball cap. The woman wore a wide grin on her face that was brightened by her pink, button down top and white pants. Neither of them wore shoes. There was a faint glow about them. There wasn't a boat nearby—just a couple sitting on a log. *How did they get here?*

"Hey, Dalton," asked Eileen, "who is that couple? They look familiar to me."

"Yeah, me, too." I steered the boat closer to the sandbar beach.

The couple waved at us as we beached *Johnny Bruce* on the sandbar.

"Hello there. How y'all doin'?" asked the lady.

"Oh, my goodness!" exclaimed Eileen. "It can't be! How is this possible?"

I stared at the man on the log. He wore an old baseball cap with a "Team Evinrude" patch on the front. *I know this man. He's . . .*

"Daddy! Momma!" shouted Eileen as she leaped out of the boat and ran to the couple.

Jake and Helen Snellgrove were standing in front of us on the sandbar. No wonder there wasn't another boat in sight. *Johnny Bruce,* our wonder boat, had unveiled another surprise for us. Jake had died eight years ago, followed by Helen four years later. Today, Eileen received a priceless gift: a visit with her parents.

"Hello, sweetheart." Helen stretched her arms out to her daughter. Eileen wrapped her arms around her mother, while her dad came over and hugged both of them.

"I don't understand," I said. "How is it possible for us to feel you and hug you as if you were really here?"

Jake knew what I meant. "We usually can't, Dalton," answered Jake. "Most times, y'all go through us. But just like when you got your visit from your dad, the love was so great between us that God let that override the physical. He created it, after all."

"I'm thankful He did!" I laughed as I reached and hugged Jake. "It's great to see you two."

Eileen was crying. "I've missed you two so much. Maybe it's a miracle. What did I do to deserve this visit?"

Helen looked at her daughter and said with soft intentness, "Eileen, you believed. You believed the truth of what Dalton told you. You knew in your heart that what he was sharing with you was real. It's your consistent faith through joy and sorrow."

"God likes to honor and reward his faithful servants," said Jake. "And you two have been faithful servants."

Jake had been diagnosed with prostate cancer about five years after Eileen and I married. Within two years, cancer had taken a toll on Jake, and he had left this earth. Eileen was very close to her dad, and in those few years, they spent even more time together. In a gray, plastic dishwashing pan, she would load up engine parts that were lying around Jake's shop. She would bring them to Jake, who was sitting in his recliner or in his bed. Jake would look at the parts and diagnose problems for improvements or repair.

When Jake died, the light in Helen died, too. Like most marriages, Jake and Helen had their share of arguments, disagreements, and aggravations with each other; but they loved each other and were committed to each other. Every now and then, I heard Helen say to Eileen, "Sometimes, he just bugs me."

Helen, Eileen, and I would laugh when she said this, but that was the extent of how negative Helen would be. They didn't share everything in common, but they exhibited how a couple complements each other. Where one was weak, the other was strong. They showed us how to take care of one another. They were like soldiers in the field living for their Lord, standing back-to-back, ready to take on anyone who might come up against them.

We could tell that Helen lacked the will to keep going on this earth without Jake, but her grandchildren kept her going. Though, she wanted to be with Jake. Four years ago, she did just that and died peacefully in her sleep.

Eileen occasionally would sigh and mention wistfully how she would like to have one more fireside chat with her parents. This visit fulfilled that request.

Both of them had lived life to the fullest. Eileen was at peace with how both left this world and entered the spiritual presence of God. She knew that both of them were together, but it didn't take grief away from Eileen. Her life felt empty without them. She was sad knowing they were no longer on this earth.

Jake stepped forward and placed a dry log over a fire pit. Immediately, a fire lit with no matches or spark from Jake. "God's here," said Jake.

I looked around to see if there was any other being present and suddenly felt a wind pass behind me as it rushed over the fire and stoked the flames skyward in a spiral.

Eileen's mouth hung open, and then she peered at me and smiled. She soaked in this casual conversation, updating her parents on how their grandchildren were growing, our busy lives, and the gratitude she had for this unexpected visit. It was the perfect visit between parents and adult children. Sally was in heaven on earth—we all were.

Jake reached out and held Eileen's hand. "We helped bring this boat to you, knowing you needed to restore the outboard. My hands were on yours as you figured out what it needed to run again. You helped restore the power to the boat so *Johnny Bruce* has the power to be with us today."

"Thank you, Daddy," said Eileen.

"Y'all need to get back to Eva and Ned," said Helen. "You give them big hugs for us and let them know how much we love them and that we are watching out for them."

Jake added, "Yep, the Son has heard our cry of protection for them, and we've seen the shields being shot out to guard and protect the kids. They look like surfboards darting through the air, then sticking to the ground around your kids like a wooden fence. Evil can't get through. It's amazing to see."

"That's the way my dad described it, too," I said.

"Y'all get going now," said Helen.

"One more thing y'all need to hear," said Jake. "Be aware of those who want to take away what you have. Remember, the enemy is deceptive and wants to take you down. I'll let you figure out the rest."

We hugged Jake and Helen again, blessed to feel their presence once more. Eileen and I got back in the boat, and Jake pushed us off. We watched Jake and Helen standing there with their arms around each other, waving at us. Then, they vanished into the air just as Daddy had in my visit with him.

We headed back to the picnic area. Eileen sat by my side with a glowing smile. I expected tears to be streaming down her face. Instead, she was in a silver glow. She clutched my hand and soaked in the warmth of the afternoon sun.

When we got back to the dock, Ned came running out to greet us.

"Mommy, Daddy," said Ned, "y'all are back so soon!"

I looked at my watch. Only thirty minutes had passed since we had left the dock—basically the travel time up Town Creek and back to the picnic area.

"I don't understand," said Eileen. "We must have been at that sand bar with—"

I held up my finger to my mouth to signal. "Shhh."

"You, on the sandbar," Eileen continued, "for like an hour. I don't get it."

I looked at Eileen and patted the gunnel of *Johnny Bruce*. "I don't either, but we aren't meant to understand everything, just accept that it is and what it is—we have a miracle boat."

Flashing through my mind was Jake's last word of warning to us about the enemy. *That's the second warning about the enemy. First from Daddy and now from Jake.*

Chapter 17

The next week, I was back to the grind at Rocket City Tech. My work at Rocket City Tech was becoming a means to provide for my family. However, I still had hope that I was being given messages and revelations for a reason. Now that I had firsthand operation experience of Green Wave, I was inclined to give another pitch on Green Wave. In the world of sales, marketing, and business development, sometimes a person has to be presented seven times with the sales pitch or advertisement for it to "land" on the consumer.

My boss had heard my ideas previously and shot them down, but I had presented them only once. I felt dejected, so I let it go. But something within me felt promise in Clyde and Herb's creation.

I pounced on Milo while he was grabbing coffee in the breakroom. He was facing the coffee pot and wall with an expressionless face.

"Hey, Milo," I said hoping my casual voice hid my nervousness.

"Hey there, Dalton," said Milo. "How's it going?"

Milo turned and looked at me as he raised his coffee cup, took a sip, and spoke in a matter-of-fact manner. "What's the latest?"

A wave of confidence and stability washed over me. "Sir, my family and I recently completed a project that we are quite proud of. We restored a twenty-year-old boat."

"Really? Sounds like fun." Milo took another sip.

"My family enjoyed the project, and now we have a boat to use. We took it out for the first time this past weekend. We had such a great time boating around Guntersville Lake. We saw eagles and loons, caught some fish, and soaked in the sunshine."

A look of disinterest showed on Milo's face as he turned away from me and walked toward the door to go back to his office. "That's great, Dalton."

I followed him. *Oh no, you don't; you aren't escaping this moment.* "What else made it great was that we tried out Clyde and Herb's Green Wave on our old outboard. It ran smoothly. No blue smoke and improved our gas mileage. It's a novel design."

Milo paused in the hallway and turned around with a puzzled look. "You tried out what—the green what?"

"It's this add-on part for outboards that works like a fuel and oil injector for older outboard motors," I explained. "It makes the outboards more environmentally friendly."

"Is this the same thing that you and Clyde came to tell me about?"

"Yes, sir."

Milo sighed and rolled his eyes toward the ceiling. "Dalton, I appreciate your ambition and perseverance, but Rocket City Tech isn't going to create more products for the marine industry. We make more money working with the companies we already serve."

"But I'm telling you, this could be revolutionary," I rebutted.

"Thanks, but no thanks. Keep up your magnificent work. We have the American Marine Manufacturers Expo coming in July to see some of our marine clients. Let's make a great booth for that and have some of our best swag to hand out. Makes those companies feel confident in us when we can shake their reps' hands and give out some coffee mugs."

Milo continued walking down the hallway back to his office. I stood still in the hallway feeling defeated, again. *Hmm, maybe this is what Jake was warning me about the enemy—the enemy was winning.*

Chapter 18

Spending time with Clyde and Herb around their outboard motors sparked memories of my love for outboard motors. As a child, I used to play with toy boats and around Daddy's Evinrude outboard in the garage. In adulthood, Jake Snellgrove taught me how to work on these outboards at his lakeside marina and small engine repair shop.

When Eileen and I were dating seriously, Jake would invite me to come help in his shop on weekends. At first, I did it because Eileen was going to be there, too, and I took every free moment for us to be together. On Saturdays, Jake wasn't as serious about his work as he was during the week. He reserved Monday through Friday to do the intense work for his customers, and on Saturdays, he was open for half days, knowing people would be at the lake and run into engine breakdowns. While he awaited new business to come in, he would fiddle with his hobby engines from the fifties and sixties.

Jake didn't get up as early on Saturdays as he did during the week. He would sleep in until six in the morning. Not much of a break, but that was what he was used to. Eileen would sleep in until about ten. Energized by my excitement to spend the day around her, I would rush over to Jake's shop to be there around eight.

Jake had an Evinrude Fleetwin that was nearly identical to the one Daddy had. Jake reminded me they had made a bunch of them, and this one needed to be rebuilt. With Jake's supervision, I rebuilt the engine by replacing worn parts with new parts to get it running as good as new. Once Eileen awoke and her lavender soap scent permeated the shop, I was not much use as a mechanic. Jake knew this and would say, "Y'all get on outta here, ya lovebirds."

After Eileen and I married, Jake and I spent more time together on Saturday mornings doing a combination of testing repaired outboards and fishing for bass. I was happy to have a father figure in my life who shared my passion for boats and fishing.

Helen was a good cook like many Southern women from her generation. She liked to make people smile by igniting their taste buds and filling up their tummies. Most of her cooking was scratch cooking—making recipes that were not store-bought, out-of-a-box cooking. That's how her mother had taught her, and that is what she was going to do as well. Her dishes consisted of roast beef, collard greens, fried squash, fresh green beans, potato salad, sweet corn-on-the-cob, spinach casserole, and chicken fried steak. Her stand-out meal was the Schofield Family Camp Stew. This was a single dish meal that contained meat and vegetables in a thick sauce. The recipe had been passed down for generations, and the key to its scrumptious taste was the time it simmered on the stove.

Helen loved to tell the story from her childhood of watching her grandmother cook this stew for large family gatherings. Helen had marveled at the big, black cast iron cauldron hanging over an open fire in the backyard.

"First, the water starts to boil," Helen described. "Then goes in the already whole roasted chicken, then a quarter gallon of tomatoes. Next is a heaping amount of sweet white corn niblets. Dump in three chopped up onions and a bulb of sliced garlic. To make it easy on the tummy, add some baking soda and some lemon wedges to sweeten the saltiness. To top it off, dump in a bunch of sliced okra. Ya know, okra is one of Gods' gifts to the South—well, that and the peach tree. Mix it all together and let it simmer over the stoked fire for six hours or when the sun begins to set—whichever comes first."

Helen told this story to whomever would listen when she made her camp stew over her natural gas stove inside an air-conditioned house. Not once did I ever see her refer to a written recipe. She did it all from memory, and that's how she taught her children to make it as well. Of course, her pot was much smaller than the one her grandmother used, and the portions were smaller. Her measurements were not in cups or spoons; instead, they were a pinch of this or a handful of that.

The Schofield Family Camp Stew was a scrumptious feast! She didn't make it often, but when she did, it was enough to feed a small encampment of children, grandchildren, brothers, and sisters.

Every meal included dessert—even if lunch was a sandwich. There were peach cobbler; strawberry pie; peanut butter cookies; and congealed gelatin salad with bananas, strawberries, apples, oranges, and peaches.

One Saturday morning, Jake and I were working in the shop, and Helen stuck her head out the door and announced, "Lunch is ready."

Immediately, Jake put down his tools and washed his hands at the sink. I kept working on removing an old gasket. Jake asked, "Dalton, whatcha doin'? Lunch is ready."

"Yeah, I heard," I replied. "Let me get this gasket off and . . . "

Jake stood next to my work bench, leaned over in front of me, and said, "I'm gonna tell you a secret to my lasting marriage to Mrs.

Snellgrove. When a meal is ready that she has spent time making, we show our respect by not makin' her wait. We drop what we are doin' and get cleaned up and come to the table because if we don't, this could be our *last* supper, if ya know what I mean."

I put my tools on the bench, got cleaned up, and followed Jake and Eileen into the house. As soon as the door opened, we inhaled the aroma of cooked beef, vegetables, and cornbread. Each of us sat down before a large bowl of Schofield Camp Stew.

With her sweet, quiet voice, Helen announced, "I made a small batch this time. On Sunday, we have a potluck dinner after church. Y'all enjoy."

We thanked God for our wonderful meal, and blessings followed by enjoying a delicious meal. Before Helen was finished eating her bowl of stew, she said, "I've got something new for dessert for y'all to try. I got this store-bought pie that looked good. I usually make my desserts from scratch, but the ladies in my Sunday school class have been telling me how good this store-bought pie is. One of 'em said it was as good as a pie she made from scratch. So, I thought I would try it. Y'all want a slice of peach pie?"

Before we could answer, she was already slicing up four pieces to serve Jake, Eileen, Helen, and myself. She placed the pie slices next to our stew bowls with the gentle clank of dessert forks on the small plates.

Jake was the first to finish eating the stew. "Great lunch, Mother Snellgrove. Thank you!"

He picked up his dessert fork and dug into his slice of peach pie. I heard the crunch of his fork as it sank into a peach, followed by the closed mouth crunching of a bite of pie. I followed suit and speared my fork into the pie slice and was surprised by the resistance of the tongs into the peach. I took a bite, expecting a warm, soft texture. Instead, I tasted cold crust and frozen fruit. I looked at Jake, who was now into his second bite. His confused eyes glanced at mine, trying to gauge my reaction to this unusually hard, cold texture. I swallowed the bite and took another.

Eileen and Helen were still eating their stew, so we could not gauge their reaction. I got the same sensation as the first bite. I pushed my fork tines into the middle of the slice and met resistance. *Ah, I know what it is.*

I looked up at Helen and said, "Mrs. Snellgrove, this pie is frozen."

Without hesitation, Jake immediately agreed with a simple, yet similar proclamation. "Yeah!"

Jake was going to eat the pie as it was and not complain a bit. He thought if his wife made it and offered it to him, then that was good enough for him. *Just be thankful.* Yet when I announced the oddity of eating frozen pie, he didn't hesitate to agree.

Helen looked perplexed, picked up her dessert fork, speared her tine-resistant slice of peach pie, and took a bite. "It sure is! My, my." She got up from the table, grabbed the store-bought pie box sitting on the counter, and read the instructions. The three of us watched her eyes as they darted over the preparation instructions.

"Would you believe it says you have to bake it first?" she said in surprise. "I thought it was ready to eat!"

"Let me see that box." Eileen grabbed the box from her mother. "Bake for thirty minutes at 325." Holding the pie box in her hands, Eileen leaned her head back in her chair and howled in laughter. "Momma, you fed us frozen pie. You have to bake it first!"

I started laughing, too, followed by Jake and, eventually, Helen.

Eileen pointed her finger at her dad and said, "You weren't going to say anything were you, Daddy?" Jake was laughing so hard, all he could do was shake his head as he wiped his eyes.

I paused in between laughs long enough to get out, "I saw the weird look on his face as he was chewing, thinkin', *Pie's frozen. Guess that's how it's supposed to be.*"

"I sure am sorry, y'all. I thought that's what you did with store-bought pie. It's ready to eat right out of the box," apologized Helen as we continued to laugh. "Let me put this in the oven and bake it properly. Y'all can have a snack this afternoon."

The Store-Bought Pie Debacle, as it came to be known, continued to bring Eileen and I uncontrollable laughter whenever we recalled the event. We did manage to enjoy a hot, baked slice of peach pie later that same afternoon.

Chapter 19

A fishing trip with Jake gave me one of the most frightening moments of my life. It happened about a year after Eileen and I married.

Numerous times before Jake and I would go boating, Helen would pull me aside and say, "Dalton, now you remember that Jake isn't always the most safety-conscious boat driver. I need you to look out for him and warn him if you see anything unsafe."

"Yes, ma'am. I will," I replied.

I was visiting Jake one Saturday morning, and he had his aluminum utility boat tied up to the dock. This boat had three bench seats that ran from gunnel to gunnel—one at the bow, one in the middle, and one near the stern. These seats combined with the curve of the hull made it difficult to stand or move about the boat from front to back. It's like being in a stadium with three rows of bleachers sitting at ground level. You have to carefully step over the bleacher seat in front of you to get to the next row.

Jake was perplexed when I arrived with fishing rods in hand.

"What's wrong, Jake?" I asked as I walked onto the dock, seeing him bent over the boat looking at the uncovered outboard engine.

"I got this one motor that I just can't figure out what's wrong with it. I thought we would use it today while we are out fishin'. A man brought it by this week, and I've been working on it ever since. I think I got it workin' right."

The outboard was painted light gray and weighed heavily on the back of this little boat. It was a uniquely branded, twelve-horsepower outboard from a retail department store that fell into decline. This was the only one I ever saw.

We got in the boat, and Jake told me, "These older engines don't have a kill switch like the newer outboards. You can start them up, even if they are in forward or reverse. If you ain't careful, when you start 'em, you will get thrown from the boat when it moves forward or backward as soon as it starts."

"I'll try to remind you to make sure the gear is in neutral," I replied.

We got into the boat. Jake turned to pull-start the engine, and I announced, "Make sure it's in neutral."

It was. Jake pulled on the starter rope three times before it started. Off we went into a deep-water, rocky cove to fish for bass. We were catching small bass like crazy with an occasional large bluegill mixed in. The sun got higher in the sky, heating the water and air as the fish-catching slowed. We were getting tired, hungry, and ready to get back to the cool Snellgrove home. I was sleepy and not very alert, and neither was Jake.

"Let's get home, Dalton," said Jake, and I agreed. He pulled on the starter rope, and it didn't start. He pulled on it again. It didn't start. Jake pulled out the choke to fully open. He pulled it again with more force, and it didn't start. Then, Jake stood up to get more leverage on the starter rope. As he placed his hand on the pull-handle and began to yank, in my stupor, I yelled, "Make sure it is in neutral!"

It was too late. The engine started, and the boat jerked forward at full throttle. With no one to guide the tiller handle, the motor turned sharply to the left. As it did, Jake's balance was thrown and flew overboard. The engine ran at full throttle in a circle. I turned around and tried to get to the back of the boat to control the engine. The bank of the boat made it impossible for me to stand as I could be thrown overboard as well.

Standing up in the boat, I grabbed a padded seat cushion that doubled as a floatation device and threw it toward Jake, who was terrified as he treaded water, watching this heavy boat and motor running near him at head level. With terror running through my veins, I crawled over the middle bench and was thrown into a roll on the back seat as I looked up to see the boat heading straight toward Jake with its sharp, spinning propeller. Jake stuck his arms out and pushed the boat's bow away from him, then dove underwater as the boat went over him. Inside the boat, I felt a thump.

I steadied myself, grabbed the throttle handle, and twisted it to OFF. Even with the engine off, the boat continued to move forward on the surface. My head jerked around, scanning the water, looking for Jake. The air was deftly silent as I saw the float cushion floating near a limestone rock. *Jake, where are you? I'm sorry, Helen. I failed you.*

"Jake! Jake!" I yelled across the silent water.

Suddenly, to the starboard side, I saw bubbles, and Jake's head shot up. As soon as he broke the surface, his eyes opened widely; he inhaled loudly as his head darted left and right looking for the boat propeller.

"Jake! You're alive!"

"Dalton, get me out of this lake!"

Jake swam next to the boat. I grabbed his arm and pulled him into the boat. Adrenaline flowed so fast through me, it felt like I was pulling his arm out of his socket while he thrashed his legs to swim-lift into the boat. He collapsed atop the center seat.

"Jake, are you okay? Did the propeller hit you?" I looked over his water-soaked body, neck, and head, looking for gashes from the spinning prop.

"I'm okay, Dalton. It didn't hit me. I dove when it came near me. I've never moved so deep so quickly!"

I collapsed in a heap on the rear seat. Out of breath and chests heaving from our sudden terror act of saving Jake's life, we lay there in the bright sunlight. Minutes passed quickly as we regained our composure. Suddenly, a shadow appeared over us. The boat had floated under tree branches. I popped up straight, knowing that if we didn't get away from these branches, we could encounter another terror we wished to avoid—water moccasins dropping into the boat from overhanging branches.

I grabbed the paddle and moved us back to open water.

"Dalton?" asked Jake.

"Yes sir?" I replied.

"I think I know what's wrong with this motor. It needs a kill switch added and a new carburetor."

I started laughing. "You figured it out, huh? Good for you. I am in agreement."

Still lying on the center bench seat, Jake surprised me. "I've never been so scared in my life. By the way, have I ever told you how proud I am that you are my son-in-law?"

I was stunned and nearly speechless as the adrenaline began to wear off. "No, sir, I think this is the first time."

"You're a good husband to my Eileen. You've passed the test."

Jake, still lying on the bench seat, turned his head toward me and looked at me sitting on the rear seat. "I love you, Dalton Russell. Thank you for saving my life." He reached out with a shaky right hand, and I reached out and shook it.

"I love you, too, old man—and you're welcome."

Jake was still lying there in recovery, and he said gently, "Dalton, let's not do this again."

I laughed as I helped him sit up straight. I put the engine in neutral, pulled on the starter rope, and fired the engine. I placed the throttle into low position, moved the gear lever to forward position, and idled out of the cove.

"I agree, old man, not again," I said as we sped toward the Snellgroves' dock to fish another day with a bond strengthened between the two of us.

Chapter 20

Fishing has always made me happy. Learning how to fish was a gift from my dad and granddaddy. For them, fishing was a means to put meat on the table for their families when they were younger. Later on in their lives, it became a way to have fun and be outdoors in the presence of nature.

Often, I go fishing and don't catch a single fish. But other times, I catch a bunch of fish, only to practice catch-and-release and throw them back in the water. And sometimes, I will go out and catch some bluegill, crappie, or "bream"—as we like to call them in Alabama—and bring them home to fry up for dinner. Crappie and bream are the most scrumptious.

I am passing this gift to my children. I don't know how long they will enjoy it, but at least, I'll have introduced it to them. A father passing the love of fishing on to their children was how my friendship with John developed into a brotherhood.

For years, I held onto Daddy's tiny twelve-foot boat for sentimental reasons. The classic aerodynamic engine cowling design of the 1956 Evinrude Fleetwin motor mesmerized me. It was like the cars of the fifties moving into the space age. It had a rounded front that rolled into the rear white-painted side wings. Blue paint mixed with white and black markings and red side reflectors made it look like the face and head of a human imaged robot. To me, it was a symbol of happier times. In elementary school, I drew pictures of the Evinrude to personalize the manila envelope that held my report card.

The sound of the engine mixed with the scent of oil and gasoline soothed me. This boat and motor linked me and Daddy as it was the engine that propelled our fishing adventures. After Daddy died, I held onto the boat and motor. Problem was, in my early twenties, I weighed more than I did as a lanky teenager.

At that point, I had graduated from college and was working my first job and living on my own in an apartment. It was May, and I had decided to take Daddy's boat and motor for a day of fishing. I kept the boat stored at my mother's house, since I didn't have a place to keep it at my apartment. I went to Mother's house and hooked the trailer to my truck. The trailer lights weren't working. I fixed them and headed to the lake. My larger, heftier frame weighed the boat down, in addition to the outboard motor and a trolling motor battery on a wide-open throttle, and the boat was plowing through the water.

"I need more horsepower to push this boat around," I muttered in frustration. I continued to fish but quickly grew exasperated with trying to get around the boat's cramped space. Finally, I called it quits and headed home.

On the way home, I realized it was time for me to let go of the boat and Evinrude. I had outgrown them. Daddy wasn't *in* these things. Machines need to be used in order to remain operational. It wasn't doing any good sitting around the garage or the yard gathering dust and rain.

I had matured and reached a healthy point in my grieving over Daddy's death. I was ready to let go of the things that connected us and hold onto the memories we had made. When I got to Mother's house, she came out to greet me.

I looked at her longingly. "Mother, I think I'll sell the boat," I said. "My day was frustrating; and I'm ready to let go of the boat, motor, and trailer."

Mother tilted her head, perplexed. "I wasn't expecting this."

I told her about the day and what I had experienced. I placed my hand on the Evinrude and gripped the throttle handle.

"She's been a happy, little outboard," I said. "But it's time for someone else to make fresh memories with it."

"As much as I would like to free up space in my garage," said Mother, "I want you to be okay with this decision." She looked directly in my eyes and placed her hand on my shoulder. "We've held on to it because I know how much it means to you. I'm proud of you, Son; you've grown up."

I smiled, reached out, and hugged her as tears of appreciation rolled down my cheek. "Thank you, but I'm ready. Thank you for loving me." I paused in our embrace and then said, "I wonder who the next owner of this fishing rig will be?"

Chapter 21

The next day, I went to church, where John served as a bi-vocational music minister. When the service was over, I chatted with John; it had been a while since we had visited. Our working lives had taken over our social lives. Plus, he was raising a family and had a seven-year-old boy and a ten-year-old girl.

I followed John around the church to turn out the lights and lock the outside doors as we chatted.

"I have started taking Patton and Amber fishing. We go down to the Tennessee River marina just south of town to fish, and they enjoy it. It's a wonderful bonding time. You should see Amber's face light up when she hooks bluegill or catfish. Patton is just happy to be casting the rod or playing with the rocks, but when he catches a fish, I hear, 'Daddy! Daddy! Daddy! I got a big one. Come help me!' You should come with us some time. I could use an extra hand helping them out. I don't even carry a rod. I'm just there to help them."

"Does it get tricky for them standing on the chunk rock shoreline at the marina?" I asked.

"Yeah, it does," answered John as he tested the lock on the sanctuary door. "In fact, we have run into too many water moccasins on the rocks, and it scares me to death. What I really would like to do is find a small boat so we can get away from the snakes and critters. That will work better for us. You got any suggestions on where I can find a small, used boat?"

Strangely, a beam of light shone through a stained-glass window onto me. There it was. The sign illuminated brightly for me to hear and see. *I wonder who will be the next owner of this fishing rig . . . You got any suggestions on where I can find a small, used boat?*

Flabbergasted, I grinned and answered, "I think I can help you out! I've got the fishing rig you've been looking for."

The next weekend, Daddy's boat and motor were hooked to the back of John's minivan on the way to the lake for the first time.

"Try it out and let me know what you think," I told John before he headed down the driveway. Later that day, I got a call from John. "It's perfect. How much do you want for it?"

"Just a chance to see y'all happy in it," I said. "The boat and motor are yours. I'm just delighted that it has found a cheerful family home to make fresh memories."

A week later, I received a check in the mail from John for one hundred dollars with a note scribbled on a yellow office pad.

Dalton,

Hey, please sign this bill of sale for me so we can register the boat.

Thanks,

John

Our friendship moved toward a brotherhood forged by our passion for fishing and boats.

Chapter 22

John and I had many bumpy fishing trips that were a mix of frightening and downright hilarious, bumbled messes.

Our first fishing adventure was in his tiny boat powered by the familiar Evinrude. We went bream fishing on Guntersville Lake on a gorgeous April day. The sky was robin's egg blue, filled with the scent of honeysuckle and fresh-cut grass. Yellow pollen coated the water's surface, while red-winged blackbirds chirped nearby.

The bluegill were in the middle of their spring spawning season. Using their tails, the fish fan out a circular spot that is typically around the size of a car tire. These circular, bowl-shaped spots provide a bed for the female fish to lay eggs and the male fish to fertilize and guard the eggs. The bluegill will create these beds in shallow water with a sandy bottom. From above, these beds look like an underwater field of car tires laying on their sides. The spring spawn is a great time to catch bluegill.

We found bluegill spawning in a muddy, isolated cove. Using live crickets for bait, John and I caught over twenty fish each. Bluegill are tasty fish to eat, but they are small, so you have to catch a large number to feed a family. We caught enough to feed John's family a tasty fish dinner.

Once the sun rose high overhead, we were ready to head home. With our live crickets for bait, John and I had caught over twenty fish a piece.

Back at the launch ramp, John backed the trailer down the ramp while I stayed in the boat to steer and drive it onto the trailer. John got out of his van, closed the door, and came to the back of the van to connect the winch strap to the bow.

"Shoot!" yelled John. "Dalton, I locked the keys in the van!"

"Check the doors," I said. "Maybe one's unlocked." They were locked.

"I am so glad I have an extra key!" John sighed as I hoped it was under a nearby rock.

"Problem is—it's safely on my key rack in my mud room!" answered a disillusioned John. "Joyce to the rescue! I will ask Joyce if she wants to be a hero after I get her on the phone—make the thirty-minute drive here and magically unlock the door!"

Yeah, magic, huh?

Here we were on one of the first beautiful days of spring. It was warm enough to wear shorts, and the fish were biting. Boaters were coming out of garages, driveways, and backyards to be on the lake for the first time of the year. Problem was, they wanted to get their boats onto the water, but our van and trailer were blocking the ramp. Piddle buckets.

A raggedy man with a long beard and cut-off shorts walked down the ramp and hollered, "Hey, what's the hold-up?"

Being the supportive friend I was, I wanted to take the pressure and embarrassment off John, so I answered, "My friend here locked the keys in the van."

"Dalton!" growled a disgruntled John as he gave me the evil eye. That was okay because I redeemed my betrayal by asking, "Would you mind giving him a ride to the nearest payphone so he can call his wife to bring the extra key?"

"Well," said the raggedy man, "what goes around comes around! Hop in my truck, mister."

Off went John and the raggedy man in a Chevy pickup. I watched them get on the highway and drive out of sight, and a sinking feeling came over me. Looking behind me, I saw boats lining up near the ramp with owners desperate to get their vessels onto trailers. Then I looked at the parking lot and saw a line growing of trucks with boats on trailers wanting to get their boats into the water. We were blocking the boat ramp for all.

In the spring as the weather warms, every boat owner is anxious to get their vessel onto the water for a relaxing day to fish, water ski, sail, or ride around the lake. Noontime on a sunny Saturday in the spring at the lake is like Friday afternoon rush hour for cars in the city. When traffic stands still because of a stalled car in the road, traffic backs up; people are anxious to get to their destination. Drivers become inpatient, testy, and uncaring of the poor soul whose car has stalled in traffic. In spring, the boat ramp consists of an even mix of residents from the city and rural areas. The city folks seem to be inpatient because of the stress of city-living. The rural folks seem to be inpatient because traffic is pretty minimal where they live, and they're not used to having to wait. Plus, the city folks make them anxious.

Sweat poured down my back as I explained again and again why our van was blocking the ramp. Securing the bow eye of the boat to the trailer winch, I grabbed the wooden paddle stowed aboard and prepared myself for battle next to the paralyzed van. The accusers gathered on the pavement, near the dock, and on boats. My face was red; my wrists were sweaty; and my stomach was empty—which was clear by its loud growling and gassy toots. Questions about our actions hurled my way.

"Why didn't ya leave the windows rolled down?" demanded a boater.

"I always keep an extra key tucked under the wheel well," shot a pickup trucker.

"Idiots, you're blocking the ramp!" exclaimed Captain Obvious.

"I'll just send this rock here through the window, and that will open 'er up to get the keys!" fired Sergeant Impatience.

"Are you crazy? That will leave broken glass all over the ramp that could puncture a tire, and then you got another mess on your hands!" I exclaimed in shock.

The crowd was gathering, and I stood my ground with a paddle, fending them off with the best charm I could muster in such an embarrassing situation.

"Yeah, it's my fault. I should have told my friend to roll down the windows," I stammered.

"Idiots, yes, we don't know how to carry a spare key," I bumbled. "Just us idiot city folk."

Suddenly, behind me, I felt a shield behind my back.

"Talked to Joyce," said John. "She'll be here in twenty minutes." John stood his ground next to me, having picked up his weapon of choice—a six-foot bait-casting rod armed with a fishing lure at its tip and dangling with treble hooks ready to enter the skin of anyone that dared attack us. Desperate times, desperate measures!

“You okay, Dalton?” worried John while he swung the Abu Garcia weapon before him. “You are soaking wet! Did you fall in the water?”

“Naw, just sweat,” I answered as my eyes darted over the looming crowd gathered on the dock and in the boats creeping closer to the ramp. At the moment, it looked like the boats were gaining in number so great that you could walk from one to another without hitting the water. Thoughts of the Battle of Leyte Gulf filled my head. In actuality, there were only ten boats nearby.

The crowd hurled insults to the two of us, some of them questioning our ancestry. Thankfully, I knew more about my family tree than these strangers in boats—especially my mother’s. Just when it seemed to get at the highest peak of disgruntlement, the clouds parted, and a ray of light shone down illuminating a forest green Mazda chariot entering the parking lot. A savior had arrived. A hero appeared by the name of Joyce the Keyholder!

“She’s here!” shouted John. “Joyce to the rescue!” John ran toward the Mazda to bow down in thankfulness at his wife’s presence, along with his two children riding in the back seat.

Joyce pulled up to the top of the ramp, rolled down the driver’s side window, and reached out her arm, holding a tiny, black wand of entry. With a simple press of the button, we heard the magic chirp of doors unlocking the van. John opened the driver’s side door, looked toward the heavens offering thanks, turned toward Joyce, and said, “Thank you!”

Joyce looked at John and asked, “We good? It’s unlocked?”

“Yes!” cheered a celebratory and appreciative John.

“Okay, we’re off to soccer practice and piano lessons,” replied Joyce. “Bye.”

With that, Joyce was off in the forest green Mazda chariot, carrying the tiny, black wand of power—er, I mean, keyless entry.

With the boat already hooked to the trailer, John wasted no time pulling it up the ramp.

"Dalton, get in!" hollered John from the driver's seat.

"Sorry, folks," I yelled to the heated crowd of boaters. "We're out of your way now."

Eager to avoid a mob attack of hurled insults that could wound us for the rest of the week, John focused on inching the van forward while I high-tailed it to the passenger side and hopped in. We didn't even bother to strap down the boat.

"I just want to get out of here," said John. "We'll pull into this gas station, put away our gear, and secure the boat to the trailer. Whew! What a mess."

Thus ended the first fishing boat adventure of John and Dalton. Thankfully, there were more to come that didn't require us to fight off rural Alabamians and inpatient city folks with wooden paddles and treble-hooked fishing rods.

Chapter 23

Uncanny occurrences happened when John and I fished together out of his boat, but sometimes, things went right. Difficulties are a part of life, and they are a part of following your passion. For us, there was more to fishing than catching fish, which made it all the sweeter when we caught fish.

John and I fished in Town Creek on a sunny, but chilly February day. We got a bucket full of minnows from Lake Front Bait 'N Grub next to the launch ramp. John and I fished there so often that the store owners became our friends. Gene and Sharon lived in a house next to the store and were always around. The store was a cinder block building painted green with a twenty-feet long window offering a full view of Town Creek and Little Mountain. We parked in the gravel parking lot and walked up the concrete walkway that led to the store's front porch, where a huge tub of water circulated to keep the bait minnows swimming lively. Gene greeted us and dipped a net in the tub to gather two dozen minnows for us.

"Sure like that boat you got, John," remarked Gene.

"Yep, I finally got it all fixed up the way I like it," replied John. "I think today will be a great crappie-catching day."

"Minnows and jig fishing," I clarified.

"Y'all be careful out on the water," warned Gene. "It's warming up, but that water is still cold. Bundle up and go get 'em."

"Thanks, Gene," I said. "Tell Sharon we said hello."

One fabulous thing about fishing in winter months is that we did not have to get up early to beat the sunrise. We arrived at the lake around mid-morning as the sun was heating the air and water. We felt well-rested when fishing in winter, but we needed it, too. The body works harder to keep warm than it does on warm spring days.

We were bundled up with thermal underwear, wool socks, flannel shirts, layered jackets, toboggans, and fingerless gloves. This was our first fishing day of the year after a winter of waiting for a warm Saturday to get outdoors for more than a quick run to the mailbox. North Alabama is in the southern United States, but it is not a tropical environment. Guntersville Lake is in the foothills of the Appalachian Mountains. It snows on occasion, and temperatures can drop below freezing for a few weeks.

As always, our time together warmed with conversation. We shared our struggles, provided each other with advice on handling situations, and unloaded our burdens. All of this mixed with the beauty of watching bald eagles soaring high on thermal drifts above the lake, seeing mist rise like pillars of steam, and hearing the wind blowing through a forest of leafless hardwoods. Fishing is about being absorbed by nature on a floating platform.

I dipped my hand into the minnow bucket of chilly water to grab a minnow for my crappie jig and chuckled. "Man, this feels great! My hand is freezing in this water, but it's great to be out here!"

"Nothin' like fishin'," said John.

We were fishing for crappie with ultra-light rods and reels with a baited hook drifting under a red bobber. The wind, with directional help from the trolling motor, drifted us around fallen trees hanging over the water. The tendrils of branches reached underwater to make ideal hiding spots for crappie.

"Hey, you smell that?" asked John. "Someone is cooking up some sausage. Mhhmm."

"Yeah, I see the smoke rising from the lakefront store," I said. "Looks like Gene and Sharon are having brunch."

"Sure smells better than the peanut butter sandwiches we have on board." John grinned.

"Yep, but we're catching crappie," I replied. "Just imagine how that will smell when we fry them later this afternoon."

Already, we had about ten crappies in the live-well from fishing in the deep water under the bridge. Enough for a decent dinner between us but we wanted more to have a veritable feast for the entire family.

"Let's anchor in this spot here, John." I gestured to the rocks and fallen trees. The tree branches of the fallen pine tree provided a structure for the crappie to gather and feed on the tiny fish feeding on the algae growth on the tree. "I think we have an excellent shot at catching some more."

"Good enough for me," replied John.

We anchored the boat so it was parallel to the bank. We started catching more crappie, one after the other. Our hands grew colder as we dipped them into the cold minnow bucket to re-bait our hooks.

We munched on peanut butter sandwiches, flicking crumbs into the water. The water was clear emerald green in sharp contrast to the brown, leafless hardwoods surrounding the lakeshore. The creek arm sheltered us from the wind of the open water of the lake. Whiffs of pine filled the air as the wind blew past the pine and cedar trees scattered among the forest.

"You know," said John, "I think I'll put on a tiny spinner bait and scout for some crappie around our boat. I'll keep a bobber fishing rod in the water at the bow while I cast around. Dalton, you mind keeping watch on my minnow rod?"

"Sure thing!" I replied.

With that, lunch was over, and we were back to fishing.

"John," I said, "it's funny how on a lunch break during a workday, we take that full hour to do things we want to do."

"Yeah," said John. "I'm usually reading my fishing magazines during lunch."

"Here we are out fishing," I continued, "and we can't gobble down our lunch fast enough to get back to fishing!"

"Not to mention"—John laughed—"How hard it is to get out of bed at six a.m. on a workday, but we bound out of bed at four a.m. on a Saturday to go fishing!"

"The pursuit of passion." I grinned.

John placed his minnow rod in a holder mounted to the side of the boat.

We got back on the boat deck to keep fishing. He sat atop a swivel seat perched at the bow and cast his spinner bait to nearby trees. I sat at the stern and crept my red bobber around the nearby tree branch, seeking a hungry crappie. Between us, John's red bobber floated near the overhanging tree. Suddenly, I saw the red bobber zoom off in front of the boat.

"John," I yelled, "you've got a fish on your minnow rod!"

John quickly put down his spinner bait rod and picked up his minnow rod. He set the hook and felt a heavy tug on his line. This was bigger than the one-pound crappies we had caught today.

"My goodness!" shouted John. "This is the biggest fish I've *ever* hooked!"

"Oh no," I yelled back. "The line has gone under the branch and log." We needed to pull the fish out into open water to get away from the branches sticking in the water. They were a hazard to the thin fishing line that can easily be snapped if it rubs against the rough bark. The hooked fish knows it is safer if it can stay in the tree brush, so it fights its way toward the tree while the fisherman pulls it away. Our boat was parked parallel to the shoreline and fallen trees.

"Get up the anchors!" John applied pressure to the fishing rod. "I've only got a six-pound test line on this reel."

Quickly, I brought up the anchors so we could move the boat near the branch. John used the trolling motor to move the boat so I could reach the branch.

"See if you can get the line free from the tree!" hollered John. "Oh man, Dalton, this is a *big* fish!"

I reached over to free the fishing line that had gone underneath the branches and log.

"It's wrapped around a branch!" I hollered. Gingerly, I tried to unwrap the line when we heard it. *SNAP!* I saw the bow on John's fishing rod snap up straight. He slumped over in dismay.

"It broke off." A disheartened John sighed. "That was a big fish."

"I'm sorry, John." I hung my head, joining John in disappointment. "I guess I should've been gentler with the line on the branch."

"Nah, it ain't your fault. Things happen."

In disgust, I glanced at the tree where John's line had wrapped on a branch. The fishing line was still attached to the branch, and the red bobber floated near the branch.

I reached over and unwrapped the fishing line from the branch.

"John!" I yelled. "There's still some weight on the end of this line!"

"Is it still on?" John asked.

Hand over hand, I carefully pulled in the fishing line. After four wraps of line, a two-foot-long largemouth bass floated to the surface with a crappie hook in the side of her mouth.

"Look at that!" yelled John. "She's still on! She ain't moving at all. Guess the water is too cold. Grab her, Dalton!"

I reached out my right hand and grabbed the lip of this bass behemoth. I lifted her out of the water. John and I burst into laughter.

"Look, I can stick my whole fist in her mouth!" I exclaimed.

"Hah-hah, what a catch." John chuckled. "Just a moment ago, I thought we'd lost her when the line snapped. Oh, thank goodness for that tree branch to hang onto the line."

"Is this the biggest bass you've ever caught?" I asked.

"Yeah, it is," replied John as he bent over to rest his hands on his knees. "Except *we* caught it. I reeled her in with the rod, and you reeled her in with your hands! How much do you think she weighs?"

The largemouth bass had a half-ball-shaped belly behind its dorsal fin, which is a sign of a pregnant fish. "She's full of eggs, looks like." I eyed the fish. "I guess 'bout seven pounds."

"Let's go weigh her at Gene and Sharon's," said John. "Then let's release her back into the lake so she can lay those eggs soon. We've got enough crappie for a fish fry, and I'm about ready to get warmed up."

"Me, too," I agreed.

After getting the boat on the trailer, we took the big bass up to Lake Front Bait 'N Grub.

"Whohoo!" hollered Gene as we walked in the store. "Looks like y'all got a giant!"

"We sure did." John beamed. "And we caught her on a crappie hook. Can we weigh her on your scale?"

"Sure," replied Gene. "Bring her right over here." Gene had a grocery store scale commonly used to weigh produce. "By Alabama Fish and Game rules, this is an official scale."

Gene placed the bass on the bucket of the scale and let go.

"Eight pounds, one ounce," announced Gene.

"Wow!" hollered John. "It's bigger than I thought."

"Let's get a picture, so we can post it to the wall over here." Gene pulled out a Polaroid, camera from under the counter. John held up the eight-pound largemouth bass and held it in front of his chest.

"Smile!" instructed Gene. *SNAP!* The photo ejected out the front of the Polaroid and we watched it develop before our eyes.

"Nice photo, but too bad you're in it," I ribbed my buddy.

Gene wrote John's name at the bottom of the photo, the date, and the weight of the bass. He added the photo to the corkboard wall of other photos taken over the years of lunker fish caught by Lake Front Bait 'N Grub customers.

"Tell me," asked Gene, "how'd y'all catch it?"

We told him the story of the collective effort of reeling in the bass.

"I'm gonna' mount this fish," declared John. "It's the biggest fish I've ever caught."

For years afterward, our eight-pound, largemouth bass hung on the wall in John's office.

Some fishing days, we caught a glorious memory but no fish. Some days, God smiled, and we caught fish and a glorious memory.

Chapter 24

The Sunday following our day on the lake with the family, I was washing *Johnny Bruce* in our backyard. Our good neighbor Ed Bartwell was working in his backyard.

"Hey, neighbor." Ed waved.

"Hey, Ed," I answered, "how are you doing today?"

"Good," said Ed. "Gettin' the grass mowed for the week. The weeds they are growin'."

"Yeah, you are welcome to mow mine, too." I chuckled. Ed walked over next to the boat.

"I see y'all have taken your boat out," said Ed. "How did she run?"

"Good. The outboard, trolling motor trailer—everything works swimmingly. Thanks for your help in getting the boat restored. I lovingly patted *Johnny Bruce* like a doting father.

"Glad to. Anything to get this beauty up and running again. Take me out with her sometime." Ed grinned.

"Absolutely!" I answered. "You know what's weird, Ed? All these years, I have referred to boats, ships, airplanes, even cars with a feminine name. I've always called them *She* but this here hunk of metal has a masculinity about it. For the first time, I've called a boat *He*."

"I've done that, too." Ed leaned against the boat. "Oops, I'm sorry. I know you named it *Johnny Bruce,* and here I come over and refer to it as *She*. Well, you know, *Johnny Bruce* is a handsome feller. I understand he used to belong to one of your best friends."

"Yeah, that's right, Ed." I dropped my head and then looked at the boat. "John was a best friend, who died a while back. This boat was a key link in our friendship."

"I'm sorry to hear that, Dalton." Ed sighed. "Sudden loss is hard, no matter what the circumstance. Has restoring *Johnny Bruce* been helpful in reconnecting with your friend?"

"Yeah, Ed," I answered. "It has. I have told no one outside the family about this, but the boat seems to have some, well, personality all its own. Kinda like therapy for me and ya know, showing me some things. I wouldn't be able to experience any other way without it. Sorry, I don't know why I'm telling you this. I hope you won't think I'm looney for thinking like this."

"Odd as it sounds," said Ed, "I understand where you are coming from. You ain't looney at all. We miss those who've passed on."

"What y'all talkin' 'bout?" came a voice behind me that made me jump.

"Oh, Mark." I turned around as the hairs on my neck stood up. "You startled me. Hey, how was your day at the lake yesterday?"

"Samfrantastic! How 'bout y'all?" answered Mark, taking a swig from the can in his right hand.

"It was a beautiful day," I said. "Whatcha' up to today, Mark?"

"Got a project in my yard," answered Mark, "and was wonderin' if I could borrow that swing blade you got? It's great for getting rid of tall grass too high for mowin'. I remember you showin' it to me one day several years ago and said it was your grandpa's." Mark shifted from side to side, glancing around my yard as if he was taking inventory.

"Well, sure," I answered, "it spends more time hanging in the garage than anything else." The voice in my gut asked me if I thought that's all he wanted, while another voice told me to be neighborly.

Mark and I went into the garage, and I grabbed the swing blade off the nail on the wall.

"You know how to use one of these?" I asked, prepared to show him how to swing the blade across our grass.

"Sure do. My uncle used to have one, and we used it on his farm when I would visit as a kid," answered Mark.

"Dalton, Mark"—Ed popped his head into the garage—"I need to get back to my yard. Y'all have a wonderful day. Nice catching up with ya, Dalton. Keep enjoyin' the boat."

"See ya, neighbor." I waved.

"Later, Ed," chimed in Mark at Ed's back. "You got that boat all fixed up and looking and runnin' good. My family's boat and motor is tickin' along. Little maintenance required. You and I have the same appreciation for boats. That there outboard twenty-five horser of yours is a classic. If you ever upgrade or sell it, let me have the first crack at it."

"Well, it will be a while," I said, "but I'll keep that in mind. I like how easy it is to work on these older outboards."

"Well, okay." Mark smirked at me with one eye wide open and the other half-closed. "Thanks for loanin' the swing blade. I'll get it back to you in a couple days."

"No rush, man," I said.

"We'll see ya," Mark strutted down the driveway carrying the swing blade over his shoulder like a lumberjack.

"Later." I raised my hand and waved, watching my neighbor walk off with my property to his house down the street.

Once I was alone, my thoughts grew loud. *That was uncharacteristic of me to say so much about what I have been experiencing. Ed seems to be a trustworthy neighbor, and I know he has been through his own struggles. I wonder how much Mark heard from our conversation. Oh well, that's rear-view mirror talk. What happened has happened.*

I put the cover on *Johnny Bruce.*

"Daddy," hollered Ned as he ran toward me in the backyard, "I want to say night-night to *Johnny Bruce.*"

"It's not night just yet, but . . . " I laughed at my exuberant son.

"But you are putting the blanket on him for the day," insisted Ned, "so it's like nighttime for him."

"Good point, Son." I pulled the tarp away by a few inches.

Ned ran up to the boat and wrapped his arms around the bow. In his soft, childish voice, he whispered to the boat, "Daddy will put your blanket over you, *Johnny Bruce.* You sleep and rest well. Mr. John, we are so glad to have you with us. Thanks for coming back to us. You make Daddy happy and me, too."

My head snapped back when I heard this. Eileen and I had said nothing to Ned about the miracle of the boat, much less about our experience from Saturday.

"Sweet dreams, *Johnny Bruce,*" whispered Ned. Then he turned his head to me. "Okay, you can cover him now, Daddy."

"Thank you, Ned." I smiled lovingly. "That was very sweet. I'm glad you like our boat. Quite a gift Mr. John left for us, isn't it?"

"Yeah, Daddy! Can we go fishing soon? Just you and me?"

"Sure, maybe we can go next Saturday."

"Yeah," cheered Ned. "I can't wait!"

Chapter 25

"Ned, time to wake up to go fishing," I whispered to my sleeping boy, still snuggled in his warm bed.

When Ned heard, "fishing," he sat up in his bed. It was four o'clock in the morning and still dark outside—early for a Saturday morning wake-up.

"I'm up, Daddy," loudly whispered Ned as he leaned over and hugged me.

"Great, let's go have breakfast." Hugging him back, I marveled at his little boy head nestled in my neck and shoulder.

We moved quietly so we wouldn't disturb Eileen and Eva. As soon as we finished breakfast, brushed our teeth, and made our lunches, we headed outside and quietly closed the door behind us.

Ned's eyes were full of excitement. He whispered to the boat, "Good morning, *Johnny Bruce*," and then sweetly kissed the bow gunnel. Seeing Ned greet and kiss the boat made it worth all the effort of restoring *Johnny Bruce*.

As we pulled out of the driveway with *Johnny Bruce* in tow, Ned turned around in his seat to watch the boat following us—just as I used to do when my dad took me fishing. As soon as we were out of the driveway, Ned's whispering silence ended, and the chatterbox was unleashed.

"Daddy," began Ned, "it's fun watching *Johnny Bruce* following us. I'm not used to having a boat behind the truck. Funny how the outboard motor turns in the opposite direction every time that we go around a turn. What way are we going to take to get to the lake? I believe you said there are several ways we can go."

"This morning, we will go over Blevins Gap to get to Highway 431," I answered.

"Good," continued Ned. "That's one of my favorite drives around the city. Did you know that we may see the sun rising as we come over the mountain? Are we going to Honeycomb or Town Creek?"

"Where would you like to go?" I asked.

"Um, I think Town Creek. Yeah, Town Creek." Ned nodded. "It's got those pretty mountains around it. Plus, maybe we can see an eagle. Maybe we can catch a bunch of bluegills. That will be fun! Now it's time to sing a song I wrote for you, Daddy.

Goin' fishin', goin' fishin',
Me and my daddy.
Goin' fishin', fishin',
Me and my daddy.
We are on our way to Guntersville,
To Town Creek.
We're going to catch bluegill,
Maybe a bass for my daddy.
But today is 'bout me and my daddy
Goin' fishin', goin' fishin'—
My Daddy and me.

"Ned!" I exclaimed with a grin. "That was great! Did you write that all by yourself?"

"Yeah," said Ned, "but I had help with that book you read to me about the boy going fishing with his daddy. I love that book; it makes me think of you."

"Thank you, Ned," I said, bubbling with pride.

Ned chatted the entire drive to Town Creek. I just listened and smiled through the rearview mirror at my little chatterbox in the backseat. I was the same way when I was his age and Daddy took me to the lake. Daddy called me his Little Chipmunk. Just chewing away at the words, while soaking up the surrounding sites like a sponge.

After a drive through the tunnel of hardwoods of Lake Guntersville State Park, we arrived at the launch ramp and Lake Front Bait 'N Grub.

We hopped out of the truck, grabbed our large, plastic and metal mesh cricket box, and walked up the pathway to see Gene and Sharon and fill up our cricket box. Ned carried the box in his right hand while holding my hand with his left.

We walked to the store, and the old-fashioned bell on the door announced our presence.

"Well, " cried Gene as soon as he saw me, "is that Dalton? Hop-diddle-doo, it sure is! How long has it been? Sharon, get in here!"

As soon as we walked into the store, Ned made a beeline to the aquarium at the back wall.

"Great to see you, too, Gene," I said as we shook hands. "Ned, this is Mr. Gene. He owns the store here."

"Nice to meet you, Mr. Gene," said Ned politely. "I love your aquarium! Daddy, look, it's got the fish in it we will catch today!""

"Nice to meet you, too," replied Gene. "I'm glad you like our fish tank. We put it in here for little boys and girls to get a glimpse of what's in the lake here. What can I get for y'all today?"

"We need some crickets, please," announced Ned.

I handed our cricket basket to Gene and elaborated, "We'll get two dozen." Gene turned and dipped a large, wax cup into a mesh caged box the size of a tall mini fridge. Inside the cage were chirping brown crickets that Gene raised on his own. This is commonly found in bait shops around the lake. He scooped up two cups of crickets and dropped them into our red and white basket.

I got caught up with Gene on our history since our last visit to the bait shop. "I've got John's boat now. He left it to me, and we have fixed it up. It's runnin' fine now."

"I was stunned to hear about John," murmured Gene. "He was such a wonderful man. I still have his photo on the wall with the big bass."

"You're kidding me!" I would've thought it had been taken down by now to make room for new photos. Ned, come over here and see this photo of Mr. John."

We went over to the pegboard next to the front door. I found the photo amongst a myriad of newer people holding their big catches.

"There's Mr. John," I explained quietly. "See that big bass we caught that day?"

"Yeah, Daddy," replied Ned. "That's the one you told me about the line breaking and you winding it in with your hands?"

"That's the story, and now you've seen the fish." A familiar, pleasant feeling washed over me as I looked at the photo—a feeling of joy, comfort, friendship, and brotherhood of fish seekers. My mind was brought back to the present when I heard Sharon's voice behind me from the other side of the store.

"Dalton," sang a surprised Sharon, "it's been quite a while since we've seen you." Sharon reached out and hugged me. "Who's this little guy you got here? Is this your son? Yeah, he's got to be. He looks so much like his daddy."

"Sharon, this is Ned. Ned, this is Ms. Sharon, Gene's wife. They run the store together."

"Nice to meet you, Ms. Sharon," Ned continued to show off his manners. "I like your aquarium and the photos here."

Remember to tell Eileen how well our son is doing.

"Thank you." Sharon beamed. "I see you brought your old boat today. I remember it very well after all of those times you and John would stop in to see us."

"Sharon, we couldn't help but stop by—especially when y'all were cookin' up sausage and eggs," I recounted fondly. "I was just telling Gene that John left the boat for me. We got it all fixed up. Today's the first time we take it out for a father and son bluegill fishing trip."

"I'll tell ya one thing, Dalton—those khaki decks make it stand out from any other boat I've seen come by here lately. Distinctive. Most boats are boring gray. What's it say on the side of the boat?" Gene puffed his chest out and crossed arms as he talked. It was the stance of a man who was confident in what he knew.

"*Johnny Bruce*," shouted Ned. "That's his name!"

"Honoring an old friend." Sharon smiled. "I miss that man, but it looks like the family tradition continues. I know y'all came out here to fish and not jabber it up with us. Has Gene gotten you fixed up?"

"Yep, here's your two dozen bluegill magnet crickets," answered Gene as he leaned over and held out the cricket box for Ned to take as he winked. Ned shyly smiled and took the cricket box.

I paid for the crickets and asked, "How long have you and Sharon been here?"

"Oh, huh, too long," answered Gene. "Seems like a lifetime. Sharon and I are talking about selling the place and taking it easy ourselves. We don't want to sell to just anybody, though, but to the right people who share our passion."

"Really?" I asked. "Someone who loves this lake and people like y'all do, right?"

"Yeah." Gene sighed as if he doubted that was possible.

"Sounds familiar," I continued. "That's how I felt when I sold an old boat and outboard to John many years ago. It belonged to my dad. I had outgrown it but wanted to pass it on to someone who could appreciate it. You know, Eileen's family has been a part of this lake for quite some time."

"Oh yeah, I remember her dad," Gene said in a far-off voice. "I always referred motor repair work to him."

"Here's my card with my cell phone number." I handed my business card to Gene. "Keep me in mind, and I will talk with Eileen's brothers and cousins to see if they know anyone interested."

"Okay, Dalton." Gene took my card and taped it to the glass case next to the cash register. "Thanks. Not sure when we will be ready to move forward with a deal, but we will be open to when the right person connects with us."

"Yep, I understand." I nodded. "Hopefully, we'll be back with another great fish tale."

"Yeah," agreed Ned. "And maybe we can help feed your fish, Mr. Gene and Ms. Sharon."

"See y'all," I called as we waved to our bait shop friends.

"Good fishin' to y'all both, especially you Ned," encouraged Sharon.

We bounded out the door, finished loading the boat with our supplies, and launched into Town Creek. Ned and I hopped in the boat ready to go, as the sun's head was just barely showing over the nearby mountain.

"Ned, you got your life jacket on?" I asked firmly. "Are your feet clear of any rope or any other obstruction?"

"Got my life jacket on, Daddy," answered Ned. "But what's an obstruction?"

"Oh sorry, I used a big word on you." I chuckled. "An obstruction is something that gets in the way. I want to make sure you have nothing tying you down to the boat should something happen and the boat sinks. I want you to float free of the boat."

"Sounds a little scary, Daddy." Ned bit his lip and peered over the edge of the boat.

"Yeah, I'm sorry, Ned. I'm just trying to keep us safe." I patted his shoulder lovingly. "It's ingrained in me from my dad, your granddaddy Sanders, who went through the same checklist with me when I was a boy fishing with him. Are you ready?"

"Ready!" shouted Ned, raising his hands in the air.

We cranked the outboard, turned the bow up the creek, idled beyond the wake zone buoys, and opened the throttle. We were on our way.

Sitting beside me, Ned's head pivoted as he scanned the horizon, looking at the short stubby mountains. His hands waved at great blue herons and jumping fish. His bright blue baseball cap shielded his eyes and his head from the sun. My son excitedly bounced up and down on the seat cushion.

"Daddy, how about that cove over there?"

"Looks fishy to me," I quipped as I turned into the cove. As soon as I shut off the outboard, Ned jumped to the back deck and pulled up the backrest on his pedestal seat.

"This looks like a fishy spot. Do you smell that? If you train your nose just right, you can smell the bluegill in the water. It's a musky scent that comes off the water when hundreds of bluegill are gathered close."

"I smell something, Daddy," shouted Ned. His nose exaggeratedly sniffed the air.

"Hey, once we have some bluegill in the live-well, you will smell it better. Then next time, you will pick up the scent of a bluegill bedding area."

"Daddy, can you put a cricket on my hook and cast the rod to a bluegill bed?"

"Sure thing, my boy," I responded, moving quickly to help my son.

I could easily bait a hook on Ned's little cartoon character rod that's the perfect length for him at four feet long. The fishing line goes through the rod and out the tip to prevent any tangles. With a practiced hand, I cast the bobber and hook to a bream bed fifteen feet from the boat. Ned eagerly grabbed the rod and placed his hands on the reel.

"Ned, get ready," I instructed. "When that orange bobber goes underwater, that means a bluegill has eaten the bait. Jerk back the rod and start reeling as we did at home." While Ned watched his bobber, I baited my rod.

"Daddy! I got one," hollered Ned. The reel drag was singing as it released the line. Ned turned the crank and reeled in the fish.

"Look, Daddy, is that a bluegill?"

"Yep, it sure is. Swing it over this way, and I'll unhook it for you."

Ned was so excited that he reeled in the flopping fish to his rod tip and swung it over the side of the boat. The dark-backed bluegill flopped around. I grabbed the rod tip and wrapped my hand around the beautiful, feisty fish.

"Way to go! You got one!" I cheered for my son in paternal pride.

"Yeah, Daddy, it's a beaut!"

Unhooking the fish, I held it out in the palm of my hand, gripping its dorsal and anal fin to keep it still.

"Can we keep it, Daddy?"

"This one's a keeper. Do you know where to flip the switch for the live-well pump?"

"Yeah, you showed me; it's over here," answered Ned as he flipped on the live-well switch. Water began flowing into the square, plastic live-well box, and I gently placed the newly caught bluegill into it. As soon as I took my hand off of the fish, it flopped, looking for water. We watched the water cover the fish while it was lying on its side.

"I think it's okay, Daddy. Let's catch another." Ned closed the hatch lid to the live-well. "It's your turn to catch one."

I laughed as I baited our hooks. I cast both lines toward the bluegill bed. Ned took his rod and sat back down in his chair. As soon as his bum hit the seat, his bobber went under, and so did mine.

"Daddy, we got a double hook-up!"

We reeled in our fish and swung them over the side of the boat gunnel.

I unhooked Ned's fish and placed it into the live-well and then did the same to mine. The water was nearly over the back of the fish already inside. We re-baited and cast out again. Bobbers continued to be pulled under.

"Oh boy," cried Ned. "Looks like Mommy will be happy with the fish we bring home tonight. You know, she loves eating bluegill. She said they are the best-tasting fish from Guntersville."

"Yep, she oughta know, having grown up around this lake," I nodded.

The catching action continued steadily, and Ned's excitement remained high. We moved around the cove to a few different spots to catch more bluegill off their beds.

"Look at the blue heron," announced Ned as he pointed to the shore.

"Yep, that's a sign that fish are nearby. The heron is out fishing for food, too."

An hour later, the fish-catching tapered off, and Ned asked, "How many bluegills do we have?

"Let's look." I opened the live-well. Ned pointed his finger at the fish and counted.

"One, two, three . . . fourteen, fifteen, sixteen . . . twenty-one, twenty-two, and twenty-three. We have twenty-three bluegill! That's good, right?"

"Twenty-three bluegill for a morning of fishing is fantastic, and each one is a good eatin' size."

"Daddy, is it bad for us to take the fish from the water?" puzzled Ned.

"Not at all," I answered.

"See, bluegills lay eggs in these beds just like a chicken lays an egg in its dry nest. Bluegills lay eggs about once a month from March until August here in Alabama because it's so warm. They lay eggs just about every time there is a full moon. If we don't catch and take home some of these fish to eat, then there ends up being too many bluegills in the lake. All of those bluegills have to eat, and if there are too many, there is not enough food for all of them. So, we catch some, along with many other fishermen. Well, er, I guess we could say fisherpersons."

"Oh, yeah, and then there is plenty of food to go around for everyone, including us who eat the fish as fisherpersons and Mommy and Eva." Ned clapped.

"You got it!" I laughed at this little boy's outlook.

"Now that we've caught a good number of fish, can we go for a boat ride?" asked Ned eagerly.

"Sure. Are you getting tired?"

"Yeah, and it's getting warm. I want to go fast, so we can feel the wind," declared Ned.

Ned placed the rods in the rod holders on the side of the boat and patted the gunnel of the boat. "Thank you, *Johnny Bruce,* for giving us a grand catching day."

I smiled when I saw his little hand pat the boat.

We continued up the creek, enjoying the boat ride. With the sun rising higher, it was an ideal time to stop fishing with a little boy. The wind felt refreshing on our faces as we raced across the lake.

In the next hour, my son would surprise me with a fresh revelation.

Chapter 26

We enjoyed our boat ride on Town Creek. I held my right hand up in the air and hollered into the wind, "Yeah! Feels good on a boat ride with my sonny boy."

Ned lifted both of his arms in the air and mimicked, "Yeah! Feels good on a boat ride with my daddy boy."

In sight was the sandbar where Eileen and I had stopped to visit with her parents. There were no clouds today. A gentle wind chopped across the water, dappling the light on the surface.

"Look, Daddy!" hollered Ned as he pointed to the sandbar. "There's Granddaddy Sanders! I was hoping we would see him today."

"What?" I replied in shock as my head snapped to look at Ned and follow his arm to the sandbar. There on the sandbar was my dad waving at us.

"Ned, it sure is!" *How did he know Daddy would be here?*

"How did you know that was Granddaddy Sanders?" I pressed.

"He came to visit me when I was younger," replied Ned assuredly. I could believe it or not, but Ned believed it; therefore it was true. "He told me he saw you not too long ago, too, Daddy. He told me that in my dream last week."

Oh, the profound acceptance and faith of children. Adults doubt more and are less trusting.

"Hey, Granddaddy," called Ned, waving excitedly.

"Hello there, Ned." My dad beamed. "It's nice to see you two. I've got some more folks for you to see."

I looked toward the crest of the sandbar and saw Jake and Helen Snellgrove.

"Oh boy! It's Grandy and Grandma!" said Ned as he waved like crazy standing up in the boat.

We beached the boat. Ned leaped from the bow and ran toward Granddaddy Sanders, who wrapped his arms around his grandson. Then he bolted over to Grandy and Grandma, and they embraced him in a three-way hug.

"Hello, my little boy," crooned Helen. "We are so glad that we get to be with you."

I looked at my dad and shook my head. "Ned has seen you before?"

"That's all part of the learning of things on this side, Son. "It's easier for us to reach children because they are more innocent and willing to believe. I've visited you over the years; you just didn't believe enough to see me. I think you do now."

"Yeah." I smirked. "I've felt your presence, but I couldn't see you."

"Part of it comes from knowing how our appearance can frighten you. God warned us to be careful about that. We have to do it when no one else is looking or when there's cameras and people wanting to report a story. Remember, when Jesus came back to life after the cross, He appeared only to the ones who already believed in Him. He didn't spend time with those who questioned Who He was. His appearance was an affirmation to those hundreds of people to say, 'Yep, I honor your belief. You have seen and believe, but what about those that haven't seen and yet they believe?' That was talking about us yet to be born. I'm not sure why God has allowed us this chance to be together, but thank goodness He has." Daddy placed his hand on my shoulder, and I looked up to the sky.

"Thank you is an understatement," I cried in a voice brimming with emotion. "Look at my son there; he is eating it up—seeing his grandparents face to face, knowing full well that . . . " My voice trailed off.

"Daddy," interrupted Ned, "aren't we lucky that Heaven has come to us?"

There it was. One sentence, by an eight-year-old boy. Heaven came to visit us! While Ned chatted with Jake and Helen, I listened to Daddy's wisdom from the world beyond as he spoke in a gentle voice to me.

"At night or early morning, when Ned was about to go to sleep or wake for the day, I would lean over his bed and comfort him to sleep. He would smile at me and point at me with a giggle. I whispered, 'I'm your granddaddy Sanders. God and I are watching you. We are here to protect you, my little boy.' When we heard you or Eileen coming into the room, I would tell him, 'Bye for now, Ned,' and disappear."

"Is that why he was crying?" I asked.

"Could be, but he also needed his mommy and daddy to be there to comfort him, too," said Daddy. "The other night, he was having trouble going to sleep because he was thinking about going out on the boat. I came to his bedroom and whispered to him softly, but he couldn't see me. I told him, 'Ask your daddy to take you fishing, and maybe I will see you at the lake.' Then, I hummed him to sleep."

Daddy continued, "Son, I don't know how long God will allow this portal to be open, but it could stop anytime. That's up to Him.

In the meantime, soak up everything you learn here, but don't tell anyone outside of your family. Not every person accepts this world beyond like you do."

I nodded in affirmation and clutched my hand over my heart.

Daddy and I walked over to Ned and Grandy and Grandma. Ned was chatting away with stories of what was in his room and how much he loved all the colors of the rainbow.

"Oh yeah," chirped Ned. "Grandy, Grandma, and Granddaddy, we caught a bunch of bluegills today! I'm so happy my dad brought me fishing. I love fishing! We will have an amazing fish fry tonight. Thanks to *Johnny Bruce*, we can see y'all today. Now, maybe Mommy and Daddy will believe me when I say I heard from y'all."

"Definitely will now, Ned," I assured him. "Can't deny it."

"See, Daddy," replied Ned knowingly, "believing is seeing!"

"I see why Jesus loved being with the children so much," I reflected. "We adults just don't always get it."

At that moment, I heard the soft sound of a bell, much like a church bell in a downtown church building. The air vibrated with each ring.

"Oh, that's our signal." Helen sighed. "Ned, we have to go now, but I am so grateful we had this visit together."

"Aww." Ned pouted. "Do you have to go?"

"Don't worry," comforted Jake, "we will still be around watching after you and your sister. We continue to be helpers to your mommy and daddy."

"Oh, okay." Ned sighed in disappointment. "I can't wait to tell Mommy and Eva we saw all of you today!"

Ned hugged his grandparents and grabbed my hand to lead me back to the boat. "Let's show them the fish."

We hopped in *Johnny Bruce*. Ned opened the live-well and said, "See! We got a mess of bluegills." Grandma, Grandy, and Granddaddy stood by the side of the boat and peered in.

"Great catch!" said Grandy. "I imagine what they will smell like when you cook them."

I pushed the boat off of the sandbar and hopped aboard the front deck. Daddy, Jake, and Helen stood on the sandbar and waved at us. Ned waved furiously and called out, "See you later! Bye! I love you!"

"We love you, too, Ned and Dalton," came their reply in unison. They vanished into the background.

"Okay, Daddy," insisted Ned, "let's go home now."

I smiled and nodded in agreement, at a loss for words. We pointed the bow toward the ramp. I looked up at the sun, and it was in the same spot when we approached the sandbar. Time stood still during these visits.

We ate our sandwiches while we rode back to the ramp.

Ned looked at me with a cheerful face. "Daddy, we have a miracle boat. I sure am thankful for Mr. John's gift."

I wrapped my arm around Ned and squeezed him tight. "I am, too, Ned; I am, too."

Sharon saw us pulling the boat out of the water. "Did y'all catch anything?"

"Yes, Ms. Sharon," hollered Ned. "Twenty-three bream! Now, we are going home."

"That's great, Ned." Sharon clapped. "Sounds like quite a fish fry for tonight. Have a safe drive home."

With a belly full of lunch, Ned was asleep in the car seat before we rounded the first turn on the two-lane road.

Thank you, God, I prayed as I glanced at his sweet, sleeping face in the rearview mirror. *Thank you for everything.*

Once we were back in the town of Guntersville, I heard my cell phone chirp. I pulled off at a gas station and checked my text messages. It was from Eileen.

> *Hope y'all are having fun. BTW, Eva has something to talk to you about when you get home. Be safe.*

I sent a reply.

> *Will do. On the way home now, Ned has something grand to tell you about. Get ready for a good fish fry.*

Chapter 27

"Dad . . . Dad . . . Daddy," a voice nearby poked through my consciousness. "Daddy! Wake up!" came Eva's voice, speaking through a fog.

I opened my eyes and saw Eva's face looking at me and noticed the garage storage shelves behind her.

"Oh, hey, Eva," I said groggily. "Where am I?"

"You're in the boat, sprawled out taking a nap," answered Eva, hands on her hips.

I turned to my right and saw the trolling motor pedal next to my shoulder and my head on a red flotation cushion. Overhead, I saw the popcorn ceiling of the garage.

"Looks like you got the boat pushed into the garage, closed the door, and collapsed on the front deck," said Eva.

"Yeah, I was pretty wiped out when we got back. Oh, my goodness, did Ned go inside with you and Mom?" I said as I bolted upright.

"It's okay, Dad," answered Eva. "He's been inside talking with Mom about the fishing morning. Sounds like y'all had quite a reunion."

"Oh, he told y'all about that?" I asked.

"Yeah, it's unbelievable," declared Eva, running her hands through her hair nervously. "I mean . . . well . . . it's like, well, Daddy, I wouldn't believe him, if well . . . "

Eva's chin dropped, and she cried—not just a brief cry, but a full-out bawling cry.

I jumped out of the boat and grabbed my girl around the shoulders and pulled her tight.

"Eva, what's going on?" I asked.

"Daddy, I got to see Grandy and Grandma, too." Eva sobbed. "How is this possible? It doesn't make any sense. I don't get it, Daddy! I mean, I'm glad I got to see them, but it's scary. I've wanted to see them for so long, and now they show up out here in the boat."

"What?" I asked. "Out here in the garage?"

"Yeah." Eva nodded. "Two nights ago, when the boat was in the garage, I woke up about two in the morning and couldn't go back to sleep. I went into the kitchen to get a snack and noticed light coming under the garage doorway. I thought someone left the lights on, so I opened the door to investigate. There was a glow around the boat, kinda like it was candlelit, except that it was very white and not the orange tint of a candle flame. I walked over to touch the side, and I heard a voice say, 'Sit inside.' So, I climbed in and sat on the back deck cushion. Then this hazy fog appeared, kinda like smoke, and out of it appeared Grandy and Grandma."

The puzzle pieces assembled in my head now that I heard Eva's story. "Ohhh, now I see. They came to visit you, too."

"Yeah, I don't know why," continued Eva. "I told Mom about it, and she told me y'all saw Grandy and Grandma on the sandbar. I mean, I was a little girl when they passed away. I'm lucky, but Ned never got to see them. Dad, why are we seeing dead people?"

I inhaled and exhaled deeply before replying, "Eva, I don't fully understand it, but you know some things aren't meant to be understood."

"What do you mean?" asked Eva.

"About a month after my dad, your granddaddy Sanders, died, I asked over and over why it happened. One night when I was crying in my bed, I heard a voice say to me, *'The past is the past—accept what you don't understand.'* At that moment, I was released from guilt and never again questioned why it happened. Daddy left this earth, and nothing I did would bring him back. I missed my dad and needed him. I stopped thinking about what I was missing and began thinking of the good times with Daddy. Today, I have a better understanding of why Daddy died. For me to understand, first I had to accept what was before me.

"When you go to the light switch on the wall, do you think how the electricity transmits from the power plant, through all the wires for miles down the road to our house, causing the light bulb to come on?"

"Well, no, Dad, I haven't thought of it before." Eva rolled her eyes. "But now, I will."

I chuckled. "You accept that by flipping the switch, the light will come on?"

"Yeah," agreed Eva.

"So, when I talk about God, I don't wonder if He does or doesn't exist, I accept that He does. I see evidence of His existence all around. We breathe in oxygen to live. Plants and trees breathe out oxygen. We breathe out carbon dioxide. Plants and trees breathe in carbon dioxide. We supply what plants and trees need, and they supply what we need. We filter each other. If it weren't for the bees, flowers can't pollinate. I don't fully understand how that works, but I accept that it does."

"Oh, okay, I get it, Daddy. But will my friends get it?" worried Eva.

"Other people don't understand things the same," I answered. "Keep this to yourself. Talk about it with me and your mom. Hold off telling any of your friends until you feel you can trust them. Sometimes, when people don't understand something, well, it can turn bad. One of my favorite bands says in a song that fear comes about when people don't understand."

Eva rolled her eyes. "You're not going to sing, are you?"

I laughed. "I'll spare you from that trauma today."

"Ugh, thanks." Eva grinned.

I asked, "What did you and your grandparents talk about?"

"They kept saying what a beautiful, smart girl I've become. Grandma kept saying that over and over. You know, it was, like, they kept saying how proud they are of me, how much they love me—you know, the usual stuff, I guess, that you hear from grandparents."

The look on Eva's face said that it bored her talking with her grandparents, but I knew she enjoyed it.

"It was great to hear it from them. I mean, I had a feeling they were proud of me, but, well, I don't know. It was just great to hear them *say* it. Probably sounds silly."

"Not silly at all," I insisted. "I know where you are coming from. My dad told me he loved me, and he was proud of me when he was around. Then, when I was your age and heading into adulthood, I wanted to hear him say it to me. I knew my dad was still *with* me, but I couldn't be *with* him. That's probably one of the hardest things about when someone dies. No more two-way conversation."

"Yeah, that's how I feel," acknowledged Eva.

"Eva, your dad has experienced some things you are already going through."

Eva chuckled and rolled her eyes. "Is this going to be another 'you should listen to me' talks?"

"Nah, I think some things you have experienced firsthand." I smiled.

"I'm glad we have this boat. It's kinda like a miracle boat. Mr. John sure has been good to us."

"He sure has. And you know what? I agree with your grandparents: you are a beautiful, smart young lady." I beamed in pride. "I'm proud of you."

"Da-aad," replied Eva as she blushed and rolled her eyes again.

As I hugged Eva, there was a knock on the door.

"Hello, Dalton, are you in there?" came a muffled voice. I answered the door.

"Hey, Ed, what can I do for ya?"

"Hello, Dalton. Oh, hey, Eva."

"Hey, Mr. Bartwell."

"Dalton, how's the boat been doing? I saw y'all took it out again today."

"*Johnny Bruce* is doing fine, thank goodness," I said. "Every day, we are surprised and blessed by where he takes us."

"Still kinda odd to me"—Ed laughed—"calling a boat he, but then again, there's the *U.S.S. George H. W. Bush*."

"Got a point there." I chuckled .

"All righty, y'all, see you later." Ed waved as he turned around to head home.

I closed the door, and Eva had a concerned look on her face.

"You don't think he heard us, do you, Daddy?"

"No, I don't think so."

Chapter 28

"Daddy, *Johnny Bruce* is gone!" Ned burst into the bathroom where I was brushing my teeth.

"What?" I replied in shock, toothbrush still in hand.

"Mom and I were about to head to school when we noticed that the boat is *not* in the backyard!" Ned continued. "Did you put it somewhere else?"

"No, I didn't," I answered. "I parked it where I usually do."

Hurriedly, Ned and I went to the backdoor, out the garage, and into the yard to see the empty boat parking spot.

"What's going on?" Eva rushed in wearing heavy eyeliner, making her look like a raccoon.

"*Johnny Bruce* is gone!" wailed Ned.

"But we had him in the garage yesterday," insisted Eva. "Daddy, didn't you park him in the backyard?"

"Yeah, I did," I answered as I hurriedly put on my shoes and rushed down the hall with Eva and Ned trailing behind me. Eileen was standing in the kitchen, shocked by what was going on.

"Ned told you that the boat isn't here?" My wife searched my eyes for an answer.

"Yeah." I scratched my head in bewilderment.

We went outside where *Johnny Bruce* should have been parked. The wheel chocks were there but no trailer wheels to block. On the ground was the trailer coupler lock with the bolt sawed through. Metal shavings littered the ground.

"Stolen—he's been stolen," I shouted as I hung my head. "And whoever took him wanted the boat enough to take the time to saw through this lock. I'll call the police. Eileen, take Ned to school? Eva, you get to school, too. Your mom and I will try to find out what is going on."

"But, Daddy," asked Ned, "what do we do?"

"I don't know, but your mom and I will figure it out," I answered.

The entire family looked dismayed as Eileen and Ned got into the van and drove to school. Eva got her backpack and left for school, as well. Slowly, I walked around the backyard, surveying the scene. I called the police to file a report.

I wasn't happy that *Johnny Bruce* was stolen. My family has become attached. This gift of a friend was more than a boat; it was its own being. A living entity and a portal of delight that connected our family with our loved ones on the other side.

I looked up from the ground and saw the backyards of our neighboring houses. One had a new fiberglass bass boat with a powerful outboard. In another was a ski boat that our neighbor bought last year. Why in the world would someone want to take a twenty-year-old boat that wasn't worth more than two thousand dollars?

I noticed the Dresdens' empty backyard. Mark hadn't brought back the swing blade he borrowed from me. *I don't think he has returned any tools he has borrowed from me.*

Chapter 29

Eileen pulled into the driveway, and the police were right behind her. She ran over to me and wrapped her arms around me.

"I'm so sorry, Dalton. What are you going to do?"

"Not sure yet, but first I'll file a report with these gentlemen. I've already called the office and told them I'll be in late."

"Are you the one who called us about a stolen boat?" asked the officer.

"Yes, sir, that's me," I said. "I'm Dalton Russell, and this is my wife, Eileen. We want to report a missing *Johnny Bruce*."

"Wait, what?" The police officer lifted his bushy eyebrows. "Is this a missing person?"

"Oh, no, I'm sorry," I apologized. "It's a missing boat named *Johnny Bruce*. I didn't mean to alarm you."

"Whew! You got me there." The officer wiped his already sweaty brow. "Big difference between a missing person and a missing boat."

Eileen looked at the officer and explained, "To our family, it's kind of like a missing person, even though it's a hunk of metal."

"Yes, ma'am," replied the officer. "I've had a boat of my own when I used to fish a lot. I'm Officer Olsen. Nice to meet you, Mr. and Mrs. Russell. Let me get some information about the boat. Do you have the registration number?"

Officer Olsen wrote all the details we had to describe *Johnny Bruce*. He finished and left to file the report. Eileen and I went into the house hand in hand.

"Gather some photos together of *Johnny Bruce* we can pass on to the police. Maybe that will help them," said Eileen.

"Yeah, maybe," I responded with uncertainty. "Eileen, you don't think the Dresdens would have taken the boat, do you?"

"The Dresdens, from down the street?" she asked incredulously. "I don't see why they would take it."

"Mark has always rubbed me the wrong way a little," I answered. "He's always borrowing odd tools from me, but I don't usually get them back. He showed up when Ed and I were talking in the backyard about *Johnny Bruce,* and I wonder if he heard some things about the boat. They have their own junkyard of an odd collection of things."

"I don't know—could have been anybody."

"Yeah, anybody who wants a twenty-year-old aluminum boat that's only true value is to us. Unless they know more about where it takes us. That's it. I'm going down to the Dresden place to see if I can find anything suspicious."

I walked down the street to Mark Dresden's house. His white Chevy Express van pulled into the driveway. Mark was a plumber, and his daytime hours were varied. He waved at me and hopped out of his van.

"Hey, neighbor," said Mark. "You picking up that swing blade?"

"Yeah," I said trying to keep an unsuspecting demeanor about myself. "What are you doing at home this morning?"

"I guess I should ask the same of you," replied Mark. "Some days don't go as we planned, do they? I had a job today, but the homeowner is sick and canceled on me. Gathering up for what's next. I'm done with the swing blade. Lemme get it for you. How's the boat runnin'?"

"Funny you should ask," I answered testily. "Eileen and I just got done talking with the police." I watched Mark's face to gauge his reaction.

"What? Why the police?" asked a perplexed Mark.

"Someone stole our boat during the night," I said.

"That's crazy. I don't think we've ever had something stolen on our street before," exclaimed Mark, running his hands over his camo ball cap. "Buddy, I'm sorry to hear that. Man, I got buddies over on Lake Guntersville that I can tell to be on the lookout. Some of 'em work with one of the marinas over there. I truly am sorry."

I followed Mark to his backyard, and he found the swing blade. "Here you go, Dalton. Thanks for letting me borrow it. And I'm sorry; I know I've got some other tools I've borrowed from you. I'll gather 'em up and get 'em back to you, too."

"Thanks," I said. "I just don't get it. There's nothing special about this twenty-year-old boat."

"People are strange; what some people think is junk is a treasure to another."

I sighed. "That boat is special to me because it belonged to a friend of mine who passed away and . . . "

My cell phone rang, interrupting the conversation I wished to end.

Chapter 30

"Dalton Russell here," I answered.

"Dalton, it's Gene at Lake Front Bait 'N Grub over on Guntersville Lake. I got your number from your card."

"Hey, Gene." I wondered why he was calling.

"Dalton, who's got your boat? Because whoever it is sure is creating a ruckus running around," replied Gene carefully.

I was confused by what Gene was saying. How did he know my boat was missing? I asked Gene to clarify.

"John's boat—*your* boat—has sand-colored decks, olive drab hull, right? With an old outboard motor on it?"

"Yeah, that's right," I said as I quickly glanced at Mark with a puzzled face.

"Your friend has been running back and forth from the bridge up the creek for several hours now, kicking up a wake that's getting my customers riled up," continued Gene. "They are trying to fish from the bridge, and he's driving them nuts. I'm about to call the marine police, but I wanted to check with you first to see if it's your boat. Don't want your boat locked up because of someone else's trouble."

I stood up straight with wide eyes looking at Mark. "Gene!" I nearly yelled into the phone. "Are you *kidding* me? My boat was stolen this morning. Are you sayin' it's over there out in front of your store?"

"Yeah," answered the unflappable Gene.

I needed more clarification, another sight of identification that would tell me that the boat Gene was seeing was *Johnny Bruce*. "Are you close enough to see the side of the boat?" I asked eagerly.

"Let me grab my binoculars. He's about to turn around and run by again," replied Gene. "Okay, got my binoculars. What am I looking for?"

"Look on the side of the boat about midway—doesn't matter which side," I instructed, pacing back and forth across Mark's driveway. "There should be a sticker on the side—same color as the decks. Read that to me."

"Okay, I'm looking now . . . Says 'SeaArk.' Oh, wait, that's the boat make; I see what you are talkin' about—says '*Johnny Bruce*.'"

"That's it!" I hollered, pumping my first into the air. "Mark, we found the boat! Okay, Gene, call the marine police; get them to stop that boat. I'll get over there as fast as I can!"

Without saying a word to Mark, I waved quickly at him, ran from the Dresdens' yard back to our house, and burst through the front door. Eileen jumped back as I scared her with my sudden entry.

"Gene found the boat!" Sweat rolled down my face.

"What? Gene? From the bait shop?" asked Eileen, who had printed out photos of *Johnny Bruce* in her hands.

"Yeah, I'm heading over there right now!" I was speaking loudly and in a hurry to the back door.

"Hey, slow down, Dalt." She grabbed my arm as I rushed by. I nearly fell over on my right side. I was in such a hurry. In the spot on my arm where Eileen grabbed me. I felt a rush of coolness like a wet rag had been placed on my arm. I stopped moving. She turned me so that I was facing straight in front of her. My head kept darting from side to side as if I was trying to find fire flames.

Still holding my arm with hers, she placed her other hand on my cheek to steady my head.

"Look at me! Look at me," she said firmly but softly. "Sshhh, I'm coming with you. It's going to be okay. Gene knows where the boat is. We just have to get there."

With her words and her touch to bring me back to reality, I relaxed; the adrenaline slowed; and I slumped over her shoulder. In my mind, a memory from John's funeral home visitation came up. I saw John's face lying in a casket, eyes closed, motionless and lifeless. Tears began to wash over me as I tightly held Eileen.

"I—I can't lose him again. We got him back, and I can't lose him again. I've got to save him."

Eileen felt the tears dripping from my cheek onto her neck. "Oh, honey, it's not up to you to save him. He's not gone anywhere from where he was before. Your job is to be dad to Eva and Ned and be my husband. We're in this together."

Even though Eileen and I had our arguments, disagreements, and shouting matches like most married couples, she knew how to keep me calm. My adage was "ready, set, go!" Hers was "ready, set, *slow*."

"Are you better now? Because I know we need to get to Gene's." She looked directly in my eyes.

"Yeah." I wiped the tears with my shirt sleeve.

"I'll call your mom to be on standby for Ned and Eva here in town."

I handed my keys to Eileen. "Here, you drive."

We turned off the lights, went out the door, hopped in the truck, and headed to Lake Guntersville.

Chapter 31

When we reached the bridge, we saw a gathering at the dock in front of Gene and Sharon's store. Gene ran toward us as we pulled in.

"They got the guy, Dalton." Gene pointed toward the dock.

Eileen ran over, hugged Gene, and exclaimed, "Thank you so much! I know it's been a while. We'll have to do all the catching up stuff later."

Sharon came running up from the dock and hugged Eileen while Gene and I walked quickly to the dock.

Johnny Bruce was tied parallel to the dock. The Alabama Marine Police's boat was parked off from the dock with its motor running, blocking *Johnny Bruce* from going anywhere. A dark-haired man was sitting on the dock with his back to us. Two police officers stood over him and were talking to him. He wore a blue t-shirt and gray shorts with sandals on his feet. One officer approached me.

"Sir, are you Dalton Russell?" he asked.

"Yes, sir, I am," I answered.

"Gene tells us you had a boat stolen in Huntsville," continued the officer. "We've spoken with the Huntsville Police Department, and this boat fits your description. Is this your boat?"

"Yes, sir, it is," I answered.

"Okay, sir, this gentleman was running the boat around here, causing a disturbance, and we stopped him."

"Who is it, Officer?" I asked.

"Sir, you can come out on the dock and see for yourself. He seems harmless," said the officer. "He keeps saying something about Andrew; he was trying to find Andrew."

Perplexed, I quickly searched my memory bank of people I knew. *Andrew? I don't remember Andrew.*

We walked onto the dock while Eileen and Sharon stood on the bank. As soon as the dock vibrated with my footsteps, the middle-aged man sitting on the dock turned his head to look over his right shoulder. I couldn't make out his face from his profile.

The police officer spoke. "Sir, stand up slowly, turn around, and face this man who is approaching."

"Yes, sir, Officer," said the man on the dock. He turned and faced me. I stopped dead in my tracks.

"Ed Bartwell?" I hollered.

"Hey, Dalton, I'm so sorry," said Ed. "I didn't mean any harm; I was going to get your boat back to you."

"Ed, you are the last person I would have thought would . . . " I shouted in disbelief.

"Take a boat. Yeah, I know. I've stolen nothing in my life until today," mumbled Ed calmly and clearly laden with remorse. His eyes were heavy with dark circles underneath. His thin shirt matted in sweat against his skin. His hair was a mess from the wind and from him pulling his hands through it. He looked sad.

"Mr. Russell, do you know this man?" asked the officer.

"Yes, sir, I do. He's my next-door neighbor," I answered. "He helped me work on the boat."

"Mr. Bartwell," spoke the officer behind Ed, holding Ed's driver's license, "please remember your rights."

"I know; it doesn't matter. Yeah, I took my neighbor's boat," admitted Ed in a manner of defeat.

"Mr. Russell, do you wish to press charges?" asked the officer as he pulled out his handcuffs to put on Ed.

A feeling caught me. It was a feeling that something was not as it seemed. It wasn't a feeling of wanting Ed to have to pay for his crime. It was a feeling that there was something deeper going on with Ed.

"Dalton, I know I did you wrong. I shouldn't have taken your boat, but I was trying to find Andrew," pleaded Ed with words in a quickening pace.

"What? Who?" I demanded.

"I heard y'all talking about how the boat had healing powers of sorts. I saw y'all put those crystals in the box and into the boat. Then yesterday, Ned was in the backyard playing around the boat, and I asked him about the fishing trip. He told me about it and how it was great to see his grandparents. I asked him if he meant Grandpa Rich and Mrs. Diane. He said, 'No, I'm talking about my granddaddy Sanders and my mommy's parents.' I asked, 'I didn't know they were still living.' And Ned said, 'They aren't. They died a while back. Our boat took us to see them over on Town Creek.'"

When I heard Ed describe his talk with Ned, my fatherly pride welled up with the same surprise of insight I had with Ned.

"When I heard this . . . well . . . er, how in the world can a boat do this? Is Ned exaggerating? Has his imagination gone wild? Then I remembered how my son was when he was Ned's age. He would tell stories to me and my wife that sometimes we thought were out there.

Then, we saw the look of certainty on his face that told us, 'Mom and Dad, this is truly what I saw.'"

"Your son?" I asked. I didn't recall Ed talking about a son or seeing him around their house.

"Yes, my son," continued Ed. "We used to fish together, too. But tragically, at thirty years young, his heart gave out, and he died. I tried to help him for so many years, but the drugs already did their damage."

"Sir," interrupted the officer, "we have to know if you want to press charges."

"Give me a minute," I said. "I need to hear Ed's story, and then I'll decide."

"But, sir, we have more matters to attend to," insisted the officer.

"I understand. Please give me five minutes. Please, *five* minutes," I pleaded with the officer in the gentlest, most respectful way I could muster.

"Five minutes, Mr. Russell," said the officer firmly.

I turned back to face Ed, whose shoulders slumped over as he looked at the dock underneath him. He looked the same way I had earlier with Eileen, except he didn't have a shoulder to bury his head into. His eyes looked similar to mine when the memory photo appeared of John's lifeless face. *He's seeing Andrew's lifeless face, eyes closed, in the funeral parlor. That's not a vision a father should have of their children.*

"Dalton, I'm sorry," continued Ed. "I didn't mean to create trouble. I just wanted to see my son again free from the damage of all of those awful chemicals he put in his body that robbed him of being him. That robbed us of our relationship. He was doing better, too. There ain't nothing like the pain of losing your child." Tears trickled down Ed's face. I kneeled next to Ed, then sat down in front of him. *Grace. You've received grace.*

"Ed," I said, looking him directly into his eyes, "was your son a drug addict?"

"Yes," said Ed softly. "I'm embarrassed to tell people about it, but yeah, he was."

I spoke softly, nearly whispering. "Did you take *Johnny Bruce* thinking you could see your son again?" I asked.

"Yes," said Ed. "These men don't have the time for me to keep prattling on about my story. They have better things to do than listen to me."

I turned around and looked at Eileen and Sharon standing on the bank watching us. Gene stood on the dock behind Officer Olsen. My eyes locked with Eileen's. At that moment, she reached up her right hand, placed it on her chest near her heart. The cool wash cloth feeling came upon my arm again. She nodded her head at me.

"Eileen," I yelled, "are you catching any of this?"

"We really can't hear anything from here," said Eileen.

I looked at Gene; he was nodding his head. He turned and looked at Sharon, and she started nodding her head. Sharon and Eileen looked at each other. Eileen put her arm around Sharon's waist. Eileen looked at me and nodded her head again as a warm smile spread over her face.

"Sir . . . Mr. Russell?" asked the officer. "Your five minutes is about to end."

"I understand, Officer," I said. "It is our decision not to press charges against Mr. Ed Bartwell."

Ed fell face forward with his head in his hands and sobbed.

"Sir, you understand this man stole your property?" questioned the officer.

I locked eyes with the officer and stood up. "I understand, that, uh, well, Mr. Ed stole nothing. He had something—er—someone, taken from him, and I told him he could take my boat to go find him. I just forgot which day it was he was going to borrow my boat." I looked down at Ed. "Neighbor, next time, you gotta communicate—leave me a note, send me a text message±just something so I'll know today is the day you are borrowing the boat." I laughed. "You created quite a stir, here, Neighbor."

Ed was still in shock, but he nodded at me quickly. "Sorry, neighbor, will do."

"Mr. Russell, if that is your decision, then we will close this case," said the officer.

"Thank you, gentlemen, for your attention to this matter and for helping us solve our mystery," I said as I shook hands with the Alabama Marine Police officers.

"Mr. Russell and Mr. Gene, let us know if we can serve you again," said the officer. "See you, Mrs. Sharon and Mrs. Russell." With that, the officers gathered their things, got into their boat, and left the dock.

"Come back tomorrow morning; I'll have some sausage biscuits waitin' for ya!" yelled Sharon.

I stooped down in front of Ed and said, "Come, man, stand up. Let's go on a boat ride."

Ed wrapped his arms around me and nearly pulled me into the lake. "Thank you, neighbor. Thank you so very much."

"You're welcome, Ed. Now let's see if there is a miracle awaiting you from this boat."

Chapter 32

Ed, Eileen, and I got into *Johnny Bruce*. I wanted Eileen to be there as a witness and my backup support if things went wrong.

"Dalton, I just kept running this boat from the bridge up the creek hoping to connect as you did," said Ed.

"Did Ned tell you this?" I asked.

"Yeah, he said he saw his grandparents up in Town Creek," answered Ed sheepishly.

I looked at Eileen with a smile and shook my head.

"No secrets with our boy, huh?" Eileen laughed.

We ran up Town Creek; and I wasn't sure what would happen, when it would happen, or *if* it would happen. I was not in control of the miracle of this boat as a vessel to the world beyond. I felt a nudge to offer Ed an experience. Our family connected with some of the dearest loved ones in our life, and that had caused healing to begin, as well as closure. The pain, the missing-ness, the life of this earth were all coming back to me. Eileen experienced it. Eva experienced it. Ned experienced it.

Eileen grabbed my arm as we continued across the water. With no words between us, just our faith, we communicated to each other that we should offer this gift to another who felt pain. A father, separated from his child, who sought closure from his loss.

One of my college professors said, "God doesn't cause bad things to happen. He uses them for our good."

In Mark 4:21, Jesus teaches that if we have a lighted lamp, we don't hide it under a bed. Instead, we place it on a table for all to see and enjoy the light it brings to a darkened room. Ed had been in a darkened room, and *Johnny Bruce* was his guiding lamp.

"Ed, what time is it?" I asked.

Ed looked at his watch. "It's just past noon. Hey, what's that over there?" Ed pointed to a giant boulder at a bend in the creek.

Eileen and I kept quiet. I steered the boat toward the boulder and slowed down.

"Over there, sitting on the boulder is . . . that . . . " Ed stopped himself, allowing the vision to come into view.

On the limestone boulder, a man stood up and waved at us. Eileen and I waved back as Ed exclaimed, "It's Andrew!" Ed looked at me and Eileen and drawled, "How is this possible?"

I shook my head and replied, "It's a gift from the One above."

Nearing the boulder, Ed jumped on the front deck. "Andrew! Andrew! I can't believe it's you."

"Hey, Dad," said the man. "It's great to see you. Grab my hands."

Ed reached out, grabbed Andrew's hands, and was pulled atop the boulder.

Ed wrapped his arms around Andrew as his body shook with sobs. "I love you, Son. I'm so happy to see you again. Let me look at you."

Andrew's eyes were bright white with pearly blue and pierced with joy! His face was clean and tan. He looked like he had been on the beach soaking in the sun.

"Oh, pardon me for my rudeness, Andrew," apologized Ed. "These are our next-door neighbors, Eileen and Dalton. They own the boat."

"I've heard about you. Thank you for bringing my dad to me today." Andrew smiled. "And yes, you are right to think, Dalton, I have been soaking in the Son—S-O-N, I mean."

"How did you know what I was thinking?" I asked.

"I don't know. It just comes to us sometimes. I can't control it," answered Andrew. "It's just something that they grant us on this side. It's different here beyond what I can explain—we just have to accept it."

"You're so healthy, Andrew." Ed beamed, looking at his son holding him with each hand on his shoulders. "So much better than the last time I saw you."

"Dad," pleaded Andrew, "I want you to know how sorry I am for how things ended. Please know that I did nothing wrong there at the end."

"What do you mean?" asked Ed.

"Dad, thanks to yours and Mom's support," continued Andrew, "I cleaned up. After ten years, I did finally stop being a user. My addiction ended, thanks to the rehab centers y'all sent me. It took me a while to want to stop. That last time, I wanted to stop. I finally saw what I was putting you and Mom through. I felt awful, and I didn't want to feel that way anymore."

"Was it the dentist visit?" asked Ed.

"Yes, it was," answered Andrew. "I went in for a visit, and they prescribed me something—well, a painkiller—I used to fool doctors into prescribing me so I could get a fix off of it, because getting legal drugs was a lot cheaper than any of the illegal stuff. I knew that I shouldn't take it, but I was in so much pain after leaving the dentist that I got the prescription filled."

"Why isn't there a record from one doctor to another about your addiction?" asked Ed. "Many times after I knew you visited a doctor, I would call them and ask if they knew you were an addict. They would usually say no. That would prompt them to cancel the prescription sent to the pharmacy."

"Yeah, and I would get so mad at you for doing that because I would show up at the pharmacy to pick up my drugs, ready for a fix, only to discover its cancellation. You were trying to take care of me, and I wasn't allowing it. Dad, that last pain medication took me right back to where I was before I was clean. But this time, my heart couldn't take it. Enough damage had been done, and it gave out. I knew better."

Tears streamed down Ed's face. "Thank you, Andrew, for telling me what happened. I was mad at myself. I didn't know you had gone to the dentist."

"I didn't tell you, Dad, and it's not your fault," said Andrew. "Please, be free from that guilt, Dad." Andrew wrapped his long arms around Ed and drew him close. "Tell Mom, too, that it's not your fault. The greatest thing you gave me was telling me stories as a boy about God and Jesus. At a young age, I became a believer. When I heard the children's stories at church and Vacation Bible School, I asked Him to save me. That's why I'm here on this boulder. I took a detour away from where God wanted me to be, but my relationship didn't end. He never gave up on me. He never left me. He offered love and forgiveness in all the mess I created. Dad, you and Mom did well!"

Eileen looked at me and whispered, "Dalton, I feel like we are intruding on a private conversation here. Are we supposed to hear this?"

I looked at Eileen and whispered back, "Let's drift back and let them have some privacy."

"Hey, Ed and Andrew, we'll be right here," I said. "But, Ed, you let me know when you are ready to go."

"Oh, I'm sorry," replied Ed. "Thank you."

Eileen and I drifted away. We saw father and son sit down on the boulder and continue their talk.

Eileen laid her head on my shoulders as we let the current drift us away from the boulder. "It's such a peaceful place here amid the valley of Little Mountain," said Eileen. "It's got healing powers just being here. It's . . . home."

Soon, we would have a visit of our own.

Chapter 33

I miss my friend John so much. Rarely do I see his children, Patton and Amber, but when we do meet up, the flood of emotions washes over us because of our connection. It's greater than my friendship with their dad because it's the bond that I am a son who lost a father to suicide and they are children who have lost a father to suicide. I've been involved in suicide prevention groups, and it just didn't fit me. That's probably the introvert in me, wanting to deal with my issues in my way and on my own rather than with a group.

When I see Amber and Patton, I hurt *for* them, knowing the pain of their loss. Amber has the emptiness of not having her dad to walk her down the aisle for her wedding. Patton does not have his dad as a sounding board for beginning life as a young man—we need that from our fathers. Both of them overcame and rose above this obstacle and made a miraculous impact on this earth. Amber was a successful business owner. Patton was using his journalism skills to keep the political powers on their toes, while teaching young men and women how to do it, too.

I occasionally talked with Joyce Millington, John's wife, and listened to her share her stories. I was helping her let go of the guilt that I once carried, thinking, *Could I have prevented this from happening*? We have to forgive ourselves so we can live in the present.

From these losses, I gained a powerful desire to live. Every time I watched Eva and Ned, the more I wanted to give them a wonderful life. I wanted them to experience the grandness of life. I couldn't shield against things, but it was comforting that I was not alone in their protection. *Johnny Bruce* had given me experiences to remind me that their loved ones were watching on the other side.

I must do everything I can to take better care of myself and Eileen, so that we can be around for many years.

Eileen and I drifted on the creek, using the trolling motor to quietly guide the boat.

"What's that, Dalton?" asked Eileen, bolting upright. "Do you hear the splashing water?" I stopped the motor.

We looked around the boat and saw nothing.

"Yeah, it sounds like someone is walking on puddles of wet pavement."

Then we saw it. The wind was calm. The surface water was smooth, except for splashes from a distance that kept appearing a footstep away from each other. There were one, two, three; and they were coming closer to us. We saw a sandal appear. The next splash, a second sandal. The next splash, human feet appeared in the sandals. The next splash, two blue jean legs appeared. The next splash, a human torso in overalls appeared. The next step, we saw a human chest in bib overalls with a carpenter's pencil and a small ruler tucked in the front pocket. The next step was right next to the boat. Shoulders and a gentle face appeared. The bearded Man with shoulder-length, black hair stood next to the boat with warm, blue eyes shining on us. A smile beamed across His face. His arms spread out wide as He bent over, lifted water over His palms, and then stood stretching His arms out to His side. The water flowed from His hands back to the lake and over the boat's gunnel.

"Hello there, my sister Eileen and brother Dalton," said the Man. "Do not be afraid, for you have brought a smile to My face."

Eileen and I grabbed each other's hands and stood speechless. I could feel trembling in her hand, and she could feel trembling in mine.

The Man laughed a little and reached out to place His hands over ours. "No need to tremble anymore, and yes, I am Who you think I am."

When His hands touched ours, warmth shot through my skin to my veins and directly to my heart. His touch was different and more human than I had felt from the hug with Daddy and with Eileen's parents. It was a solid skin touch. That's when I noticed the holes in each of His hands.

The scent of honeysuckle quickly filled the air. I looked at His face and noticed the back light beaming around His head. Comfort and peace replaced my trembling.

"I . . . I . . . I can't believe it," I said.

"You . . . you look like a carpenter," said Eileen.

Said the man, "My father is the Builder. He is your Builder, too."

"Ah, right, and Your Father, here, was a carpenter, and so were You," realized Eileen.

"Ding! Ding! Ding! Now you are getting it, Eileen." The Carpenter smiled.

"Tell me, Sir, how do we deserve this visit?" I asked.

"Dalton, you sound just like my first students, who were fishermen, too." The Carpenter. chuckled "Sometimes, you have to accept the gifts given to you, but you have always been an inquisitive child. Dalton, it is what you did for your neighbor Ed today. It was your forgiveness for his actions. Then, you went beyond that, and you gave something away that is special to you by giving away the gift we gave you. Look at him over there, happily talking with his son. That's something he has missed since his son's passing over to this side. You didn't have to do that, Dalton, and no, We were not testing you. That's not the Builder's way. It is as you say. 'He doesn't cause bad things to happen. He uses them for your good.' If people would just stop blaming the Builder for bad things on this earth. Why don't they take responsibility for their human decisions or other humans' decisions?"

"Well, You know; You were around a few of these stubborn people," I said.

The Carpenter laughed. "Ah, yes, Peter and James didn't get it until later on. Not until they had to teach others. Peter matured into quite the teacher and leader himself. He was a raw, unfinished block of wood when we met, but I shaped him into a beautiful sculpture."

"I love the story of him sitting on the roof fasting when the vision of animals on a blanket came down from Heaven," said Eileen. "God was saying, 'Peter, I made all things on this earth, so it's okay to eat them.' Then the next day, he went to the Gentiles' house and entered inside. If not for that vision, he would not have entered the man's house."

"It's because of things like that, Eileen, that you have been granted this visit." The Carpenter nodded. "We have outstanding things ahead for you and Dalton, too."

"Really, what things?" I asked eagerly.

"Ah, ah, ah, not so soon, Dalton," intoned the Carpenter. "I will reveal it when the time is right. Trust Us. We won't guide you wrong. If we tell you now, you will worry and make your plans. Be ready and on the look-out for when the Builder has you act."

"Yes, sir," I said. "I get it."

"Why were we given the gift of this . . . well . . . miracle boat?" asked Eileen.

"The full revelation of this gift will come in a visit later on," promised the Carpenter. "But one of the principal reasons is your faithfulness and willingness to listen and act on what you hear. Many of your brothers and sisters pray to ask for things, but they don't listen to the answers given. What stands in the way is they are seeking answers in the manner they want to have happened—the outcomes they expect, not what is best for them. They allow their human selves to block the Builder's guidance and direction. Then, they get off-track and it's the grace of the Builder that keeps working to keep them on track. We don't give up on them. The Builder has unlimited grace."

"Does He ever get angry?" asked Eileen. "I know as a parent, I love my children unconditionally; but sometimes, they drive me crazy and make me mad when they just won't listen to me. My daughter liked this boy, but I could feel that he wasn't good for her and I told her. They dated, anyway, and lo and behold, he hurt her."

"Yes, our Builder gets angry in a righteous way," explained the Carpenter, "but He loves His children just as you love yours. He is saddened when His children make free will choices that are hurtful. Tell me, what happened to Eva when the boy broke up with her?"

"She came running home crying. I hugged her thinking, *I tried to warn you,* but I didn't say that. I held onto her. Then she said to me, 'Mom, I should have listened to you,' which made me smile, but it also broke my heart because I don't like to see my children hurt."

"What happened the next time she was interested in a boy?" asked the Carpenter.

"She was more careful," said Eileen, "and she would tell me more about him and then have me meet him as a test. "

"So, she learned, and the next time, she listened and took to heart your guidance?" prompted the Carpenter.

"Yes," answered Eileen.

"It's the same with the Builder," said the Carpenter. "Each of you was created in His image with the ability to make your own choices and decisions. Some lessons you have to learn on your own, and some are more painful than others; but the Builder and I are molding you and allowing these things for your good."

"Dalton and Eileen, my time before you is limited. I do not make many of these visits, though I am always around."

"Hey, speaking of that, when we have these miracle moments between these two worlds, why does my watch stop?" I asked.

"Ah, that," answered the Carpenter. "Time is precious on earth. Visits with your loved ones are precious. We want you to be free to spend as much time as possible with your loved ones without taking more time away from your earthly world. Our Builder stops earth's time when *Johnny Bruce* bridges the gap between the two worlds. Time stops for you and others in those visits, too."

"Amazing!" cried Eileen. "How is this possible?"

"Oh, Eileen," said the Carpenter with a smile of delight beaming on His face. "Certain things that come from the Builder you have to accept, even if you don't understand. It's a gift. All of this is a gift. Your service to others is far-reaching. When you joined the Team, you were made to be a valuable person to Our Three Persons. I was on this earth briefly, but in that time, I prepared and trained twelve others to continue with the service. I breathed onto them the breath of the

Spirit. Each of them had unique gifts, unique roles unmatched by any other, that work in synchronicity. In the same manner that mammals breathe in oxygen breathed out by plants, the plants breathe in carbon dioxide breathed out by the mammals of this earth.

"Even though the body has many parts, it is all made to work together as one body. If the entire body were an eye, where would the sense of hearing be? If the entire body were an ear, where would the sense of smell be? But in fact, the Builder has placed the parts of the body, every one of them, just as he wanted them to be. There are many parts, but one body."[2]

"Oh my," I said with an exhaled breath, "those are the words of Paul from First Corinthians. So, that confirms Paul's words."

"Came from the Builder," said the Carpenter with a smile. "We entrust you to make the most of your gifts and talents."

The Carpenter reached into the boat, grabbed an orange bobber from the floor, and tossed it into the water. Concentric circles rippled from the bobber. "I have placed you to be a ripple effect on those around you. As that ripple spreads—as it has from the ripple of the bobber—the effect you have on others widens and spreads. Do not keep this to yourself—this love, this additional wisdom, and this experience. You have a choice to use it for good or for bad—or worse, for nothing at all. The character that we have seen from you shows us you will use it for good. Your life experiences are for a reason—every one of them—even that time when John Millington locked his keys in the van. Eileen, even that time that you wanted to go into town and go dress shopping, but your dad had you go out to the dock first. Dalton,

---

2 1 Corinthians 12:12-20

your motor broke down at the same time. Coincidence? No, it was part of a plan."

Eileen squeezed my hand, and I heard her sniffle. We always thought it was meant to be, but how many people get to hear confirmation from Heaven?

"My Lord," I asked, "does this mean we are to share this boat with the world?"

"Oh, no," answered the Carpenter, "this is to be kept very quiet. Otherwise, the entire world will be at your doorstep hoping to see their loved ones that have passed over. Some for good reasons, a lot for not good intentions. The boat would be stolen from you in no time. Keep this to yourselves."

Eileen asked, "Will we always have these visits when we go out in the boat?"

"Visits between Heaven and earth—no one on this earth can make those experiences happen. They are granted by the Builder, the Spirit, and Myself. There will be times when you will sense the right thing to do to share this gift with another outside of your family. You know that in your heart what you *are* to share with others. Tell them your story. Tell them My story. Tell them of the love given to you and that you want that love shared with them. Do your best to guide them."

Eileen and I nodded and continued to listen rapturously.

"If I stand atop a mountain and use a signal mirror to send you a message in Morse code to you down in the valley, you are immediately ready to mobilize into action to those in the valley rather than waiting on Me to climb down the mountain to give you that message or having to climb up to the mountaintop to receive the message from Me. I can remain atop the mountain top receiving messages from above and from hundreds of miles around the mountaintop because my vantage point is high. As signals come from you to be atop the mountain, I can send those to the Builder."

"Dalton, you heard the messages from the boat. You and Eileen acted on it. You were in pain and lost in your grief, and Eileen was doing everything she could to comfort you, but it had to come from above. Because you listened and acted in that direction, we gave much to you."

The Carpenter paused and then continued, "The greatest gift you have is salvation. But We have also given you the gift of each other and the gift you have together of raising Eva and Ned so they will come to know and understand more about our Builder. You are a lighthouse on this earth to your family and friends. Continue to let the light shine. Your time is not complete. Look ahead and apply your experiences for use tomorrow.

"Dalton, you have been the gift of writing and speaking. Take what you have experienced in life so far and share it in words and speech. Go beyond the traditional methods where messages are usually given. Go to the marketplaces or wherever people are gathered seeking relief from their suffering."

The Carpenter smiled at us, as we hung onto His every word. "There are people today who have lost a loved one similar to you. Boldly tell others how you got beyond those first days. Give the message of hope so it will not tempt them to follow the same escape.

"Eileen, you have the perspective of a mother and spouse who has battled depression within your home. You have overcome it, so share your story with your authentic way of storytelling. I know you are not comfortable on stage, but you can share your story and what was helpful to you."

"Be a megaphone for the Builder's Word—for my Word. Be a lighthouse, helping others to safety, promise, and hope."

"I get so nervous when I speak to groups," protested Eileen.

"So do I," I chimed in.

The Carpenter looked upward, then looked at us, pointed upward, and said, "That's when you have to depend more on the Spirit and the Builder to guide you, more than your abilities. When that sense of nervousness comes over you, something is about to be done through you. Pray up, too, because it also means that the enemy is about to derail you."

"How long can You stay?" Eileen questioned the Carpenter eagerly.

"I'm always with you, even though you cannot see Me. Be ready. As soon as I leave, someone will come to undo the good you are doing."

With that statement, the Carpenter reached down with His hand and sank the bobber below the surface. The bobber floated back up, but it was farther away from Him with rougher ripples.

"Trying times may come; rough waves may rock the boat; but our Builder will always surface."

"Dear Lord," said Eileen, "we have so many more questions. There is so much for us to learn, and we need to know . . . "

"Ask your questions, and be ready for the answers. I cannot answer everything today. I cannot give you all-knowingness, which is up to the Builder. Draw on each other; We put you two together for a reason. The two of you united are stronger together than you are as individuals. Make the most of it. Fight away the battles when the evil one tries to pull you apart."

"The evil one. Interesting initials, E.O.," I commented.

"Yes, I don't think he is worthy to mention his name," declared the Carpenter. "He just keeps nipping at my heel, and I just keep stamping his head."

"My child Eileen, my child Dalton, I must go now." The Carpenter stood up.

"Can I hug You?" pleaded Eileen.

"Why, yes." The Carpenter smiled, extending His arms.

Eileen and I both reached over and wrapped our arms around this Man—the Man, this Carpenter, and this Son.

"Thank You!" we said together. "We love You so very much."

"I love you, Eileen and Dalton," assured the Carpenter. "Know that more experiences are in store for you because of *Johnny Bruce*. Go now and continue to make more students and teachers."

The Carpenter stepped away from *Johnny Bruce,* and just as He'd appeared to us, He vanished in the same way.

Chapter 34

Eileen and I held onto each other as tears streamed down Eileen's face. I thought I would cry, too, but I was filled with such a great feeling of warmth and happiness. We got to see and talk with the Carpenter—Jesus Himself! I kissed the top of her head. Words were not spoken between us, and I felt great love for this woman.

Eileen broke the warm silence. "We have been searching and seeking guidance for so long, and now we have it!"

I replied, "I'm blown away."

"It will take a moment for this to sink in." Eileen sighed. "But I guess we should pick up Ed."

"Oh my!" I yelped. "I almost forgot. I was so wrapped up in it all."

"Yeah, me, too." Eileen smiled.

We headed to the boulder, where Ed and Andrew were sitting and laughing. They waved as we got near them.

"Mr. and Mrs. Sanders, thank you for bringing my dad here today." Andrew grinned as he winked at us. "I hope you had an enjoyable visit here at uh, Town Creek, as much as Dad and I did."

"Andrew, it's been our pleasure and quite a day for us, too," I replied cheerfully.

"Dad, I have to go, and you need to get back to Mom." Andrew sighed. "Your neighbors here need to get back to their children."

Ed and Andrew stood up, and Ed embraced his son as he said wistfully, "I wish I could take you with me to see your mom."

"Dad, you are taking me with you—I'm always with you," declared Andrew. "Tell Mom about today and assure her I am with her, and I am good. I'm right where y'all wanted me to be. Hug her for me. I love you, Dad."

"I love you, too, Andrew," replied Ed. "I feel so much better. Thank you, Dalton!"

"You're welcome, neighbor," I said. "But you need to thank the Builder, too."

"Thank you, God!" Ed yelled as his voice echoed through the valley.

Ed stepped into *Johnny Bruce,* and Eileen embraced him. We drifted away as we waved at Andrew. When I turned downstream, Andrew vanished.

"Thank you, Eileen and Dalton," said Ed. "I am sorry I stole your boat, but I found what I was looking for. Let's go home now. I have so much to tell Andrew's mom."

All three of us were in a daze as we absorbed the beauty of the low, green mountains.

I broke the silence as I yelled over the sound of the outboard, "Hey, Ed, check your watch."

Ed looked at his watch and quickly turned his head to me. "What? It says 12:44 p.m. Did my watch stop?"

"Your watch didn't stop," I answered.

"But we were here for hours. I don't get it," Ed said in confusion.

"God gave you a gift without losing time on earth."

Ed peered up and shook his head with a grin.

After we got back to the ramp, we asked Ed to tow the boat back home. Eileen and I didn't feel that he would take it anywhere else except for our house after today's experience. We were right. We had an even more loyal neighbor than ever.

Chapter 35

We followed Ed on the highway, staying at a leisurely fifty-five miles per hour.

Eileen exploded, "How incredible, how absolutely, without a doubt, gratefully blessed, amazing!" Eileen pounded her fist down on the armrest.

"Did we really just see the Son Himself? I mean, am I dreaming, or did this happen?"

"Eileen," I drawled, "It *really* did happen! I don't think anyone will believe us if we tell them, but . . . "

"Our children will believe us," insisted Eileen. "And so will Rich and your mother." "But"—Eileen checked the rearview mirror, as if afraid the cars behind us were listening—"we can't tell others about it. When Jesus performed a miracle, He said, 'Don't tell anyone.' Then they told people. How could they not? It's written for generations to know the works of Jesus on behalf of His Father. He trusts us with something mighty." Eileen ran her fingers through her hair as she spoke, excitement radiating from her fingertips.

"When something great happens, we want to *tell* others. When I was holding Eva and Ned for the first time, I wanted the entire world to see my babies, even though babies are born to parents every day. When I married you, I wanted everyone to know I was marrying my soulmate and fulfilling the dream of a little girl. It wasn't about the wedding to me; it was about us partnering in life together! When Dad and Mom died, I didn't want the world to know I was grieving because I didn't want anyone to see me cry. I only wanted them to see me smile."

Elaine could not be contained; she spoke in an excited cadence of excitement.

"Dalton, you have this incredible gift of writing and speaking. It comes so naturally to you. I've got to help get you back on that stage to share the story of how God and His Son have affected our lives. To tell people, 'Hey, God is real! Jesus is real! He loves *you*! Are you going to love Him back?' Wow, right there is your message! I just got goosebumps."

"So did I," I replied peering at her out of the corner of my eye while also focusing on the road. I smiled broadly in pride and joy in seeing my wife with so much vibrance.

"Dalton, He's right; I'm good with children, and I can tell a children's story like the best of them," continued Eileen. "I'll keep telling children the same thing, and children will love Him back! Oh wow, we are onto something. Are we going to have the money to do these things?"

"Now, you are being practical." I laughed. I slowed my pace as Eileen paused for the first time since we had started driving. I inhaled and replied to her question.

"Eileen, God wouldn't give us a mission without being able to provide. In *Field of Dreams,* Kevin Costner and his wife were about to lose the farm for the money he put in to build the ballfield instead of harvesting corn. No one else was building a baseball field with lights in the middle of rural America. Then, the ballplayers started showing up. There was a line of cars and people coming to pay to see *that* ballfield. No more worries about their farm. I'm not saying we should sell tickets for rides in *Johnny Bruce,* but God provided gold for Mary and Joseph through the gift of the wise men. He will provide for our needs. How? We will see."

Eileen looked straight out the windshield toward the road ahead of us, took a breath, raised her fist to her chest and said, "We believe and trust that He will."

Then a silence came between us as we allowed this to sink in. The wind rushed past our moving truck, and then Eileen's gasp broke the silence.

"Oh, my, I forgot to let Eva know we found the boat. Let me text Eva and Diane to let them know we will be home soon. I'm sure they are eager to know that we have the boat back. Yeah, see, I've gotten several messages from Eva about it. We were out of cell coverage in the state park." Eileen's fingers flew as she texted her daughter and mother-in-law the good news.

Within thirty minutes, we were home. Ned and Eva were waiting for us in the backyard. Ned jumped up and down as Ed pulled *Johnny Bruce* into our backyard.

Ned ran to Ed's truck door. "You found it, Mr. Ed! You found it! Thank you!"

Mr. Ed sheepishly kneeled to receive an enormous hug from Ned.

"Ned," said Ed with remorse, "I'm sorry to say that—"

"I forgot that I offered to let Mr. Ed go fishing with *Johnny Bruce,*" I interrupted. "He just hadn't told me which day he would take him out." I explained how Mr. Ed got an unexpected day off work and took the offer of "anytime" to mean whenever he wanted.

Ed's face was puzzled as he looked at me. "He let me know that next time, he will leave us a note or send a text message to avoid scaring any of us." Eva and Ned hugged Ed.

Ed told them, "I have a better feeling why *Johnny Bruce* means so much to you. I'm so sorry I scared you."

Ed and I unhooked *Johnny Bruce* and put the weather cover over him. I invited Ed to come inside and join me for a well-earned ice cream sandwich and ice-cold soda. Ed declined as he was anxious to get home to Debby and tell her about being with Andrew.

Ned heard me and asked, "Daddy, may I have a root beer?"

"Yes, Ned," I answered. Eva grabbed Ned's hand. "Come on, let's go get a soda." Off they went toward the house hand in hand.

Before Ed went home, he embraced me and said, "Thank you. I don't know how I can ever—"

"Neighbor, it's a gift. We are supposed to share our gifts," I replied knowingly.

Ed hugged Eileen, got into his truck, and drove the scant distance home.

Chapter 36

Over the next several nights, I could not sleep well. I tossed and turned so much that I left Eileen in our bed and went to our spare bedroom so she could sleep undisturbed. The events of the past week rolled through my head, while I wondered how to carry out the plan that the Carpenter gave us. *How do I balance that while working for Rocket City Tech?*

After multiple nights of tossing and turning and being drained, a Voice whispered, "Remember your purpose, and remember what We said about the enemy."

A light bulb lit in my mind. *The great deceiver—he is trying to wear me down and knock me off God's path!*

I sat up in bed and looked at the clock. It was eleven past one in the morning. I spoke softly, "In the Name of Jesus Christ, Satan, get out of here and leave me alone. You have no place here. Leave my house and leave my family alone. Release your clutches on Eileen, Eva, and Ned. I am a follower of Jesus, and He is stronger than you! Stop nipping at His heel."

I flopped back on the pillow, feeling relief with eyelids so heavy that they closed and didn't open again until six o'clock in the morning when the alarm went off. I sat up, dragged my legs over the side, and prayed, "Thank you, God, for these hours of rest."

I ate breakfast alone in the dining room. The house was still asleep. I heard the Voice whisper again, "He will hear you out. Confidence. God's work comes in threes."

I left the house encouraged. When I walked into my office at Rocket City Tech, there was a clear, plastic bag with the Green Wave part inside. A handwritten note read:

> *Dalton, here's an improved Green Wave for your outboard motor. Toodles, Clyde.*

Now, I knew what the whisper meant. I wasted no time thinking it through. I knew what action I had to take.

Twice, I had presented the Green Wave to Milo. He didn't buy it. It was time to make the third presentation. Not to Milo, but to Bob King, the owner of Rocket City Tech. He was the man who had hired me years ago. He was in the office. When I arrived this morning, I saw his prized possession parked in the lot—a four-door 1967 Plymouth Belvedere.

I bolted out of my office back to the parking lot to get a good look at Bob's Plymouth. Bob and his son had spent a great amount of time restoring this car. It was his parents' car that sat in a garage for decades until Bob had the money and time to restore it. It was glossy, light blue and gleamed in the sunlight. Bob wanted to restore it to factory condition.

I slowly walked around the Plymouth to get a good look. I looked at the rubber-stamped writing on the tires. They were white sidewall tires, and it said, "Goodyear Eagle." *Wait a minute, the Eagle tires didn't come out until the eighties.* Then I remembered Bob talking about the difficulty finding a replacement carburetor. Instead of restoring the original carburetor, he had found a modern carburetor with an electronic chip to give it electronic fuel injection. He was so proud of that carb as he bragged on the savings on fuel mileage in addition to the power punch of the engine. Original restoration or not, it was a beautiful car that highlighted the muscle car era. *Okay, I found what I needed to see.*

I walked back into the office wiping the sweat from my brow with the sleeve of my shirt. I got to Bob's office down the hall and knocked on the door.

"Come in."

"Hey, Bob, you got a minute?"

"Sure, Dalton," said Bob. Bob sat at his desk with his right hand moving the computer mouse, but as I entered, he reached out to shake my hand. Bob was in great shape for a man in his sixties. He still had a thick head of cotton-white hair, tan face, and pearly white teeth that showed with his broad smile. He wore wire-rimmed glasses and a navy blue golf shirt. He looked like he had just come off the golf course.

"Please, have a seat."

I sat down in front of Bob's desk and took a quick glance at the credenza behind his desk with the framed family photos of his wife, children, and grandchildren. Amid the family photos was a photo of his 1967 Plymouth Belvedere sitting next to a trophy he had won from a car show.

"How's the family doing?" Bob tilted his head and smiled.

"The family is doing great," I replied. "I don't want to take you away from what you have planned today, so let me jump straight to it."

Bob nodded his head and leaned back in his chair. "Okay."

"We have an opportunity coming up soon to make a splash with our products at a trade show in Orlando for the marine industry."

"Oh yeah, we've got a booth there, don't we?" Bob peered at the calendar on his desk to find the date for the show.

"Yes, but I think it's time to go bigger," I continued. "I've worked at these booths in the past, and it's great to meet people who already use our products and meet new prospects. However, these are tire-kickers who are coming by to chat more than listen or pay attention to what we have. Let's have a booth this year, but let's schedule a special announcement from Rocket City Tech."

Bob sat straight up in his chair and leaned forward on his desk. "We've never done that before. That's a bold move," said Bob. "Do you think this will help us grow? What will we tell them that's different from what we have already told them?" His eyes were fixed on me now.

I took a deep breath. "Bob, I saw your Plymouth this morning in the parking lot. Tell me, did you restore it yourself?"

"My pride and joy," said Bob as he leaned back in his chair. "That is, next to my kids. That Plymouth was my mom and dad's car. It was the family car we traveled in. Lots of memories. Yeah, my son and I restored it ourselves. It took me a while, but it became a family project."

"Can I buy it from you?" I asked with a smile.

"Hah-hah. I'm sorry. It's not for sale." Bob shook his head. "No amount of money can replace what that Plymouth means to me. Plus, I put in a lot of sweat equity to restore it. It's special for my son, too. I just want to drive it, enjoy it, and keep it running for as long as I can."

"I understand. Besides, I don't think you pay me enough to be able to buy it from you." I laughed. "By the way, I believe you told me you installed a new carburetor on it. How's that working out?"

"Yeah, I had to replace the carb." Bob shifted forward, engaged in his story. "And I added an electronic throttle body fuel injection system. It allows me to use today's unleaded gasoline and gives me incredible fuel mileage compared to the old carb. Belches out less smoke, too. I guess it's what you call "more environmentally friendly." She's running as good as can be."

I leaned forward and put my hands on my knees. "What if I told you that Rocket City Tech has a product that can do the same for old outboards that your new carburetor electronic fuel injection did for your Plymouth?" I asked, my palms sweaty against my slacks.

"Really? When did this come about?" Bob's eyebrows raised, and his eyes widened. "Herb Ericson and Clyde William came up with it. We have been testing it out on numerous outboard motors aging from the 1950s to the 1980s. All of them were made with gasoline-and-oil-mixed fuel tanks that belched smoke and dumped unused gas and oil into the water. Now, the product is ready to launch, and no one else is making it. Rocket City Tech is ready to break ground in the marine industry. It's a bolt-on replacement part just like your EFI carb for your Plymouth."

Bob checked his cell phone, and I worried the moment was lost. But then, he set the phone down and motioned for me to continue.

"It's called the Green Wave, and I have personally been running it on my outboard all spring. Let's leap into the marine manufactures world and make an enormous splash at this summer's expo. What do you say?"

Bob leaned forward and put his elbows on his desk.

"Interesting," said Bob. "I like the things that Clyde and Herb come up with. Can I see it?"

"Sure, Bob. Come on back to the production area." I wasn't expecting this, and I wasn't sure if Clyde and Herb were here today, but I went with the flow and said a prayer. *Okay, You got me into this; see me through.*

Bob followed me out of his office and into the production area. As soon as we entered, I saw Clyde and Herb at their workstations. *Whew, thank you!*

"What's going on, Boss?" asked Herb as he stepped away from his tinkering.

"Hello, gentlemen." Bob shook their hands.

"Hey, Bob would like to see your Green Wave in action. Can y'all do an impromptu demonstration?"

"Sure thang," said Clyde. We walked over to the roll-up door, where an outboard motor was mounted in a barrel full of water. The engine was visible as the cowling was removed. Clyde handed a Green Wave to Bob and described how it worked. He showed him where it was mounted on the engine and told him that it took only about thirty minutes to install on an old outboard.

Bob turned the Green Wave in his hands as he peered at it and then inspected it on the outboard. His eyebrows were taut over his eyes as he stepped back and asked, "Let me see it run."

Clyde started the engine. It fired immediately, and no smoke came out of the exhaust. Clyde throttled up the engine. Still no smoke. Bob took a closer look, stood back, and waved his hand across his neck, indicating to cut the engine. Clyde stopped the outboard. Bob held the Green Wave in his hands, nodded his head, and smiled as he looked at Clyde, Herb, and me. "Pretty impressive! Y'all came up with this yourselves?"

"Yes, sir," replied both Clyde and Herb.

"Is there anything else like it on the market?" asked Bob.

"No, sir," answered Clyde and Herb.

"I like it," Bob said with a smile as he leaned back on his heels. "Keep up the great work on this. Can I take this Green Wave to my office?"

"Sure," said Clyde.

Bob thanked them and shook their hands, turned to me, and said, "Come back to my office Dalton."

I followed Bob to his office, and he closed the door. Holding up the Green Wave, he said, "This little thing is impressive, and I see the promise of getting it on the market. And the sooner we do it, the better jump we get on the competition."

"If there is any competition right now," I replied.

Bob took a deep breath. "So, you are saying a big presentation for all attendees, almost a center-stage kind of announcement?"

"Yes," I answered. "Then in the back of the room, we will have our people ready to take orders."

"That's audacious, but who are we going to get to do this? I don't know if we can have this ready in time."

"I'll put a plan together, craft and deliver the message. Trust me, Bob, it's time for us to be leaders and action takers—rather than followers, but I have to have your blessing first to get everyone on board to make it happen."

"Dalton, you are a good one-on-one salesperson, but I don't know about captivating a large audience." Bob sent a stunning blow that a month ago would have emotionally knocked me down. Not today. His comment caused me to rise up and be bold.

I stood up and walked toward the door. I turned around and pushed aside the chair I had been sitting in. I looked up at the ceiling and then directly at Bob, whose eyes were following my movement. Filled with a sense of warmth and purpose, I smiled and said, "You haven't seen me in action, Bob. I used to preach at a small church every Sunday, but it's been a while since I did that."

I took a breath. "This vision came to me this morning during breakfast after several nights tossing and turning. I walked in here two hours after the idea landed. I am your guy to make it happen. I'll build a team to put everything together. We have the team here—they just don't know it yet. President Kennedy challenged this nation to go to the moon when we didn't have a rocket or spacecraft to get there. This is a much smaller scale, and we can do it—trust me." My confidence swelled, and I held my fist to my chest.

Bob flopped back in his chair, reclined backward, breathed out, and asked, "What does Milo think about this?"

"Sir, he's heard about it but hasn't seen it in action. He knows that the decision is up to you." I peered into Bob's eyes.

I stretched the truth, but it was time to make bold moves.

"My mind is saying no, but my heart is shouting yes. Let's do it. You have my blessing. Make it happen!"

"I'll get to work! Oh, and one more thing, I need my entire family to come along with me on the trip to Orlando. They will be part of the presentation and working for the company that week. I need you to cover their expenses, too."

"Ah . . . well . . . okay." Bob shrugged his shoulders. "You are full of determination and asking for the moon, but my instincts still think I should go for this."

Encouraged, I continued to press my luck. "We need a suite, so we have space for our teams to gather and complete our plan, and a place to park a trailer boat."

"Uh, sure, you got it, Dalton," agreed Bob, still in shock that he was agreeing to my requests. "I'll get Steve to make the reservations for y'all at the host hotel. Plus, I'll tell Milo and the entire team to get behind you."

"Thanks, Bob," I said. "Your blessing and decision is about to launch Rocket City Tech to new heights. It's so important."

And with that conversation, I had committed my family and the entire company to this project and got someone else to pay for it. *Thanks, God!*

I walked out of Bob's office with a saunter in my step and an enormous grin as I passed Milo in the hallway.

"What are you grinnin' about, Dalton?" asked Milo.

"Get used to hearing the name Green Wave. It's about to make enormous waves around here," I answered as I walked down the hall, not stopping to talk to Milo.

From Bob's office, I heard him say, "Milo, is that you? Please step into my office."

I called Eileen and told her I was bringing home takeout for dinner. "I've got some exciting news to share with y'all." I grinned into the phone.

Chapter 37

"Get everyone together. Time to eat." The four of us gathered at our rectangle dinner table. Ned sat to my right. Eva sat across from me with Eileen to her left.

"Daddy, what is it?" asked Ned, his small body radiating with excitement.

"Yeah, Dad," seconded an unemotional Eva. "Mom said for us to come out of our rooms as soon as we heard the garage door open. Did you get a promotion or something?"

"You are about to find out. Let's thank God for our food," I answered.

We all held hands and bowed our heads as I prayed, "Dear Heavenly Father, thank You for all You provide for us—our home, this warm food, our clothes, but most of all, each other. We live for You and because of You. May we use the blessings You have given us to be blessings for others. In Jesus' name, amen.

"This morning, I arranged for our family to have an expense-paid trip to Orlando this summer!" I announced.

"Woohoo! Where's Orlando?" hollered Ned.

"Yeah! Disney World?" shouted Eva with wide eyes.

"Yes, I believe a trip to Disney World will be part of our trip." I grinned. Eva and Ned both celebrated this news by thrusting their arms in the air with huge smiles.

"Whoa, how did you pull that off?" asked Eileen.

"Well, there is a catch." I tilted my head and glanced at Eileen.

She rolled her eyes. "Ah, I should have known. Here we go, kids."

Ned and Eva's heads fell forward in disappointment. "You're going to have to work, aren't you?"

"It's a working trip for all of us. Bob, the owner of my company, has agreed to pay for the hotel and meals, even put us in a suite at an Orlando hotel. In exchange, we will get to attend the nation's largest marine trade show. When I say *working,* I mean we have work to do between now and the show."

"Daddy, I don't get it," moaned Eva.

"Yeah, clue me in, too, Dalton." Eileen patted my arm supportively.

All three of them looked puzzled, as we heaped Chinese food onto our plates.

"All of you were instrumental in getting *Johnny Bruce* restored, and we are taking him with us to Orlando as part of Rocket City Tech's display and presentation. Our company is launching a new product line of parts to restore the used boat industry. Eva, remember that new part you and your mom installed on our outboard?"

"Yeah, the little computer chip valve box." Eva's interest piqued as she looked up from her plate.

"At the trade show, we will introduce this to the marine industry." I grinned, my food untouched.

"How does *Johnny Bruce* fit into this?" asked Eva before taking another bite of spring roll.

"He will be our example of how a family can enjoy a low-cost restoration project of used marine equipment," I continued. "Most of the electronic and mechanical things made today aren't built to last. Our boat and outboard motor will last. All we had to do was change some worn or rusty parts. A family shouldn't be burdened with the rising cost of recreation, such as boating. It cost us less than two thousand dollars to get the parts to restore *Johnny Bruce*. I want y'all to tell folks how much fun it was. Do y'all want us to sell our boat and get a brand new one?"

"No, not at all. *Johnny Bruce* forever!" shouted Ned.

"Yeah, I love that boat," piped up Eva. "I love it as much, if not more, than my car."

"Exactly!" I said. "Eva, you drive an old car that has 150,000 miles on it, but it's yours and still runs, right?"

"Yeah, it's old, but I'm going to keep it as long as I can," Eva said. "It's still in pretty good shape. The seats are comfortable. We put in a new stereo, and it needs new tires. But other than that, I love it! I even got to paint it my favorite color—candy apple red."

"You customized it and restored it to make it your own," mused Eileen as she caught onto the idea. "You probably wouldn't have done that to a brand-new car."

"Absolutely not," insisted Eva.

I peered into each of their eyes and inhaled. "We need to do a better job of preserving God's world. Stop being a throwaway society. That's what we are working on at my company to work within the marine industry. This vision came to me, and *we*—the team at Rocket City Tech joining forces with Team Russell—are taking action and making it happen." I beamed, placing my right arm on Ned's shoulder and reaching across to grab Eva's hand.

"Way to go, Daddy!" Ned clapped in celebration as he reached across the table to grab Eileen's hand.

"I'm in, Daddy!" cried Eva, placing her left hand on Eileen's shoulder.

"Dalton . . . " Eileen sighed with a look of concern. "I'm uneasy that you didn't talk to me about this before committing our family to such an audacious task." She exhaled. "But this is such a bold move that I haven't seen in years." All eyes at the table were fixed on Eileen. She shook her head and laughed. "However, you got us a free trip to Disney World, so why should I complain?"

Eileen peered into my eyes. "I have one question. Was this caused by what *He* said to us?"

I smiled, showing my teeth, tilted my head, and nodded. "Absolutely."

Eileen nodded at me and grinned. "Okay, count me in, too. I trust Him." She pointed upward.

I exhaled, dropped my head toward Ned's shoulder and exhaled in relief. "Thanks for your support, Team Russell. Now, before we get to work, let's enjoy our meal."

"Ooh, sesame chicken is my favorite," approved Ned.

"Please pass me the broccoli beef," requested Eva.

"Beef?" Eileen glanced up in surprise. "I haven't seen you eat meat in quite some time. What's got into you, girl?"

"Mom." Eva rolled her eyes. "I haven't been this active in a while."

Eileen glanced into Eva's eyes. "It looks good on you." Eva leaned her head onto her mom's shoulder.

Our dinner chatter continued as Team Russell made the first action step to fulfill the Carpenter's mission.

Chapter 38

My family committed to the mission; we went to work preparing for the summer expo in Orlando. Rocket City Tech was gung-ho, and Bob gave me all the support we needed to put this together quickly, since time was of the essence.

When I told Clyde and Herb that the company was ready to take their Green Wave into production, they were both flabbergasted and pleased to see one of their new designs go into production. They had become used to the same old thing with Rocket City. Finally, their tinkering in Rocket City's research and development department was moving out of their shop.

I encouraged them to cash in their favors with their friends that were testing Green Wave. "Call them, text them, or visit them and find out how they are performing. Get as much test data as you can."

Clyde and Herb nodded and rushed back to their desks. I stood in the production area of Rocket City Tech and slowly looked around. There was the hum of the machines—drill presses, metal being stamped, even plastic wrap being unfurled to hold down the pallet shipments. Even with this noise, it still seemed oddly quiet to me. There was not much time from now until the expo. *Don't you think you've gotten in over your head? Look at how much there is to get done. Maybe now isn't the time.*

I recognized those doubtful thoughts, and I silenced them by looking around and saying aloud, "You take your clutches off of me, you evil one. You're not getting the best of me today. In the name of Jesus Christ, leave me alone."

A voice spoke from behind a row of boxes. "I'm sorry; I didn't quite hear everything. Are you talking to me?" It was Sharice, one of our shipping and receiving clerks. She had surprised me, and I apologized and said I was not speaking to her.

Sharice peeked her head out from behind the row of boxes, and our eyes met. She looked timid, but there was a glow about her as she spoke these words of strength to me: "Actually, Dalton, I heard every word. I've cried those same words to my Lord. Call away the devil; he's got nothing on us. Sir, I don't know what it is you're doin' back here, but I got this feelin' in my gut that something good is 'bout to happen. Whatever it is, sir, you go get 'em. We're behind you."

Hearing her words, I glanced down at the stainless-steel work bench. Appearing in the sheen of stainless steel I saw the faces of Eileen, Eva, and Ned as they looked on our family boat ride in *Johnny Bruce*. Then appeared an image of a *Saturn V* rocket in flight with a long fire trail behind it. I smiled and looked toward Sharice. I didn't know her that well, but at this moment, I felt like her brother.

"Sharice, today, you are God's messenger. That's what I needed to hear." I ran over and startled her with a hug.

"Stop what you are doing and gather up with everyone," I announced as I leaped into a run to my office. Once in the hallway, I slowed to a fast walk. I knocked on Bob's office door and entered. He looked up at me. "Bob, you ready? It's time to tell the team."

Bob smiled, nodded, and said, "Let's do it."

I closed his office door and bolted to my office

"Dalton, hey, I need to speak with you.," Milo cried when I passed his office, but I kept going. Milo rushed to follow me into my office. I got behind my desk and reached for the phone when Milo said, "I can't believe you fooled the old man into following you. I still think you are leading us away from where we need to be."

I looked at Milo. My face flush and short of breath, I looked into his eyes and said, "Milo, either lead, follow, or get out of the way. I don't have time for naysayers." I picked up the phone handset and pressed the intercom button.

"Attention all Rocket City employees, this is Dalton Russell. In ten minutes, please join us in the high bay building for an all-hands meeting. Again, join us in ten minutes for an all-hands meeting in the high bay building. Thank you!" I placed the handset back on the cradle, ending the intercom announcement.

Every employee of Rocket City Tech gathered in the high bay area. Some brought chairs, and some stood. The first one there was Bob King, greeting everyone with a smile and a handshake. He called everyone by their first name, being the personal, caring owner he was. The employees mumbled and milled about, some wondering if there was a lay-off about to happen.

When I walked up, Bob motioned for me to stand beside him.

"All right, ladies and gentlemen, thanks for being here today. First, know that no one is getting laid off. The doors of Rocket City Tech will be open for quite some time."

There was a sigh of relief from the team, and I could feel them all relax.

"We have some exciting news to share with you, and we need your help to make it happen."

Bob announced what we were doing and how soon we needed to have everything ready for the Marine Expo. He called out Clyde's and Herb's Green Wave design. He charged all of them, "Give Dalton, Clyde, and Herb everything you have. Listen to them. Let's make it happen, folks! We are on to something good here and will make a giant splash! Now, I want to turn this over to Dalton Russell, who got all of this in motion. Dalton, the floor is yours."

"Folks, you have heard Bob. Do you have any questions?" I asked as my palms began to sweat against my slacks. *Be strong, courageous. God is with you.* My eyes met Sharice's, who was standing in the back of the gathering.

I met some resistance from some of the team that wanted to know the full plan; but I told them that we must make the most of each day, be flexible, and carry out our work to the best of our ability. We were taking it day by day, but I *didn't* tell them that I didn't know the full plan.

"Ladies and gentlemen, you know that Bob King founded Rocket City Tech based on the culture of following God's plan. You don't have to be a believer to work here, but you know that it is part of the mission statement to be a part of God's mission. All of this came from a place higher than us. Trust me. He will give us what we need just when we need it."

All eyes were fixed on me as everyone sat or stood motionless.

"It may seem daunting, but anything worth doing comes with hard work. We can do this, ladies and gentlemen. If we need to outsource some of the work to get it done in time, we will. We will go on back order if we have to after the expo, but we gotta make the most of this gathering of the movers and shakers of the marine industry. It's our time to shine because if we wait another year, the opportunity may be gone. Believe in yourselves. Believe in each other. Believe Bob. Believe me. Believe God is about to do an amazing thing. Faith is taking that first step up the stairs, even though you can't see the top of the staircase."

Everyone stared at me in silence for a moment. Clyde broke the silence and spoke loud enough for everyone to hear, "Well, I think we've just heard from a preacher. You heard him, everyone; let's follow the man."

Sharice yelled, "Let's do this, people!" She began to quickly clap, and everyone joined her. I looked over at Bob, and he was clapping and beaming. He reached out and clapped me on the back as he shouted, "Let's get to work. That is all, ladies and gentlemen." With that, the Green Wave Project was launched at Rocket City Tech.

There were days I awoke and wondered where our focus should be. Each day, a plan was given, and we kept marching forward. I put all of my trust in His plan and followed the guidance from the Carpenter. My traveling stopped, and I spent my time in Huntsville working on the project. I was home every night with my family. At Rocket City Tech, we wrapped up the day before five in the evening and didn't have to work overtime or weekends. We were efficient and effective.

Then the restless nights crept back. One night, I awoke and spoke aloud, "In the Name of Jesus, evil one, leave me alone. Release your clutches from me and my family and my team of workers!"

I wasn't able to get back to sleep. Getting out of bed, I went to the kitchen to get some water and eat a snack. In the glow of night lights, I heard a whisper. "Go back to where it all began."

"What?" I whispered back.

"Go back to where it all began," repeated the whisper.

I looked outside the kitchen window into our backyard. There was a glow emitting underneath the boat cover on *Johnny Bruce*. It grew bright and faded back to darkness as soon as my eyes recognized it.

"I hear You," I whispered back, "and I see what I need to do."

I went back to bed and fell into a hard sleep. At breakfast, I told Eileen, "I heard a whisper last night."

"Dalton, sounds like you have heard a lot of whispers these past few months," replied Eileen as she peered at me with a look saying that she had heard this before. She placed her hand on my cheek and listened.

"Yeah, but the second time I heard it," I continued, "I saw a glow coming from *Johnny Bruce*. The voice said, 'Go back to where it all began.' I know what I have to do today." Eileen's eyes widened as she leaned back.

"You need to go to Town Creek, don't you?" Eileen sighed.

"Yes," I answered. "How did you know?"

Eileen wrapped her arms around me. "We are in this together. The Carpenter spoke to both of us."

"I feel like I need to go today," I said. "But what do I tell my team at Rocket City?"

She laughed in astonishment. "Don't you see it's connected? *Johnny Bruce* is a part of all of this. Tell them you are testing Green Wave."

"You're right," I replied. I picked up the phone and told Bob to tell the team I had some product testing to do with *Johnny Bruce*.

"Understand," said Bob. "We've got this, Dalton. The team has some follow-up to finish from Thursday's work." It was comforting to hear Bob referring to his employees as "the team."

The team was working hard with their head down, focused on the mission at hand—Project Green Wave. They were stamping out metal, assembling parts, creating product packaging, and deciding on the best print fonts and colors for Green Wave. Each day, there were raw materials being shipped in of aluminum casting blocks, raw plastic tubes, and rubber hoses ready to be created into Green Waves. Rocket City Tech was a hustle and bustle of activity under the leadership of Bob, Clyde, Herb, and me. Even Milo jumped in to do his part—mainly because he felt pressure from Bob that if he didn't fall in line, he may not be with Rocket City Tech much longer.

Hearing Bob's words of assurance, I hung up the phone, kissed Eileen, hugged the kids, and towed *Johnny Bruce* to Town Creek.

Chapter 39

Town Creek holds many special beginnings in my life. It was the sight of my first boat ride, where I met my wife, the first place I took the restored *Johnny Bruce,* and where I encountered the miracle of John's boat. This is what was meant from the whisper, "Go back to where it all began."

Once on the water, I checked my watch, which had become a tradition every time I took *Johnny Bruce* out on the lake. It was a reference point.

It's 10:30 in the morning, I noted and texted Eileen to mark the time.

I added the latest Rocket City Tech Green Wave valve chip to the outboard. There was no smoke. I smiled and remarked to myself, "I need to tell Herb about this."

This visit, I was expecting something. I went up the creek a bit, pulled into a cove, and grabbed my spinning rod. I used the tiny spinner bait that I liked to use as a bluegill search lure. John taught me that trick. If fish were nibbling at the little spinner bait, then there were fish bedding there that would bite a hook baited with a cricket or worm.

I heard a voice behind me say, "It's still a great way to find some fish, isn't it?"

Startled, I jumped. "Oh!"

When I turned around, he was sitting on the boat's back deck.

"John Millington!" I shouted. "You are here. You are the voice I was hearing this morning."

"Well, yeah." He chuckled. "Along with other voices."

I dropped my rod, wanting to leap to hug my best fishing buddy, but I knew from previous visits that I couldn't always have physical contact with these forms.

I plopped my hindquarters on the edge of the front deck, dropped my head, and just cried.

"Oh, Dalton, don't be sad," exclaimed John, emotion choking his words.

"Oh, I'm not sad," I replied. "I'm so relieved and grateful to see you. Thank you for giving us this boat," I said through my tears. "We needed it."

"What you are doing with the boat is fantastic," said John. "God the Father and the Son are delighted with you and your family. I saw what you were going through and wanted to help because I know I left suddenly. I petitioned God to do something a little special for you and your family. Your dad assured me you would amaze us."

"Wow!" I said. "I didn't understand what things are like on that side of Heaven."

John grinned at me.

I sat on the back edge of the front deck in awe that John was here. "It's so special for you to visit me. Your boat is a miracle!" I patted the deck with my right hand, as my emotions began to change. This is what I had been wishing for—one more conversation with John Millington. Now it was happening, and it was time to ask the hard questions.

I looked at John as I wiped away the tears with my sleeve. My eyes narrowed at him. "Why did it have to come out this way? If you hadn't left us, I wouldn't have needed it to recover. Instead, you would have kept fishing with me and frying fish for our families. You didn't get to see my children being born or growing up. I got to see Patton and Amber grow up without their dad."

I looked directly into John's eyes. The pain of the past several years came rolling out.

"Why did you put your family through this?" I fumed. "You saw what my mother, my sister, and I went through after Daddy took his life. You arrived on the scene a month after it happened—soon enough to realize the pain and difficulty it placed on a mother raising teenagers." My head jerked from left to right as I unloaded on John. "Patton and Amber were young adults starting their careers, and they needed their dad. Much less, the guilt placed on Joyce." Spit flew from my mouth.

My cadence increased. "What happened, John? I didn't *know* you were depressed. I didn't *know* about what occurred in Idaho. I thought you were honoring a commitment to Joyce to get her back closer to her family." I glared at John, demanding answers to *years* of questions.

The entire time I unloaded on John, he listened. Years of sadness, grief, and anger at losing one of my best friends just poured out of me. Instead of yelling it to the wind and hearing nothing back, I was channeling it to the man who had created the situation.

His kind, blue eyes glowed. There was a warmth in the way he looked at me.

"Dalton, I never, ever meant to hurt you, Joyce, Amber, or Patton," explained John. "There were just the right ingredients for the perfect storm."

John peered at me. For the first time, I heard what led to him taking his own life.

"In the world of Christian service, we carry the mark of the cross, and the demons see us as a target. It's the enemy trying to undo the good being done in the name of Jesus. The enemy looks for weakness to do his work. Remember that he used humans to carry out Jesus' death on the cross.

"I was in a weakened state of compassion fatigue—that's what it was. The clients I served dealt with a great deal of suffering, pain, and anguish. Being a servant of God, I felt a great deal of empathy for them. I poured my heart into helping them. Just like a pitcher of water, when you pour the water into a glass, there is less water in the pitcher. When you keep pouring, you fill the glass and empty the pitcher. You have to replenish the water in the pitcher."

I nodded my head as I understood where John was coming from. His next statement revealed a secret that he had kept from me and many others. It connected him back to a six-year stint that he had served as a chaplain in the United States Air Force. Right out of graduate school, he was commissioned as an officer. He never talked much about his air force service, but it gave him his start into counseling.

"Dalton, what I am about to tell you is not known by many people. I trust that you will respect the reason for the secrecy of this information as I do not want it to harm the lives of anyone else on this earth. The reason I was called to Idaho was because of my experience in crisis counseling, especially with post-traumatic stress syndrome—PTSD. Near Idaho Falls, there is a government facility, more like a ranch or resort. We called it 'The Ranch.' It had nice rooms, a cafeteria, corral for horses, a tennis court, and a nearby river to go fishing or fields to hunt. The Department of Defense was bringing back soldiers here who had served on the front lines of duty in Afghanistan and Iraq as part of the Second Persian Gulf War and Operation Enduring Freedom. These men and women volunteered to be part of research on PTSD so we could better assimilate, counsel, treat, and help these men and women return to civilian life."

My mouth dropped open in surprise. Now, I understood why my phone conversations with John were few and far between once he moved to Idaho. He *couldn't* always talk to me.

"Due to my service in the air force, the Department of Defense wanted to renew my security clearance so that my expertise could be utilized. When I got the call about what had happened, my heart told me I had to go and help. The Department of Defense kept a tight lid on things to protect the privacy of the men and women involved."

John described how these young men and women were deeply disturbed by what they had experienced in combat in the Middle East. It affected their mental and physical state. For some of them, they were paralyzed to function beyond eating and sleeping. John spared telling me the details of what he had witnessed as he didn't want my mind haunted with the horror of some of the tales of what he had heard.

"I sat at the bedside of the suffering soldier and fell back into my role as a military chaplain near the front lines. I listened to them pour out their heart for how much they loved their families, gave instructions of what to relay to their spouses and children, and asked me about Heaven. Underlying all of this was the threat of suicide to end the nightmares and the pain from battle injuries. Some succeeded in their attempts; thankfully, we saved many more. That's when I was called in for the next step to be a grief counselor to the families who had lost a husband, wife, or parent."

In astonished silence, I listened to John's painful story. I broke the silence by asking, "Could you tell anyone else what you were dealing with?"

"No, I had to come home, usually by five every day, because the Department of Defense didn't want it to look like anything unusual was going on. Joyce would ask, 'How was your day?' and I would answer emotionlessly, 'Another day at the office.'"

To help John get a better understanding of what the soldiers were experiencing, he was sent on a two-week-long visit to Iraq to get an up-close look.

There was so much suffering happening in a short period of time that John didn't take time to take care of himself. He dove in fully to help those people through the crisis. Not only were the soldiers dealing with PTSD, but so was John.

"I was giving, but no one was giving back to me. I was emptying myself with empathy and compassion for these women and men. As the weeks and months wore on, I became less effective. Yes, compassion and empathy fatigue and issues of PTSD from what I had witnessed."

This gave me a better picture of what had happened in Idaho. I remembered reading a story about people who worked in meat processing plants. There was at least one person who had to take down the animals when they came in to make it possible to process meat for food. The workers in the role to carry out that final act were rotated every several months. After a few months, watching animals come to a final demise—it took a toll on them, and they needed to do something else. It sounded like this is what John experienced, only he was not being rotated out. He just kept serving, and they let him whittle down to ineffectiveness.

There was more to it than his profession; there was also an external element—long, dark, cold winters in Idaho Falls. He reminded me that the fishing season is from May twenty-seventh through November thirtieth of each year.

"Dalton, you know how much I like fishing in the fall and winter. The water may be cold, and the fish may be deep; but when you find them, you can catch a bunch of them."

"Did you use your boat much?" I asked. John's answer surprised me, but it helped solve the puzzle.

"Maybe three to four times a year. Idaho is a blue-ribbon destination for trout fishermen. The Snake River teems with fish, but I just couldn't get into wade fishing. There is something special about getting in a boat, floating on the water, getting away from all hard, physical contact with rock and soil. My favorites were Henry's Lake and Island Park Reservoir. It's a beautiful landscape in the Snake River Valley, in the shadow of the Tetons and Yellowstone. Joyce and I did some outdoor things, but really all I did was work."

His boat sat in the driveway not being used. When he did take it to the lake, he spent more time making repairs due to rain, snow, oil, and grease that froze and thawed in the elements. By neglecting his boat, he was neglecting himself and allowing burnout and depression to creep in.

"The demons came to play in my weary state. I didn't make any new friends in Idaho. Patton and Amber were back east, finishing college and about to start their careers. It was just me and Joyce trying to conquer the world in this beautiful Rocky Mountain state, but I couldn't make it feel like home. I was giving, but no one was giving back to me. I was emptying myself with empathy and compassion for these families. As the weeks and months wore on, I became less effective and lost hope."

With my elbows on my knees, I leaned over, listening intently to my buddy.

"I was worn down to a frazzle, and I realized another reason it was hard for me to really enjoy the beauty of Idaho—what I was missing the most." John leaned toward me and looked directly in my eyes. "You—you weren't there to help me enjoy it. I missed my best friend."

I dropped my head in sorrowed surprise. It took a split second for me to think through this. We humans need companionship. Our spouses fulfill a lifelong role in walking through this life together. Our children and grandchildren mean the world to us. In addition, we need friendships. Me being a male human being, I need friendships with other men. Since John's death, I had been missing that brotherhood with my fellow fisherman, lover of nature, devoted servant of Jesus, and mentor.

John touched my knee with his hand, and it brought me back out of my brief trance. He said softly, "I was trying to fight the demons myself. Joyce knew a little, but I asked her to keep it to herself and let me handle it. I was foolish because I wasn't strong enough to handle it on my own."

John's body wore down. He felt such great empathy for his clients' pain and suffering that he had taken it on as his own. He became depressed, and it affected his ability to help his clients. His supervisor talked to him and expressed concern that he was spiraling downward.

"My boss even told me, 'John, the best thing you can do is go fishing with a friend—just get away and fish.' I didn't do it. The first snowfall came, and I took on the emotion of wintertime darkness and cold.

"Then, the Department of Defense told me that my service with them had concluded, and my crisis and PTSD work was complete. They told me it was time for me to move on to something else. It was great that they provided financial support for Joyce and me to stay afloat, but they didn't help me transition to the next thing. It was up to me. I felt used and discarded when they got everything they needed from me."

For the first time in his life, John was let go from a job. That will send anyone into a depression. I thought the reason they moved was to get back to Nashville to help with Joyce's aging parents. That was an important part of the move, but not the only reason.

He looked up, and his eyes gazed at the surrounding hills. "It was time for Joyce and me to leave Idaho behind and get back to our roots." There was a deeper feeling when he mentioned Joyce. "Joyce flew to Nashville and found a job teaching while I got the house ready to sell."

"You never told me that!" I exclaimed. "I thought you decided to return to Tennessee on your own terms."

"I know, Dalton, but I couldn't tell you what was going on. I had to maintain a happy front amid my inner turmoil. I decided to get back to being a church pastor. I love music, and I love sharing God's Word with others. I had gotten away from that. At least as a pastor, you see people in the hospital and give funeral eulogies, but you also get to be a part of the joys in life. Officiating weddings, visiting newborn babies, and seeing and hearing children running through the hallways full of life and energy."

"But you applied for some openings in the Nashville area, right?" More puzzle pieces connected.

"Yeah, I applied for several church positions," said John. "I even applied for a high school counseling position at a local high school. Both rejected me. I thought my depression and PTSD battle from Idaho was haunting me in Tennessee. I knew better because I worked with a classified case that wouldn't be leaked. But when you are in the valley of depression, the demons have a field day with you. Then, that last morning, I received a rejection letter from one of the churches where I had interviewed. They said they were going in a different direction and that I didn't have the pastoral experience they were looking for."

"What?" I asked. "You had decades of experience at that point."

"Yes, but it didn't seem to matter. I was low." John dropped his head and looked at me. "Joyce was at work and didn't know about the letter; I figured I would tell her when she got home. Dalton, realize when you are down and have idle time, things get dark. When I was in Idaho by myself and Joyce was in Nashville, I had idle time. Then in Tennessee, I had more idle time when Joyce was teaching at school. Idleness can be the devil's playground."

"Why didn't you tell me about this?" I asked, guilt-ridden. "I was only two hours away. We could've fished, walked the river, or met for coffee."

"You seemed so happy having met Eileen," replied John. "I didn't want to be a burden to you. I knew what you went through with your dad, and I thought I could help myself because I had helped so many other people. I was wrong."

"The weather that day was clear; but all I could see were clouds, rain, and darkness. The whiskey and Coke probably didn't help. I heard whispers—loud, indistinct voices speaking lies to me. 'Your last chapter is complete. You can't rise above this. You're too old. They want someone younger. You can't make a difference. You've passed your prime.' It was terrible, so I decided to end it."

There it was again, the flat lack of bitterness in his voice. Hearing John tell of what led to his final moments surprised me in how direct, succinct, and final it became.

"At the end, all I could see was the bottom of the pit, the deepest part of the sea, the darkest cloud. I didn't want to continue to be a burden on my family. I wanted out. I even checked my life insurance policy and took the last step as painlessly as I could."

"Do you know about the call that came the next day?" I asked.

"I know now that Joyce talked to another church where I interviewed and preached," continued John. "She told them I had died the day before, and they told her they wanted me as their pastor. My experience as a counselor combined with leading music and serving as a bi-vocational pastor was a good fit for them."

"Yes, I didn't hear about that until later, too," I said sadly as I shook my head. If John had hung on for one more day—*one more*—he may still be with us on earth, and none of this would have happened. Tears began to well.

"Once I made it to this side of Heaven, I stopped feeling the emotion of disappointment, hurt, anger, or sadness. I am free from human hurt. I have complete forgiveness for all involved in it—except for what the enemy did, but I know that the Carpenter has already taken care of him and defeated him, too."

I snapped back when I heard him mention the enemy—that there can still be a sense of frustration with the enemy once you crossed over into Heaven. *Ah, he's a spirit, too, that was in Heaven before God kicked him out.*

John got onto his knees on the floor of the boat. "Dalton, listen, you have survived two suicides. Go back and spread this message. Don't give up! Hang on to God! Share your struggle. It's part of your story that can help others."

I sensed this message was coming from a place greater than John—a heavenly message of guidance. And then, John finally released me from the burden that I had carried since the day he died.

"Dalton, it's not your fault. You didn't know. You even called me that day, and I ignored your call. I am sorry for what I put my family through. I'm sorry for what I put you through."

I fell forward on my knees in front of him. My body went limp. With these words, I felt a great weight lifted from me. The dam burst, and the flood of sobbing tears came. I held my head in my hands, and that is when I felt the warmth of John's hand on my shoulder. "Dalton, you are my brother; you are going to be okay. I love you."

There was a long silence between us as my tears subsided and I heard the birds chirping even the distinct call of a red-winged blackbird. Honeysuckle scent filled my nose.

John patted my back and told me, "Almost as soon as I arrived in Heaven, I saw your dad. He welcomed me and told me who he was. Then he said, 'Thank you for being there for my son. You helped him through tough times. You took the place of a fishing buddy that I left vacant.' He and I kept a close watch on you and my family. We saw the potential. I told him about the boat I left you. Your dad said, 'That's it; I have an idea about that. Talk to God.' He owns the boat and did something with it only He can do.

"Soon, you must gather Joyce, Patton, and Amber together in *Johnny Bruce* so they have this opportunity that God has granted you."

I got off of my knees, sat on the front deck, and wiped my face with a towel that was laying atop my tackle bag. I looked at the top of the nearest hill, breathed out a sigh of relief, and promised John, "I will. Your family deserves that."

John smirked at me. "I know what you are thinking—get past the expo first. Ask them to join you. Check your email soon. There is an invitation waiting for you."

"What is it?" I asked, confused.

"Uh-uh, not yet. Some things have to remain a mystery." John chuckled. "Great job on the expo prep. You listen well, and when people hear your story and what you are offering, it will amaze them. Through all of it, give thanks to the One Who gave you the direction, gift, and ability. Allow Him to speak through you."

My head fell backward with a great sigh. "Oh my, the weight of responsibility, John; it's growing."

"Hey, Dalton, God wouldn't give it to you if He wasn't going to help you with it. God is taking the unhappy and unpleasant experiences you have been through and using them for your good."

"God always wins, doesn't He?" I looked to the sky and smiled.

"Yep, which is why He crushes the head of the enemy," answered John. "Now, my friend, I must get you back to the work you are doing on earth. We will see each other again. Fight for life, fight for light, fight for goodness, and fight for wellness."

"Thank you, John," I said. "I'm sorry I was so angry with you when you appeared."

"Nonsense." John smiled. "I forgive you. Besides, you earned the right to be angry, and I deserved to hear it from you. I'm glad we talked it through, the same way we talked through things in this boat together. That's why I needed you to be back here at Town Creek. I know I don't have to convince you to come here."

I nodded my head. "I miss you, and I'm glad you're in my life."

John scrunched his face and waved his hand back and forth from left to right. "Ah, thank the Lord." John beamed, pointing upward.

I leaned toward his face and said what we always said at the end of a fishing trip: "It's been great being with you today, my friend." I looked into his bright blue eyes and he into mine.

"It sure has, Dalton. It sure has. I love you, my friend." John's eyes glistened as he reached and shook my hand. Warmth passed from his hands to mine.

"I love you, John, the best fishing buddy a friend could have," I replied.

With that, John disappeared. My body went limp as the adrenaline left as quickly as it had appeared. I looked at my watch; it was an hour before noon. As always, the visit seemed to go on for hours. Back to this beautiful side of Heaven.

Chapter 40

Eileen and Ned were playing in the backyard when I returned home.

"Daddy!" shouted Ned.

We hugged each other. Eileen hugged me, too.

"Better?" asked Eileen.

"Much better!" I answered.

"Enlightening?" she asked.

"Very much."

Ned ran off to play with his soccer ball. Eileen looked up at me, pulled my cap back, took off my sunglasses, looked into my eyes, and asked me intently, "Did you see John?"

I nodded my head as tears streamed down my face and I melded into my wife's arms, burying my crying eyes in her neck.

"Eileen," I cried, "an enormous weight is lifted. I feel myself again. Each visit, I felt lighter, but this one . . . this . . . getting to hear his voice, yell at him, ask questions, understand the 'why.' I miss him so much, but I see that he is all around me in the memories we made together in this miracle boat."

"Yes, he is all around us." Eileen squeezed me tight, and I felt the same warmth I felt when John shook my hand, only this time I could feel Eileen hugging me back. I glanced around at our backyard and saw Ned happily running along, chasing after his ball. A father's pride filled me as I watched him.

"I'm proud of you. I'm proud of our family. Look at our little boy—he is happy. He has his daddy back. I want every family to have this. I don't want anyone else to have to go through what we went through."

"Keep following and listening to His voice; keep following your heart; keep trusting. I love you, Dalton Russell."

"I love you, Eileen Snellgrove Russell."

Eva pulled into the driveway, coming home from school. She looked confused, like an investigative reporter seeking answers to questions. She was such an inquisitive young lady, but that's how she was learning. I sensed she had some doubts. She walked over carrying a notebook in her hand and asked, "Dad, did you and *Johnny Bruce* go out today?"

"Yes, we did," I answered. *What does she know?*

"You got to see Mr. John, didn't you?" This surprised me. *How did she know?* I gave Eileen a perplexed glance.

"Uh, yeah, I did."

"In my class before lunch, I was doodling in my notebook. Suddenly, I saw a face on the page, and I drew it out with my pencil. The first face was you, Dad. The next face . . . well, it matched up to a photo from a while back you showed me of you and Mr. John together. Except in the picture, you were wearing exactly what you are wearing right now. Then, I heard a whisper say, 'Together again.' Here's the drawing."

Eva handed me her notebook. I was stunned. At the top of the page was today's date. Below it, a sketch of John and me sitting in the boat, talking and smiling.

"Dad, your friend lives on, and we're in this together." I hugged Eva tight.

"Dalton, go check your email," said Eileen. "I think you will find something interesting. I got an invitation, and so did you."

I went to the computer, opened my email, and read the message:

To: Dalton Russell, Eileen Russell

From: Amber Millington

Subject: Invitation to Fundraiser

Dalton and Eileen,

I invite you to an evening fundraiser on Sunday night June 26th at Orange Community Church in Orlando, Florida. Dalton, we would like for you to be our keynote speaker that evening to share your story of being a survivor of two suicides.

The audience will be suicide survivors from across Florida. Some of them are recent survivors looking to make it through the early stages of grief and people who have been survivors for many years. Dalton, we want to hear how you kept going, despite the devastating loss of your dad and your close friend.

Please RSVP as soon as you can so we can prepare for this important event.

Sincerely,

Amber Millington

President

U.S. Suicide Prevention

Eileen entered the room as I finished reading the message. "It's the night before the expo." Eileen smiled knowingly. "We will already be there, and it's close to the hotel."

I looked at Eileen and knew what to do. I quickly replied.

Amber,

We accept your invitation.

Sincerely,

Dalton and Eileen Russell

Chapter 41

The weeks passed quickly until one day, we were in Orlando for the American Marine Manufacturers Expo and the Florida Suicide Prevention event.

On Sunday, June 26, we arrived at Orange Community Church. Everything was ready at the convention center for the marine expo. *Johnny Bruce* was displayed near a staging area for all to see. This twenty-year-old boat sat among shiny new rigs, from aluminum bass boats to the enormous fiberglass yachts found in the marinas of Miami Beach.

Eileen, Eva, Ned, and I walked into the church dressed in our best church attire. A booming voice filled the air. "The Russells are here!"

Amber Millington ran to us with her brother, Patton. Her blonde hair highlighted her royal blue dress, which pulled out the blue of her eyes that she had inherited from her dad. Patton, with his short cropped light brown hair, looked handsome in his navy suit. I forgot how much he looked like his dad.

"Thank you for coming!" Amber squealed as she hugged all of us.

"Is this Eva?" asked Patton as he hugged us and shook our hands. "I still see you as a five-year-old girl."

"This must be the handsome Ned," crooned Amber.

"Amber, it's great to see you," gushed Eileen as they hugged. "You are just as beautiful as always."

Then I saw her, the woman who must feel as though the weight of the world was on her. She had sandy blonde hair, wore a tailored green dress, and was beaming brightly with glowing green eyes. "Joyce." I exhaled as Eileen and I both encircled her with our arms. "It's great to see you. I have some news for you, but now may not be the time."

"I know." Joyce nodded and hugged us tight. "I'm glad y'all are here. Your family's been deep in my thoughts ever since Amber told us you were coming."

We continued our family catch-up greetings throughout dinner, and then it was time to address the crowd of survivors. It thrilled me that John Millington's family was here, mere miles away from our miracle boat. We were all together for the first time in years.

Amber took the stage, and the murmur in the room died down "Good evening, fellow survivors. Tonight you are in for a special treat of a message of hope from a man who, to me, is a brother and a second dad. When he was thirteen years old, his dad took his own life. That same summer, he met my dad. Over the years, John Millington and Dalton Russell became friends, fishing buddies, and brothers-in-fishing tackle. Dalton's lovely family is with us—the beautiful Eileen, stunning Eva, and handsome Ned. Thank you so much for joining us tonight, Russel family. Without further ado, here is Dalton Russel."

I jogged on stage, strangely energetic, and hugged Amber. She whispered in my ear, "Be God's megaphone, Dalton. I love you!"

The applause died down as I stepped to the podium. Using a wireless mic, I was free to move around. I launched into my message. I was on fire before I had even begun.

"Thank you, Amber. Let's show our appreciation to Amber and her amazing leadership. Her passion for helping others comes directly from her mother, Joyce, who is with us tonight, and from her dad, whose tragic loss is the reason Amber gathered all of us here."

I saw many in the audience nod their heads in agreement. I saw Joyce sitting close and smiled as she reached out and grabbed her children's hands. They leaned their heads on her shoulder for a moment.

"Folks, you are here tonight because you lost a loved one to suicide. Each situation is unique, and grieving varies from person to person, so you may not relate to all of this. You heard my story. I have been a suicide survivor for years. I saw my dad's slow demise into depression until the very end. Afterward, it took me years to come to terms with what happened. I miss him terribly. He wasn't there for me in my teen years or as I moved into adulthood, but I finally got to a healthy place. Then whammo, out of left field, my best fishing buddy, John Millington, took his life. I didn't see that coming, and the grief of his loss knocked me on my butt."

At this, many people shook their heads in disbelief at the ordeal of being a double suicide survivor. I felt that many understood because they had been there.

"Tonight, I'm here to tell you I'm off my butt and standing firmly again, fully alive." The audience laughed as I stood fully erect, with my arm outstretched like Lady Liberty.

Encouraged and energized by the audience's response, I began to take a turn from the dark and head toward light.

"Instead of being paralyzed by grief of what I have lost, today, I celebrate the experience. I have my lovely wife, Eileen, two beautiful children, a mother who is a ten out of ten on the side of positivity, and many friends who walk alongside me in this life together."

"Les Brown, the inspirational speaker, once said, 'The graveyard is the richest place on earth because it is here that you will find all the hopes and dreams that were never fulfilled, the books that were never written, the songs that were never sung, the inventions that were never shared, the cures that were never discovered, all because someone was too afraid to take that first step, keep with the problem, or determined to carry out their dream.'[3]

"I've been lucky enough to hear voices from some of these graves, and they say, 'fight to live.' Do everything you can to be alive and stay alive. Just like our loved one, we are susceptible to being dragged down by the enemy, the devil, the angel cast out of Heaven. If he can fool people of earth to put the Son of God on a cross of death, we are just as susceptible to a similar temptation of darkness."

Sweat began to form on my palms as I brushed them against my pants. For a split second, doubt and voices of insecurity whispered, *You can't escape it either.*

I quickly glanced at Eileen, who sensed my insecurity. The audience began to look at each other, wondering what was happening. She placed her fist across her chest and over her heart, nodded, and smiled at me. I closed my eyes and prayed, *In the Name of Jesus Christ, take your clutches off me, my family, and my friends, Satan.*

When I opened my eyes, I saw Eileen, Eva, Ned, Joyce, Amber, and Patton all holding their right fists across their chests and over their hearts and holding their neighbor's left hand as a shield of strength. I smiled at them and took a sip of water.

---

3 Les Brown, "Les Brown Quote," Goodreads.com, Accessed September 7, 2021, https://www.goodreads.com/quotes/884712-the-graveyard-is-the-richest-place-on-earth-because-it.

"Don't give in, and don't let him win. Instead, draw on strength from God to keep going. Today may be gloomy, and darkness may surround you, but you have to be there for your friends and family. Aren't they worth fighting for to get through the ominous day?"

"Yes, they are!" shouted a man in the audience, followed by a collective amen.

This got me going.

"After a rainstorm, the rainbow comes, and the sun shines. Laughter eventually follows pain."

"Mmm-hmm! Tell it brother," came from the crowd.

"My friend, John Bruce Millington, battled depression and didn't tell me. His mind and body wore down. Then, his job ended, and he was out of work. He packed up and moved his family to a different town. He received rejection letters from employers who interviewed him. Demons of doubt filled his mind. He kept it to himself, thinking he was strong enough and knowledgeable enough to get better. He was a mental health counselor. Outside, the sky was glowing, but within him were storms. He gave in to the voices of doubt.

"The day after his death, he received a phone call from a prospective employer who wanted to tell him they wanted him to join their team of counselors." My voice cracked in grief as my throat swelled.

"Ah, no, no, he didn't," came from the audience.

"One more day would have made the difference, and he may still be with us. One. More. Day. I wish he had waited one more day. Someone might wish you had waited one more day."

"That's right—one more day, brother," said someone in the middle.

"Now, don't feel guilty about it, thinking, 'If I had just called my friend, been there with them.' Uh-uh, it's not your fault."

"No, it ain't," hollered an audience member.

"Our loved ones made this decision. Stop blaming yourself for not doing enough because God doesn't want you carrying that guilt."

"Let it go, fellers!" shouted another.

"God doesn't cause bad things to happen. He uses them for our good."

At this, some in the audience clapped, stood, and shouted, "Thanks be to God. Right on it, brother."

"My dad's death strengthened me into a compassionate person who reached out to every classmate and friend who lost a parent, grandparent, friend, or child. I have been to countless funerals because I felt like I needed to be there." Flashing quickly through my mind were the images from funerals of high school friends who lost a grandparent and college friends who lost a parent. Empathy welled up.

"It caused me to dive deep into studying the causes of depression so I wouldn't repeat the cycle of pain my dad went through. Demons crept over him and turned a very talented engineer into a man who could hardly function."

"That's not right, Dalton," shouted one.

"It created pain and discord within our family. After he died, God used the experience to help me, my sister, and my mother to live life to the fullest. When you are down, turn to the ones who love you the most and be there for them when they are down."

"You're here for us now!" shouted a man in the crowd. A woman said, "And we're here for you, baby."

"Aren't we grateful that Amber took her experience and made it possible for us to gather in a place where we don't have to explain what we are going through?"

Many clapped their hands across the room. I saw Amber beaming with pride and humbled with tears.

"All around us are people who are going through it." My voice cracked again at the sight of so many audience members wiping their eyes.

"Raise your hand if you are a survivor of fewer than six months." A bunch of hands raised.

"Raise your hand if you are a survivor of one year." More hands raised.

"Raise your hand if you are a survivor of five to ten years." More hands raised.

"Look around. Draw on the strength of the people in this room. I know that in the early days, the early weeks, the early months after a loss, it's hard to get past one morning without being paralyzed by how much you miss your loved one."

People looked around. Those raised hands joined hands with the hand raised by a neighbor. People patted backs.

"Some of you are years past it and to the point where thoughts of your friends are just about the good times. We never get over missing them, but we are able to make it through the days better as time heals our loss."

"Yes, sir!" shouted a young voice.

"Years after losing my dad, I was on a path to success and happiness on this earth, making the most of life when John took his life and I stopped living life to its fullest."

"Ah no, that's aint' good," shouted a woman.

"I'm done being that guy. I've got my family to live for. I'm not taking my riches to the grave. I'm planting them in the soil to sprout, grow, and thrive in the light of this world."

Numerous people jumped to their feet, clapped, and stomped their feet as someone shouted, "Look at you now, Dalt; you got a fine family."

Hearing this, I laughed, and my voice got louder as I walked back and forth across the stage. I spotted a young lady on the third row wearing a green dress with a print of tree branches across it. I called her up on stage, "Y'all, look at this young lady's beautiful dress. Y'all see the tree?"

"We see it, brother. Beautiful!" came a reply.

I motioned for her to stand center stage for a moment. "Every oak tree starts as a seed in the completely dark, damp soil of earth before it can sprout into the sunlight. Once it reaches above the surface, its growth is limitless, having planted solid roots. In the years to come, it will be taller than a house, solid as concrete, flexible enough to weather storms, and growing toward the sun."

I noticed a diamond ring on this lady's finger and said, "Tell me about your ring."

She held up her ring hand to display her big diamond. Several ladies responded, "Look at that!"

I held the microphone to her mouth. "I'm engaged to marry Gerome."

"Oooohhh, what a lucky man," replied a few men.

"Is he here with you tonight?" I asked.

She looked at me and smiled proudly, "Yes, he is, right over there." We all clapped and congratulated the young couple.

"What's your name?" I asked.

"Stephanie."

"Stephanie, will you please hold up your ring hand again, so everyone can see your diamond engagement ring?" She held it high for everyone to see. There were oohs and ahhs.

I continued, "The most precious of all gems starts as a lump of coal burdened by high pressure and exposed to high heat. As the years pass, this lump of coal becomes a diamond that can sharpen iron to perfection and is sought as an ornamental symbol of love and connection. Each of us is an oak tree at various stages of growth. Each of us is becoming a diamond."

"You nailed it, brother Dalton," shouted an older woman as many clapped. A few men stood up, twirled in place, outstretched their arms, and shouted, "Look at me, I'm an oak tree. I'm a maple."

A lady who looked to be in her eighties stood up wearing an aqua dress and flower-adorned hat, grinned broadly, and proudly announced, "Look at me; I'm a diamond."

We all burst out in laughter, and I said, "You sure are. You sure are! Let's hear it for these oaks, maples, and diamonds."

I put down the microphone and joined in the applause at these many brave, strong trees and diamonds. Then I bounded across the stage, watching the audience.

"Let your beauty shine. Go. Act. Take your experience. Make the most of it. Write your stories for books, magazines, plays, movies, TV shows. Draw, paint, mold, and sculpt your experience for others to see. Speak about it, as I am here today to inspire, support, and lift others. Be a vessel of good for God's people. Act, live, and be."

I stood center stage and lowered the microphone, and everyone jumped to their feet amidst a mixture of shouts from the audience.

"Amen, brother. We'll paint. We'll write. We'll sculpt. We'll sing."

The audience quieted down, and I motioned that I had one final thing to share.

"I'm no longer allowing my grief to take away from living life to the fullest. That is not what John Millington wanted. He left me a gift, his boat. My family has restored this boat, and it is a miracle. It brought our family together. It helped restore me to who God created me to be. Tomorrow, we will announce to the world what we are doing with this gift.

"If you can, join us at the convention center for the American Marine Manufacturers Expo, where you can see John's boat, which we have named *Johnny Bruce* in his honor.

"Yeah, I realize this is a shameless advertisement for the Marine Expo, but it does connect the Russell and Millington family." I lifted my arm and pointed toward where the Millingtons and Russells were sitting.

The audience laughed. "Not shameless, Dalton," shouted one man. "You just followin' your mission."

"We'll follow you," announced a lady.

I was flabbergasted everyone was still here. No one had left. My pace slowed, and the room was quiet as I concluded, "Survivors, you are here for a *reason*. Fight like survivors. Jesus left His disciples behind so they would continue to tell His story and the miracles He performed. Through them, the Holy Spirit continued to perform miracles. Now, it's in our hands to keep telling about His miracles on earth. In all of it, know you have my support, the support of the Russell family, the support of the Millington family, and the support of this tribe of suicide survivors.

"All of you are oak trees. All of you are diamonds. All of you are created in the image of God, lifted by the love of Jesus, and guided by His ever-present Spirit. Let *your* strength and beauty shine!"

With my last word, I smacked my hand on the podium and headed to the steps. The crowd got on their feet and erupted in applause! Amber grabbed me and brought me back on stage. We joined our hands, raising our arms and pointing upward. Joyce, Eva, Ned, Eileen, and Patton rushed the stage.

Amber handed me an envelope and said, "We have something for your family."

Eileen, Ned, and Eva leaned over me as I opened the envelope, and we saw Mickey's ears.

"Tickets to Disney World for two days—for all of us!" I announced, "Thank you!"

Amber grabbed my hand. I grabbed Eileen's hand, who grabbed Ned's hand, who grabbed Eva's hand. The Millington and Russell families' hands outstretched to the survivors in the audience. Across the room, we joined together in one continuous chain of hands.

Patton Millington, blessed with his dad's singing talent, broke into song.

Blest be the tie that binds
Our hearts in Christian love;
The fellowship of kindred minds
Is like to that above.

Quickly, the audio-visual person got the lyrics to the hymn "Blest Be the Tie That Binds" on the screen behind us. The Millingtons, Russells, and survivors sang together in a capella.

Before our Father's throne,
We pour our ardent prayers;
Our fears, our hopes, our aims are one,
Our comforts, and our cares.

We share our mutual woes,
Our mutual burdens bear;
And often for each other flows
The sympathizing tear.

When we asunder part,
It gives us inward pain;
But we shall still be joined in heart,
And hope to meet again.

Patton pointed to his head, and everyone was silent as his lone voice echoed throughout the room.

Blest be the tie that binds
Our hearts in Christian love;
The fellowship of kindred minds
Is like to that above.[4]

There were tears, laughter, and smiles. Most of all, there was love.

---

4 Johann Naegli and John Fawcett, "Blest Be the Tie That Binds," *The Worshipping Church*, Chicago: Hope Publishing Company, 1990. Public domain.

Chapter 42

The next morning, I arrived at the convention center before the doors opened to the attendees. Eileen, Eva, and Ned were sleeping in, recovering from last night's event.

Marine product companies were setting up booths. The boats were displayed in neat rows lined up by bow tips evenly pointedly toward the aisles. In some spots, the boats were aligned so close side by side that you could leap from one boat to the next and not touch the floor. The big, open exhibition hall was filled with the new boat aroma mix of fiberglass resin, vinyl, varnish, wax and brass polish. I saw outboard companies like Mercury, Yamaha, Honda, and Suzuki. Electronic companies were flashing their wares of fish finders, navigation systems, and trolling motors—Humminbird, Raytheon, Lowrance, Garmin, Motor Guide, and Minn Kota.

Boat manufacturers filled most of the space with everything from kayaks to small, yacht-size behemoths. It was a mix of boat styles and types familiar to boat aficionados—sailboats, bass boats, flats boats, bay boats, ski boats, pontoon boats, and more. There was everything from human-powered, paddle-driven to outboard-powered, to stern-drive-powered boats on display.

Since Florida is a peninsula in the United States at near sea level, it is loaded with lakes and rivers in the interior surrounded by the Gulf of Mexico on the west and the Atlantic Ocean on the east. It's a boater's paradise of freshwater and saltwater. It is probably the best place in the U.S. to have a marine expo for the pleasure boating industry.

SeaArk was there, and I stopped at their booth to see their latest aluminum models. One of the key salespeople saw my event badge and noticed Rocket City Tech's logo.

"Hey, you're the company here with one of our older boats, aren't you?" asked Ken from SeaArk.

"Yes, that's right," I said. "It's my boat. I'm Dalton Russell."

"We are excited to hear what Rocket City is unveiling this afternoon. I saw your boat, and it sure looks great. What is it—about five years old?"

I chuckled and said, "It's over twenty years old."

"You're kidding. Twenty years?" responded Ken in surprise. "You have maintained it well."

"Thank you." My chest thrust forward with pride as I felt our hard work was paying off. "You will hear more about it today. SeaArk builds a hull that will last a few lifetimes. It's already on its second lifetime within my family," I announced as I kept walking down the aisle to the next booth.

"Good luck this afternoon."

Ranger Boats displayed a boat from the 1974 Bassmaster Classic. It was in pristine condition with its beautiful, gold-painted Johnson outboard hanging on the transom.

When I saw the Flamingo Boats booth, I felt compelled to stop. At their booth, they had a pool of water about one foot deep and twenty feet long. Floating in the pool was their prototype, "Crevalle," from the late nineties—about the same year that John bought his boat brand new from a SeaArk dealer. Placed around the boat were yardsticks showing how shallow the boat floated in the water. The outboard on it was only ten years younger than the outboard on *Johnny Bruce.*

I stood next to the boat I had seen in many episodes of the famous fishing show, *Everglades Adventures.* This Saturday morning show captured what John and I felt when we were fishing. The stunning videography drew us in even deeper. Most of the shows were from saltwater fishing adventures, but it was the feel of the show that kept us watching season after season.

I gasped when I saw the one and only Topher Stevens standing in front of me. He was the host of *Everglades Adventures* and the founder of Flamingo Boats.

I wanted to speak to Topher and meet him face to face. Everyone seemed to have the same idea, and people surrounded him. I moved on, thinking, *Maybe I'll catch him later when he isn't the center of attention.* Besides, something else had snagged my attention. Gleaming in the bright lights of the convention center, tucked away in the back of center stage, sat *Johnny Bruce.*

Herb dusted *Johnny Bruce.* Clyde shined the outboard with a coat of WD-40.

"Hey, Dalton, welcome to the show." Herb waved his white dusting cloth in the air to greet me. Clyde looked up beaming with pride.

I stopped walking the floor, absorbed this scene, placed my hands on my hips, took a deep breath, and exhaled. "This is the most beautiful sight of the entire show. All of those bright, shiny boats look great, but this one has history, and he's mine. There are only two other boats here that have that history, like *Johnny Bruce.* He looks great!"

"We are ready to go," said Clyde. "You like our sign?"

In front of the Rocket City Tech booth was a four-by-eight sign that said, "Why is this 1997 SeaArk here, amid the latest and greatest of the marine industry? Join us here at 1:30 today to find out."

"There you go." I grinned. "I love it!"

At the bow of *Johnny Bruce* was a 1956 Evinrude, 7.5-horsepower outboard mounted in a clear running tank with a fuel line connected to a red pressurized fuel tank. It was just like the one Daddy had. Next to the stern of *Johnny Bruce* was a 1975 Johnson fifteen-horsepower outboard in a clear running tank. Even *Johnny Bruce*'s outboard had its lower unit in a tank of water. All three were ready to run.

In a flash of pride, I envisioned the brain film of Daddy guiding our boat across Town Creek, Jake Snellgrove tuning a Johnson outboard at his dock, Eileen grinning at me as she wiped sweat from her brow to repair my rented outboard, John sticking his tongue out at me as I snapped a photo of him running his boat, and the laughing faces of Eva and Ned as they peered at loons in *Johnny Bruce*.

For *Johnny Bruce*, Rocket City Tech, and the National Marine Industry Expo, we were ready to open the doors.

Chapter 43

The doors to the expo opened, and people started pouring in. Booths were visited by movers, shakers, designers, engineers, and salespeople of the marine industry.

Around noon, Eileen, Eva, and Ned arrived.

"Y'all ready to go?" I asked.

"I've got this, Dad," said an annoyed Eva. "I've got everything in place for my weird entrance." I recognized this emotion, as it is similar to mine in its raw form. She is in the creative mode of an artist about to perform, and you don't interrupt their concentration. She will bite your head off, just like an Olympic gymnast preparing to perform across the show floor, who suddenly has a camera or microphone thrust in their face. I quietly walked away to avoid breaking her concentration.

The time approached, and I announced to the team just like a director of a play, "Places, everyone."

Ned perched himself on the bow seat of *Johnny Bruce*. Eileen stood near him at the trailer tongue, which marked center stage next to the microphone. I placed Bob King just outside the exhibit space near the loading docks, along with Eva. I held up my fist high in the air with a thumbs up and looked at each of our performers, who gave me a thumbs up in reply.

Show crowds gathered in bleachers in front of the boat display and the floor area surrounding the Rocket City Tech booth. The crowd abuzz with conversation and anticipation of what this small, little-known electronic company was about to announce to the onlookers of the marine industry.

I stood next to Eileen, peered into her smiling eyes, nodded, squeezed her hand, and then disappeared in the shadows.

Eileen grabbed the microphone and announced, "Ladies and gentlemen, welcome to this year's American Marine Manufacturers Expo! I am Eileen Russell and part of the family here at Rocket City Tech. It thrills us to have you gather here, and I am sure you are wondering, 'Why is this little tech company here talking to us?'"

I glanced at Eileen's shaking left hand at her side. She was nervous, but her voice beamed with confidence.

"Amid these shiny, new boats, motors, electronics, and hardware, there is deep within each of you a story of how you came to love the water." The audience nodded in agreement.

"My love of the water came about because my dad owned a small marine outboard repair shop on Guntersville Lake in Alabama. We lived on the lake." Many in the crowd murmured to their neighbor that they could relate.

"My love for boats began following my dad and watching him repair outboard motors. He taught me how to do it, and to this day, it is second nature to take a rough-running engine and get it running right again."

The audience gasped, and one woman hollered, "Pretty impressive for a woman, I tell ya."

"That's actually how I met my husband." We heard a collective, "Aaahh," from the crowd. I was surprised and pleased to hear this as Eileen had practiced this introduction on her own.

"Ladies and gentlemen, there is much joy a family can get from fixing up old things and making them new again. It can bring the family closer together. This boat next to me is *Johnny Bruce*. It's over twenty years old, but our family came together to make it new again. My eight-year-old son and sixteen-year-old daughter had enormous smiles when they were working on it." Eileen gently placed her left hand to her heart as she said this. Her hand was not shaking anymore as she found her voice. A tear formed in my eyes as I proudly recalled those moments.

"As fun and exciting as these shiny, new vessels are, I wouldn't trade any of them for the experience that *Johnny Bruce* gave to us and what he means to our family. But speaking of fixing up old things, I turn this microphone over to my husband, Dalton Russell." The audience laughed, appreciating the marital banter. "He is Rocket City Tech's Director of Marketing. Here is Dalton Russell."

I high-fived Eileen; she hugged me tight and handed me the microphone.

"Let's hear it for my beautiful wife, Eileen!" I said amid the whistles and applause. "Like Eileen was saying, there is beauty in restoring old things and making them new again. How many of you love old cars?"

On cue, an engine revved behind the crowd, and everyone turned to see a gleaming 1967 Plymouth Belvedere rumbling slowly down the aisle toward our booth.

"Here is Rocket City Tech's CEO, Bob King, in his pride and joy." Bob parked the Plymouth in front of the booth and got out to cheers from the crowd.

"Bob, tell us about your Plymouth." I gestured toward the gleaming vehicle.

"Sure," chirped Bob as he took the microphone. "This was my mom and dad's car, which we kept for many years until I restored it five years ago. My son and I did most of the work myself, but it carries so many fond memories for me, and I am glad to still have it in running condition. It's the car I drive to work every day."

"Thank you, Bob!" I continued. "Not all of us have a classic muscle car in the garage. Some of us have something we have passed on to our children once they start driving, such as this."

A highly polished, candy apple red Honda Accord quietly rolled down the aisle with Eva behind the wheel. Eva parked the car behind the Plymouth. I heard some in the crowd say, "That's more like it."

"This is my beautiful daughter, Eva, and this car is her pride and joy now that she has become a driver." Eva got out of the car amid applause and whistles of her own in her beach print summer dress. Eva's face turned red in embarrassment.

"Hey, now, calm down; remember, this is my daughter."

The audience laughed, and one dad in the crowd announced, "Gotta be proud of her, Dad."

I brought the microphone to Eva. "Eva, tell us about your car."

"Well, Dad," announced a nervous and timid Eva as she brushed her dark hair from her eyes, "it used to be Mom's car, but, you know, she gave it to me to drive to school." The high school dancer and background play performer in Eva began to appear as nerves subsided. She glanced at Ned, who was giving her two big thumbs up.

"It meant a lot to me that y'all entrusted me with such a valuable thing. I want to take care of it."

"How often do you wash and vacuum it?" I asked.

"Every week, of course." Her eyes wide, she asked, "Isn't that what we are supposed to do?" The crowd laughed.

"How often do you wax it?" I asked.

"I've only waxed it twice, but it's been six months apart." She nodded at me, and someone said, "Great job, girl!"

"How often do you change the oil?" hollered an older man from the crowd.

With confidence, Eva looked at the man. "Every three thousand miles and I do it myself, with the help of Mom, you know. She's the real mechanic in the family." The crowd laughed again and nodded. They were enjoying themselves.

"She's right," I confirmed as we both looked at an embarrassed Eileen. "Eileen has the skills. Eva, how long do you expect to keep this car?"

"As long as I can keep it running," replied Eva. "It's my shiny apple, and I love it!" Eva continued, "Not only do I love it, but so do Grandmother and Grandpa."

Suddenly, the Accord back doors opened, and my mother and Rich jumped out. I wasn't expecting this!

"Surprise, Dad!" announced Eva. They hugged me, and Mother grabbed the microphone and said, "This here is a family deal," and handed the microphone back to me.

"Sorry, folks, this *is* a surprise to me. I wasn't expecting my mother and stepdad to be here. All of these people had a part to play in what I am about to tell you." I waved my hand across the show floor in the direction of my family, Bob King, and the team from Rocket City Tech.

"Behind me, you see this beautiful 1997 SeaArk boat with a vintage outboard. Both have been renovated and customized by my family."

The crowd oohed and ahhed. "It's a beauty," yelled one woman.

I described the history of *Johnny Bruce* and what he has come to mean to us because of our family coming together in his restoration. I told of how he created lifetime fishing memories. "We could have bought a brand-new boat and motor, but it would not have had the same heart. In its restored condition, it's bringing new memories for our family."

With the surprise by my mother and Rich, my knees began to feel like gelatin. Eva and Eileen saw me wobble, and they gently came to my side to steady me by standing on either side with their arms at my waist. *You aren't grieving anymore, Dalton. Rise above. Blaze a new trail.* Strengthened and steadied by these women, I continued.

"Our family could not afford to buy a new boat, but we did have the funds available to restore *Johnny Bruce.*

"As I have traveled across our country, I've seen boats sitting dormant in yards, driveways, and carports. Families bought them intending to enjoy them, but the focus in life changes. The vessels decay over time."

Many in the audience voiced their agreement. Some said aloud, "Yep, that's me."

"Today, there is a resurgence in restoring older homes and cars to modern glory. It's fueled by TV shows on home and auto restoration. It's more affordable to restore or renovate compared to the cost of starting new. You can do it a piece at a time or dive in for complete restoration. The property and auto values nearly double when complete." My eyebrows lifted at this fact.

"Restoration brings a family together because they have restored the heart and soul of the home or car. They bring it fresh life, creating space for fresh memories to last a lifetime."

A man in the crowd suddenly yelled, "So what's this got to do with boaters?" The crowd laughed and mumbled in agreement they wanted to know, too.

I laughed and looked at the man and smiled. "I'm glad you asked! Here at Rocket City Tech, we are launching a new product to bring back the heart of the old boats and outboards gathering dust!"

"That'll be great!" hollered one young woman with a toddler on her lap.

"On display at this year's expo is an original Bassmaster Classic boat restored to showroom condition. There is a fishing boat displayed that runs in the shallow water of the Everglades, that is maintained in its original running condition. There is a wooden boat that appeared famously in an Academy Award-winning film. These three boats alone revolutionized the boating industry. The owners show them with pride, and it's lighter in the wallet for the cost-conscious boater. We want more people focused on enjoying time rather than it remaining a daydream."

The crowd mumbled in agreement, and a voice said, "How true."

"How is Rocket City Tech doing this? By helping old outboards meet modern standards of emissions to preserve our water resources."

On cue, Eileen pulled the starter cord on the 1956 Evinrude. A puff of white smoke belched out the exhaust.

I continued, "A common problem for older outboards is the gasoline and oil mix in the fuel tank. This puts oil in water every time you run the engine. Rocket City Tech has developed a computer chip regulator to make these older outboards much more environmentally friendly. It's like an electronic fuel injection for your outboard engine. We call it Green Wave."

Bob King pulled the starter on the 1979 Johnson outboard. No smoke came out. The audience was in awe of the lack of smoke that they expected to belch out.

"This outboard is fitted with Green Wave. As you can see by the outboard started by Rocket City Tech's owner, there is zero smoke. No oil or gasoline is coming out of the exhaust."

The audience craned their necks as they inspected the back of the outboard looking for white smoke.

"We have done tests, and the exhaust comes out cleaner than this little engine has ever been. It's getting enough oil to the power head to keep it regulated with no excess to dump into the water.

"Crank up *Johnny Bruce*!" I shouted, exultation evident in my tone.

Ned proudly pressed the starter button on the outboard on *Johnny Bruce,* and it started cleanly with no smoke emissions.

"Ladies and gentlemen of the American Marine Manufacturers Expo and the movers and shakers of the marine industry, I present to you Green Wave by Rocket City Tech!"

Applause thundered across the floor of the exhibit hall. I paced the floor, placed the microphone in my armpit, and clapped my hands as I faced our team from Rocket City Tech.

"I challenge all of you to join Rocket City Tech in creating a wave across the marine industry. Join us in helping more families enjoy their time on the water without breaking their bank account. Join us to create a Green Wave of restoration for the boats and motors of old."

The audience erupted in applause, and those who were standing stepped in for a closer look at the outboards fitted with Green Wave. They were eager to get an up-close look of their own. I motioned for the audience to quiet down.

"Don't worry, in a moment, you can look at Green Wave at our booth. Behind you, there are three order stations with Rocket City Tech team members ready to take orders.

"Join me, Dalton Russell, the Russell Family, the King family, and the family of Rocket City Tech and be a part of the Green Wave!"

Applause and cheers thundered the exhibit hall. A mob gathered around the old outboards and *Johnny Bruce* to look at Green Wave.

At the stations, people lined up to place orders for Green Wave to ship to their marinas and parts stores.

Bob King put his arm around me with pride. "Dalton, when you came to me with this proposal, my brain said, 'No, gather more data.' My gut said, 'Yes, let this guy loose; something great can happen.' Looks like my gut was right! Look what you've done! You've created a firestorm of interest in this little company!"

"Sir, when God breathed air of life into Adam, He filled up his gut with God's breath. Our gut instincts come from God's guidance. Thanks to God for all of this. Thank you, sir, for believing in me."

I felt a hand on my shoulder. A familiar voice said, "Hey, Dalton."

I turned around. It was Topher Stevens.

"Oh my, Topher Stevens!" I nervously exclaimed.

Topher held his hand at his shoulder with his thumb pointing behind him. "Great presentation. This is quite a revolution ya got here. How long are you in Florida?"

"Until the end of the week. We are going to Disney World tomorrow."

"Can you spare a day and come to Titusville to fish for some redfish with me?"

I looked at Eileen. "Eileen, come here. Hey folks, make room for my wife, please."

Eileen stood next to me and saw the legend of the Everglades and practically squealed, "Topher Stevens! My husband has been wanting to meet you for years."

"Nice to meet you, Eileen." Topher smiled. "May I borrow your husband for a day of fishing later this week before you head back home?"

"That will be great!" Eileen beamed. "He's earned it."

"How about Thursday morning on the Indian River?" asked Topher.

"Sounds great!" I replied in shock, nearly bouncing like Ned would. "Here's my card; text me the address and time, and I will be there."

"Will do!" said Topher. "I look forward to Friday."

Eileen hugged me and looked around the crowd. No words were spoken between us. Our embrace and the Spirit said it all.

With my right arm around Eileen's waist, I placed my hand on the gunnel of *Johnny Bruce* and absorbed the sight of activity. Nearby, Eva talked with show visitors about her candy apple red car. Ned spun in the bow seat of *Johnny Bruce*. Bob King proudly opened the hood of his Plymouth. Clyde and Herb surprisingly had taken off their ball caps and were showing visitors how Green Wave worked. At a table nearby, Rocket City Tech team members took orders for Green Wave.

Behind the table stood one man who saw me look at him—Milo. At first, his face was expressionless. When he caught my eye, he held his fist high in the air, smiled, and gave me a thumbs up.

"Eileen"—I exhaled—"we did this as a team. All thanks to our miracle boat here. All thanks to God."

Chapter 44

The working part of our trip to Orlando was complete now that the expo was over. We took the next several days for our family to play. We spent two full days at Disney World. I know that Ned and Eva had an extraordinary time, but I believe Eileen and I had just as much fun. It had been a long time since we had a family vacation getaway.

For lunch on our second day, we were at Epcot, and I asked Eva to keep close with Ned so that her mom and I could have a nice lunch together—just the two of us. I have always wanted to take her to Italy, but since we hadn't made it yet, I planned to do the next best thing without leaving the United States. We went to the World Showcase and had a romantic lunch in an Italian restaurant. It may have been hot and humid in Orlando, but sipping espresso was refreshing in the air-conditioned restaurant. It was rejuvenating, sitting across the small, round table from beautiful Eileen. A permanent grin spread across her face and her eyes aglow with joy, she said, "Thank you for taking me to Italy."

After lunch, we rejoined Eva and Ned at the test track, where they had just come off a fast ride. They were holding hands, laughing, and skipping. I have to say, I felt like skipping, too, while holding Eileen's hand. They ran up to us with delight, talking a mile a minute about all they had experienced since we last saw them.

I squeezed Eileen's hand, looked up to the beautiful, cloudy sky, and mouthed, *Thank you.* The next day, we went to Sea World and added to our incredible holiday.

On Friday, I awoke early while everyone else slept in for a well-deserved relaxing day at the hotel in Orlando. Topher Stevens sent a young man to pick me up in Orlando and drove me to Titusville to meet him at a boat launch on the Indian River. Illuminated by the dock light glowed the famous white hull of Topher's boat—the same boat I had seen in numerous episodes of his fishing show. It floated next to the dock with Topher standing aboard ready to begin our adventure. Topher greeted me warmly and welcomed me to come aboard.

"Today, I'm your guide, Dalton. The Indian River is yours. How about some redfish, maybe some snook, and a jack crevalle or two?"

That launched our terrific fishing adventure of catching all of the fish Topher said we would. By the end of our time together, my arm was sore from fighting and reeling in so many fish. Topher even piloted the boat into Mosquito Lagoon so I could see the launch pads of NASA's Project Mercury, Gemini, Apollo, and Space Shuttle. The Vehicle Assembly Building towered over the landscape as did the launch pads. With this site, I made the connection from Daddy's work at Marshall Space Flight Center to the actual launch pad gantry. It was a delightful bucket list day for me. I returned from Orlando a very happy man.

Chapter 45

Once we were back in Huntsville, Ned excitedly rehashed his adventures at Disney World. Each morning since we had left Orlando, he would crawl out of bed and walk through the house snuggling tightly to his Pooh Bear, plop down next to Eileen or me, and lay his head on us. The walls of his room began to fill with Ned creating drawings of a boat with a smiling girl, grinning woman, a clapping daddy, and a happy boy. Above the characters, he labeled, "Sister. Mommy. Daddy. Me." On the side of the boat was labeled, *Johnny Bruce*.

On one of these drawings, I noticed he added some more characters. One was a man sitting on a nearby island smiling at the boaters, while Another floated above the water looking down on the boaters. He was the only One in the drawing colored with white clothes that contrasted His dark hair. There was a label next to him that said, "TC."

Curiously, I asked Ned about this character, and Ned said matter-of-factly, "Oh, you know Him, Daddy; that's the Carpenter. He looks like I always saw Him and just like how you and Mommy described Him." When I heard this, my heart swelled with pride and amazement. "Of course, Ned, of course."

Every time that *Johnny Bruce* was uncovered in the backyard, Ned would climb into the boat, sit on the back seat, grab the tiller handle, and pretend he was on a boating adventure. Through him, I saw myself doing the same thing decades ago with my dad's boat and motor.

For Eva, the month of July was a chance to visit with friends without the interruption of classes and homework. Surprisingly, many of her friends came and spent time at our house. The draw was Eva, but I believe the access to a pile of snacks in the kitchen might've had something to do with it. Teenage girls may give the appearance that they avoid certain food and snacks when in the watchful eye of girls they don't know or a boy that has their interest. That all goes out the window when they are amongst close friends and family. Place them in front of bags of chips, nuts, and crunchy cereals, and they go to town munching away as much and as fast as they can. It was more affordable to buy snacks and know where they were than filling up Eva's car with gas for them to be cruising about.

Once the school year began, these visits and snack sessions continued during weekends and after school. I was pleased they found our home to be a sanctuary to let loose and be themselves, until boys started being added to the gatherings.

There was one boy Eva invited to the house who was good friends with her girlfriends. His name was Isaiah, and his name told me a lot about his parents.

Eva introduced me to him one day when I got home. "This is Isaiah. Isaiah, this is my dad."

Immediately, the young man stood up, looked me straight in the eyes and reached out to shake my hand. "It's nice to meet you, Mr. Russell." He looked to be seventeen years old, was taller than me, lanky, with short, cropped, blond hair.

I was pleased with his politeness and manners. *Good first impression around my daughter and these girls. Now, are you going to keep it up, or is this just for show?*

"Nice to meet you, Isaiah. I like your name."

"Thank you, sir. My parents named me for the prophet in the Old Testament," he replied. I maintained a hard edge around this young man because he was a boy hanging out with my daughter.

"Dad, Isaiah is in Boy Scouts," said Eva.

I looked at Isaiah and nodded. "Really? What rank are you?"

"Sir, I just attained Life rank, and I'm beginning plans for my project so I can become an Eagle. I just haven't decided what I want to do yet."

"My dad is an Eagle Scout, too," said Eva as she gave me the facial expression message saying, *Dad, please don't ruin this and launch into your Scout stories.* I got the message.

"Ladies and gentlemen, y'all enjoy your snacks. Isaiah, it was a pleasure meeting you." I headed out of the kitchen, but before I got to the door to the hallway, Isaiah said, "It was a pleasure to meet you, sir. Umm, I like your boat, Eva's told us how you fixed it up. Can I get a close look at it some time?"

Surprised, I turned back toward this teenage boy, who seemed more mature for his age. "Certainly, Isaiah." I left the room so Eva could be alone with her friends.

One afternoon after coming home from work, I saw Isaiah's car parked in front of our house, and he was waiting in the driveway staring toward the backyard. He seemed to be in a trance as I pulled into the driveway and jumped when my truck pulled up behind him. I rolled down the window and asked, "Hey, Isaiah, you lookin' for Eva?"

"No, sir, uh, um, well, I came here to see you. Uh, I was wondering if you could show me your boat today."

"Sure." I smiled, got out of my truck, and walked with him to the backyard. "What were you looking at when I pulled up? You were pretty focused and didn't seem to hear me drive up."

"Oh, sorry sir. I was, well, I, uh, was looking at your boat. I like boats, and something about yours intrigues me. Ever since I was here last, I keep picturing the boat."

This puzzled me. *What has Eva told Isaiah about* Johnny Bruce?

I pulled back the cover of *Johnny Bruce,* and his eyes got big. "I've never seen someone build a wood floor like that on a modified v-hull."

Ah, this young man knows something about boats.

He put his hand on the bow and ran his hand down the gunnel to the stern. His eyes fixated on the interior as his face glowed in delight.

"My dad was going to get a boat for us when he got back from Afghanistan."

I leaned against the gunnel on the other side from Isaiah. "When is he coming back?"

Isaiah's eyes looked at the outboard motor. "He didn't make it back."

My heart sank. "Oh, my goodness, Isaiah; I am so sorry." In a flash, watching this young man and hearing his story, I pictured myself at the same age telling someone about where my dad was.

"It's okay, Mr. Russell. Um, I know where he is, and he was serving our country. It's part of a soldier's duty." He turned his head toward me, looking straight in the eye. "I miss him, though. We had some good fishing trips together."

I shared with Isaiah the story of losing my dad when I was close to his age and how we used to fish together.

"Yeah, Eva told me a little about that."

Immediately, I felt a gut nudge, and by now, I was familiar with who was nudging me. "What you got going on this weekend?"

"Nothing, sir," he replied as he placed his hand on the outboard and rounded the stern of the boat.

"How about going fishing with me in this boat?"

His head jerked toward me, grinning widely. "Really? I would *love* that!"

"I need to talk to your mother first and make sure she is okay with it."

"That shouldn't be a problem at all, Mr. Russell."

I got his cell number and his mother's as well. I told him that I would send him details about our Saturday plan after I talked with his mother. Isaiah kept looking at the boat with intrinsic interest when Eva came out to the backyard and greeted Isaiah.

"Your dad invited me to go fishing!"

"He did? Well, that's great, Isaiah."

I pulled Eva over to the side, and we turned our backs to the boat. I whispered, "What have you told him about *Johnny Bruce?*"

She whispered back, "Nothing other than we have a boat we fixed up. I didn't say anything about, well, you know, Dad. Not a thing." Eva gave me bug eyes, and I knew she was telling the truth.

"Did you know his dad died in Afghanistan?" I asked, still whispering.

Eva gently nodded at me and then whispered, "Dad, he doesn't know the story of *Johnny Bruce*."

I nodded at her and winked an eye. "Good girl."

"Mr. Russell?" asked Isaiah as we turned and faced him. "Sir, um, thank you for showing me your boat. I'm sorry, but I have to get home. Mom just sent me a message saying dinner will be ready soon.

Nice to see you, Eva. I'll let Mom know you are going to be calling her. She's going to be so excited."

"You're welcome." We waved at Isaiah as he left our yard to go home.

The next Saturday, Isaiah and I had an incredible fishing trip to Guntersville Lake. Knowing his story, I expected to get a visit, but we did not. It doesn't happen every time. Besides, I needed to get to know more about this young man. My gut told me there would be more fishing trips to come.

The rest of Eileen's summer was spent gathering parts and tools in our garage. Working on our outboard motor, visiting her parents, and seeing Ned's curiosity for building things reignited her passion for working on engines. She set up a hands-on children's workshop to teach elementary age children how engines work. She and Ned would drive around neighborhoods and pick up old lawnmowers that people were discarding.

She invited Ned's friends over during weekday afternoons to teach them how to drain the oil, disassemble the engines, and clean the parts. With small engines, these eight- to eleven-year-olds would learn about our Creator, our Builder, through hands-on science and technology.

I would go into the garage; and the aroma of motor oil, rubber, and a hint of gasoline permeated the space. With grease on her hands, a spark in her eyes, and excitement in her voice, Eileen glowed as she taught these children what her dad taught her. Three or four children sat in front of their own folding plastic TV trays—their workstation or desk—with engine parts in front of them.

During one session, she held up a carburetor to the children and said, "This is the heart of the engine. Just like our human heart, the life fluids flow through it to make the rest of the engine, or our body, work. It has some tiny parts that if not maintained well can keep the engine from working right. Let's take it apart. Grab your screwdrivers and take a look inside."

The boys and girls in her classroom eagerly went to work disassembling their carburetors when one girl asked, "Mrs. Eileen, are we gonna get it back together?"

With Eileen's hair pulled back in a ponytail, she brushed away a strand of hair across her forehead, leaving a grease mark on her skin. "We are, honey. Not only that, but we're also going to make it better with new parts. First, let's take a look inside."

Standing behind the boys and girls, I caught Eileen's eyes, held my fist to my heart, and mouthed, "I'm proud of you." She nodded, lifted a finger pointed to the sky, and mouthed, "Thank you."

Her lesson continued, "Boys and girls, God created us in His image. That doesn't mean we are little gods, but He created us with the ability to create. These engines were created by another human. You, too, have the ability to create."

Immediately, the children began firing off what they had created. "Ooh, I created a painting of my house . . . I created a birdhouse out of popsicle sticks . . . I created a picture of my grandparents out of crayons . . . I created a sandcastle at the beach . . . I got to help create dinner for my little sister . . . My mommy says I create a mess everyday . . . "

There was so much enthusiasm among these children taught by Eileen using her knowledge to pass on to them what she knew. Some nights when the workshop ended, she would come into the house grinning, but exhausted, and say, "I have no idea what I am going to show them next. I don't know if any of them will come back except

Ned. God knows. Every morning, I pray, asking God to use my hands and feet."

"Eileen, I would kiss you, but you have an oil smudge on your nose and chin."

We laughed as we peered out the window to our backyard and saw *Johnny Bruce* parked in the grass. In the late afternoon light, a bright glow appeared under his cover and then dimmed.

Chapter 46

At Rocket City Tech, there were so many orders pouring in for the Green Wave that Rocket City Tech was back-ordered for two months. Calls flooded in from marine companies wanting photos of *Johnny Bruce* to see what products they could make for boat restorations. Product demonstration requests came in from all over the country to see the Green Wave.

My email box was full of speaking requests from U.S. Suicide Prevention chapters across the country for their fundraisers and events.

Eileen and I agreed that I would go to meetings that were a reasonable driving distance from home so I would not miss very much of our family life. I told Bob King that I would train an eager travel team of salespeople. This team would present in the same spirit from the marine expo.

One day, Bob King called me into his office and handed me an envelope.

"Open it up, Dalton," instructed Bob. "I'm making you marine division chief, and I'm offering you a partnership in Rocket City Tech. In addition to my family, you are our only partner. You showed more guts and leadership than I have seen from anyone in this company. We needed that boost and fresh life pumped into us. You earned it, Dalton."

"Wow, Bob," I gasped. "I . . . I . . . well, thank you from the bottom of my heart. I accept your offer."

"You are officially part of the family. Dalton, you can do what you want now. Follow your passion and profit from what you create."

When I came out of Bob's office, Milo was waiting for me.

"Hey, come into my office for just a moment," said Milo.

He had two boxes on his desk he was filling up with personal things.

"Dalton." Milo sighed. "Congratulations! I was wrong about the Green Wave. I was wrong about you. Bob told me he was offering you partnership in the company, so I guess you are my boss now. To save you the trouble, I will get out of your way and resign because I'm sure you don't want a naysayer around."

"Stop right there, Milo," I said. "I need you around here more than ever. You sharpen me. Yeah, we may butt heads, but that's part of growth. You want to sharpen a knife; you rub it against a hard stone. You are more valuable to Rocket City Tech than ever. The launch of Green Wave came about by us working as a team. You are part of that team. Now, as your leader, I'm asking you to stay, if you desire to stay. Do you?"

Milo paused, looked out the window and then directly at me. "Yes, I want to stay and work *with* you," replied Milo eagerly.

"Great, then put everything back on your desk and help keep this team afloat." Milo shook my hand.

That same week, I received a phone call from Amber Millington.

Amber said, "Dalton, your story needs a broader audience. Would you write a book on your experiences and how you survived and rose above the two suicides of loved ones in your life? U.S. Suicide

Prevention will publish it and give you a fifty-thousand-dollar advance. You can promote and market it wherever you like."

"Amber, I would love to," I answered, "but with two conditions—part of the proceeds of each book sale goes to suicide prevention. Second, you, your mom, and your brother come over to Huntsville and spend a weekend on Guntersville Lake with *Johnny Bruce*. Someone is waiting to see you. Deal?"

"Deal!" answered Amber.

"You won't believe what his boat has done for us," I replied knowingly. As I hung up, I knew that another grand adventure awaited us through the spirit of *Johnny Bruce*. That is a story for another time.

From that moment forward, Eileen and I did not have to worry about finances. God provided beyond our wildest imagination.

The book we wrote for U.S. Suicide Prevention is the one you are reading now. All of this happened when the miracle boat, *Johnny Bruce*, came to us. God doesn't cause bad things to happen. He makes the most of those bad things.

Prayer is more than giving thanks and laying our requests before God. It is about listening for God's answers. It's about being ready to take action when His direction is given. It's trusting that His way is better than our way.

Our life adventure to this point has been grand. The adventures that lay ahead are limitless and will be extraordinary. What adventure awaits you?

Rise! Pray! Listen! Act! Be!

Acknowledgments

Thanks be to God, Jesus and the Holy Spirit. One of my professors, Dr. Robert Smith, taught me that God preaches through our personality.

A monumental thank you to my wife Tracie who tolerated a lot of weekend mornings toiling over writing and editing *Miracle Boat*. Thank you for all of your love and support.

Thank you to my family and friends who cheered me along in writing this story and for your support in getting it published.

Thank you to the entire team at Ambassador International for working with me. Thank you to Dr. Samuel Lowry who had the willingness to publish *Miracle Boat* and share the story with the world. I am very grateful to Susanna Maurer whose editorial skills helped take this block of raw wood to trim it, shape it, sand it, varnish it and polish it so that it became something worthy to read.

Thank you to Mara Hamner, Carol Mitchell, Chris Siggins, and Brent McDougal for reading drafts of *Miracle Boat* and offering advice on improvement.

Thank you to the Williams Family for decades of love and support. We share a bond of being survivors of suicide. My hope is that by sharing the story of *Miracle Boat* will help prevent more suicides.

Thank you to you—the reader—for taking the time to read this story and briefly making it a part of your life. Please share it with others and shine on!

For more information about
Dean Allan Johnson
and
Miracle Boat
please visit:

www.deanallanjohnson.blogspot.com
www.facebook.com/Dean-Allan-Johnson-108973651040827
YouTube: Dean's Devo channel

For more information about
AMBASSADOR INTERNATIONAL
please visit:

www.ambassador-international.com
@AmbassadorIntl
www.facebook.com/AmbassadorIntl

Thank you for reading this book. Please consider leaving us a review on your social media, favorite retailer's website, Goodreads or Bookbub, or our website.

More from Ambassador International

When newlyweds Jonathan and Betsy became involved with a radical, charismatic group, their encounter made Christianity seem more vital and scriptural than the fundamental denominations in which they were raised. Instead, they found out the hard way that things which appear to be spiritual and godly might be deceptive underneath, and they experienced firsthand the natures of demonic influence and mental illness. Here is their story . . .

Sean Winter is burdened by a heartrending past he can't share, and any faith he had has been eroded. At twenty-four-years-old, he has a bachelor's degree and works at one of the top customer service firms in Oklahoma City. A new job and post-college life bring new opportunities for friendship and even love. What happens when one of those new acquaintances turns out to be a Christian? And is Sean ready for any kind of romantic relationship?

After his wife dies, Marco finds himself lonely and desperate for companionship. Katie is an abused woman, who is now tied to caring for an invalid husband. When Marco and Katie meet, they form a bond quickly. Realizing they are walking a line outside of God's will, Marco returns to his life in New York with Katie telling him to forget her forever. But she is never far from his mind. Does God bring beauty from ashes? Can God repair what has been broken and "make all things new"?

Made in the USA
Columbia, SC
27 August 2023

22173082R00152